Ripple

Ripple

---

a novel

L.D. Cedergreen

Cover design by Robin Ludwig Design Inc.,
www.gobookcoverdesign.com

ISBN: 978-0-9893783-1-4
ISBN: 978-0-9893783-0-07(ebook)

For Melissa

Prologue

I stood at the cold dark water's edge, my reflection staring back at me from the glasslike surface. The reflection of a girl that I no longer knew. I breathed in the overwhelming scent of pine and recognized the tranquility that surrounded me. The soft hum of the city in the distance, the echo of an eagle's cry overhead, the steady drum of my heart—the only sounds that could be heard in the quiet serenity that was present all around me.

Inside an entirely different scene existed. Whirling thoughts, like hurricane-force winds, blew through my mind while a dark, thunderous storm was raging inside my soul, cutting the power to the central organ of my existence—my heart. I was destined to weather this storm on my own. After all, like Mother Nature, I was the controlling force behind these conditions.

I threw a stone into the mirrored surface of the water before me and watched the small circular wave expand from the point where it broke through the stillness.

It was hard not to think of the stone as the choice I had made, the choice that inevitably created waves in the smooth waters of my life. The first lie, like the first ripple in the water, seemed so small but quickly became more significant. Each wave growing in size and depth, impossible to stop. The effect from that one choice spread through my life like the ripple moving across the surface of the water.

I longed for the stillness.

Home

It has been said that the past has a way of catching up with us. That we can't run from it no matter how hard we try, but I had hoped that didn't apply to me. I had hoped that the blood, sweat and tears that I had poured into creating a new life for myself, that my will to keep moving forward and to never look back, would somehow save me from this age-old notion. But inevitably—usually when it is least expected—the past has a way of staring us right in the face.

~

There were reasons why I avoided this town, the place where it all began, the place that I called home for the first eighteen years of my life. I had been born and raised in the confines of this rural setting, the place that a whopping 1800 other people called home. I had accumulated a lifetime of memories—some good, some bad—in this small town, but the ones that kept me away, the ones that I had been running from for the past ten years, were the only memories that I could recall while I parked my rental car across the street from the largest church in town.

Damn, it was cold, I thought, pulling my jacket tighter around me as I walked from the car to the church. One of the many things that I did not miss about this place was the freezing-cold winters. At twenty-eight, I was now living happily on the warm shores of Southern California. I had become comfortable with the constant seventy-degree temperature, gladly forgoing the extra layers needed in winter here in eastern Washington.

I glanced down the desolate street lacking any sign of life this time of year and noted the lack of color as well. Everything was frozen in place. Not just from the plummeting temperature but also frozen in time. Not much had changed since I had left home. Small towns were like that. I could see the drugstore still painted in the same red-and-white color scheme, matching its striped awning, and run by the same family. The few taverns still opened their doors each afternoon to, sadly, some of the same patrons that had become "regulars" years ago. The small family-owned restaurant where I had earned many paychecks during summer breaks remained, as did the car dealership that my grandfather had owned for as long as I could remember. Although now the showroom sat empty, and the large windows that once showcased new shiny sedans were covered in dust.

I sighed at the thought of my gramps. He was the reason that I was home. He had passed away last week, and I now found myself walking across this cold desolate street with a heavy heart to attend his funeral. I was asked to say a few words about him. My grandparents were such a big part of my life. My gram left us just last year. She had been suffering from Alzheimer's for quite some time. I think that my grandfather died of a lonely heart; he lost his whole world when he lost my grandmother. They would have celebrated their fiftieth wedding anniversary this year.

My family already waited inside for me. I had stayed behind a few extra minutes to write down the thoughts that I wanted to share today. I really just wanted to speak from my heart but at the last minute had decided that I should write something down so that my emotions didn't get in the way. I didn't enjoy speaking in front of people. I could feel a lump rising in my throat just thinking about it, the weight of the folded paper in my pocket feeling heavy like a brick.

I stepped inside to see my family gathered in the lobby holding onto one another for support. My mother, so young and full of life. My older sister, Marie, her husband, Reid, and my younger brother, Scott. My dad would not be here. It was odd since it was his father we were mourning, but he had been estranged from us all for some time.

I quickly hugged my mother, trying to draw warmth from her as my hands and feet were nearly frozen.

"Are you ready to go in, Kendall?" she asked with concern in her eyes.

I softly nodded. Only my mother called me by my full name. Everyone else called me *Kendi*. I removed my coat and slung it over my arm, as we all filed into the church and found our seats in the front pew reserved for family members. I let my eyes drift across the first few rows of the church to the rest of my family. My uncle Mike, aunt Margaret and aunt Natalie, along with my many cousins and their children, were seated among us. Although the circumstances were incredibly sad, I smiled at the sight of the many relatives that I had known my entire life.

While I was growing up, we were such a large, close-knit family. All my childhood memories were branded with their faces. Every birthday, holiday and summer vacation spent at our family's lake cabin included them. My grandfather had been at the helm, the one who held us all together, despite where our lives seemed to steer us. It was hard not to notice how much we were all drifting away, caught up in our own lives, since Gramps had lost his strength to pull us as one. And now he was gone.

As I rested my back against the hard wooden pew, my eyes scanned the front of the church, taking in the beauty of the various colored flowers surrounding the altar—the deep red of the roses, the red and white amaryllis, the white calla lilies, and the beautiful array of yellow, pink and purple freesia. Suddenly my breath caught in my throat, and I froze, my eyes taking in more than my heart could bear. Marie must have felt this new tension within me and reached over to squeeze my hand. I could not turn away to look at her, my gaze fixed solely on what was only a mere ten feet from where I sat.

It was him.

He was sitting in a chair near the altar, facing us. He had his head bent down deep in thought. I would never mistake that hair for another's. A complete but beautiful mess of thick dark wavy locks. I knew instantly that he was nervous, as I watched him pull a long curl down over his forehead and roll it between his fingers. I knew more than I cared to remember about him. At that moment, he released the lock of hair in his fingers and looked up, his eyes squarely meeting mine, as if he had sensed that I was there. I should have known that I couldn't run forever, that there was something completely inevitable about the moment. The moment when my past caught up to me. I looked into his familiar blue eyes, lost in their depth, as it all came rushing back.

The Beginning

I strolled into Spanish class and sat down at my usual seat.
He was sitting in the desk next to me with a smug grin on his
face. Mrs. Samson, our Spanish teacher, instructed us to pair
up for conversation practice, and he immediately reached out
and pulled my desk over to him. I knew him well, as I know
everyone in this small town. But in my sixteen years of life
he had never paid that much attention to me, until now. I
looked over at him, shocked by his forwardness. He
introduced himself as Manuel, his Spanish name in class,
although his real name was Adam. He began sitting next to
me in this class a few weeks ago, which was the only class
that we had together, since he was a year older than me and
this was an elective.

His flirting was becoming more and more obvious,
and my playing-hard-to-get role was getting weaker every
day. He was the only guy that I had ever deemed beautiful—
knowing that this was not a label that most males were

comfortable with nor were they worthy of it. He was tall with an incredible athletic build, deep blue eyes, dark hair and a smile that reeked of confidence, but his matching deep-set dimples removed any trace of arrogance.

Feeling a bit flustered, I continued our conversation in Spanish and, after what seemed like several minutes, responded with my chosen Spanish name, Isabel. I blushed at the sound of his laugh, feeling like he had caught me getting lost in my own thoughts, hoping that he couldn't sense they were of him. I hated that he had this effect on me. He was "that" guy, and I was just me.

I had many close friends, and had dated a little here and there, but I wouldn't call myself popular. I was an average student, with great "academic potential" according to my guidance counselor. I had dabbled in sports when I was younger but decided that I wasn't coordinated enough to pursue anything seriously. Adam, on the other hand, was everything that I wasn't. He was popular, his flawless athletic ability placed him as a starter on all the varsity teams, and he was a great student. And of course, his yumminess attracted every female glance in the school. I didn't want to be one of "those" girls—the girl that swoons over him every time that he walks into a room. I had far too much self-respect for that, didn't I? If he wasn't so nice, it would be easier.

The flirting continued and eventually evolved to friendly lunch dates. Our high school had an open-campus policy, so we were free to drive to nearby food establishments for lunch. It was a relatively warm fall day. Adam was backing out of his parking space in the student lot. We were heading to lunch, as we had countless times before, and I was scanning through radio stations trying to find a good song to listen to on our short drive to the diner. Adam didn't seem to be himself; he was more uptight than usual and—if I didn't know any better—nervous.

"Can't you just leave it alone?" he asked, clearly

annoyed with my obsession to find the perfect song.

One of my habits that drove him absolutely crazy and usually earned a few minutes of harmless banter whenever we were in the car.

I gave him an eye roll and continued to scroll through the stations. Satisfied with the new Garth Brooks song that was playing, I turned up the volume and settled back in my seat.

Adam reached over and turned down the music a few seconds later.

"Hey, I like that song," I complained, as I batted his hand away from the volume control.

"Relax. I just wanted to talk for a minute."

I looked over at him, giving him my full attention. I was surprised by his serious tone. *This was new*, I thought to myself.

"So what do you think is going on here?" Adam asked. He reached over and placed his hand on my thigh, a more-than-friendly gesture that sent chills down my leg, as he glanced over at me.

"What do you mean?" I asked in return, not sure where he was going with his question.

"I mean, between us."

I could feel his hand brushing softly up and down my thigh. I instinctively put my hand on his, and he laced his fingers in mine. We were getting so comfortable with one another, but I still felt butterflies in my stomach every time that he was this close to me.

"I really like you and can't stop thinking about you. It drives me crazy to be around you and act like you're just my friend," he continued with a huge grin on his face. "I was just wondering if you felt the same way."

"Um…I'm definitely feeling the same way," I said a little too quietly as I swallowed the lump in my throat. I squeezed his hand reassuringly and could hardly contain the ridiculous grin that spread across my face or the warm blush that I felt on my cheeks.

He let out a loud sigh as he glanced back at the road. "Well, now that we've straightened that out, I was wondering if you wanted to go to homecoming with me? You don't already have a date, do you?"

Wow. Homecoming. "No date yet. I don't know though. I'll have to think about it," I teased, drumming my fingers against my lips, as if it was a difficult decision. I was ecstatic, but I wasn't about to let him know that. He playfully pinched the inside of my thigh as I squirmed away from him, trying hard to contain my laughter.

"Well, don't leave me hanging for too long."

Warmth spread throughout my insides as I took in his apprehensive expression. His feelings were becoming clearer by the minute.

He pulled into Susie's, our favorite lunch spot, a small diner known for its great burgers and shakes. After helping me out of the car, he grabbed my hand and led me inside to our usual booth. My best friend, Morgan, and Adam's friend, Rick, were already seated in the booth, waiting for us. They had become friends by default now that Adam and I were spending our lunchtime together. We ate as a group often, but most of the time Adam and I went to lunch on our own. I got the feeling that Adam preferred to be alone with me, but I felt much more comfortable when I had Mo— as I had nicknamed her years ago in elementary school—to help keep things on the lighter side.

"What took you guys so long?" Mo said with a teasing look in her eyes that only I would notice.

She had been interrogating me for days about what was going on between Adam and me, with my reply always the same. "Nothing, we're just friends." She had insisted that he had the "hots" for me, and, after Adam's conversation with me in the car, I knew that Mo was right. I still couldn't wrap my head around the idea that Adam was interested in me in that way, so I pushed aside these thoughts.

"Sorry, I had something important to ask Kendi, so I may have taken the long way to get here," Adam said.

"What was so important?" Mo asked with questioning eyes directed straight at me.

When I was silent, Adam filled her in. "I asked her to go to homecoming with me."

"Homecoming, huh?" Mo asked, raising her eyebrows at me.

Adam nearly interrupted her, admitting that I hadn't given him an answer yet and hinting that maybe she could convince me to go. Feeling completely embarrassed with the table's attention solely focused on me, I elbowed Adam in the ribs. He grunted, holding his side while flashing me a dramatic hurt expression. I rolled my eyes at him. Another habit of mine that drove him crazy.

"Why don't we all go together?" Rick suggested. Turning to face Morgan, who was sitting beside him in the booth, he lowered his voice to inflect a more sincere tone. "Morgan, will you go to homecoming with me?"

"I would love to go with you," Morgan said with perfect composure as we all laughed at Rick's lame proposal, although the look she flashed me screamed excitement. We both knew that she had been anything but impervious to his boyish charm and rugged good looks. She had been overly supportive of my new friendship with Adam, shamefully admitting to me her long-standing crush on Adam's best friend.

"Well, there you have it, Kendi. Now you have to go with me," Adam said, raising his hands in the air to imply that I didn't have a choice, his dimples melting me in my seat.

"Well, I guess if I have to…" I toyed with him in hopes that he knew that my answer was yes all along. I had already admitted that I liked him, but that was enough honesty for one day.

After lunch Mo whined about needing girl time and asked if she could drive me back to school. I watched the guys drive away in Adam's newer black BMW as I hopped into Mo's beat-up red Honda Civic. As soon as the doors were closed, she leaned back in her seat and let out a long sigh. "Oh, my God, do you know how awesome this is going to be?"

Morgan had been my best friend for as long as I could remember. She was pretty and full of contagious energy, always wearing a radiant smile. She had the most beautiful long blond hair, lying perfectly down her shoulders in large ringlets. I was always envious of her hair. While my dark hair was long with natural blonde highlights that most people would pay good money for, it was very fine and couldn't hold a curl despite how much product I tried to train it with. Morgan had flawless skin and eyes the color of the Caribbean Sea. She was the same height as me but a little heavier.

It was an ongoing joke between us that, if we could combine her face and hair with my body, we could be one helluva supermodel. I had been blessed—although at times it felt like more of a curse—with a body that would make a cast member of *Baywatch* proud. Not to say that my face didn't hold some sort of beauty, but I was very ordinary in the looks department.

Mo was very daring most of the time and was always convincing me to do crazy things with her. I think that this derived from her stern parents and strict upbringing. She was definitely rebelling against their authority at every turn. Typical teenage stuff I guess.

My mother was very open and trusting, and I lived on a much longer leash. That is not to say that I didn't get myself into a bit of trouble as well, but my mom was much more understanding than Mo's parents. My mother's one policy that was never to be broken was that I must always be honest with her. She loathed dishonesty and reminded me constantly that lying would always be my worst offense.

I think that my father had a lot to do with this. He wasn't a faithful husband, and his constant infidelity and lies were what ultimately had ended their marriage. He wasn't a very good father either, but I tried not to dwell on that. I was fortunate to have at least one dependable—and pretty amazing—parent who made up for my father's absence.

"Thank you," Mo said, kissing me on the cheek.

"For what?" I asked, wiping her lip gloss from my face.

"You know. Thanks to you, I'm going to homecoming with Rick."

"He asked you all on his own, Mo. That had nothing to do with me."

"Whatever." She shrugged. "What's with the playing-hard-to-get? We both know how much you like Adam. Come on, just admit it," she said, elbowing me in the arm. "You so want him."

I could not conceal the huge grin that swept across my face as I pictured Adam and me dancing close and spending an entire evening together. I could feel the heat brush across my cheeks again, and I tried not to look at her. Normally I wouldn't hesitate to tell Mo every thought that passed through my mind, but I was feeling very possessive of Adam for some reason, wanting to keep my relationship with him and all thoughts of him to myself.

I rolled my eyes at her buoyant prodding. "Can we just head back before we're late for English?"

"Fine," she huffed, feeling defeated. She started the car and as she pulled out into the street, we both erupted into a fit of giggles, unable to contain our happiness.

~

The rest of the week flew by. At lunch on Friday, Adam asked me if I wanted to hang out after his football game. We settled on watching a movie at my house. The idea of spending time with Adam outside of school and our daily lunches, under the cover of darkness, had my heart drumming in my chest the entire day.

It was an exciting football game. I sat with a group of friends and cheered on our team. Although inside I was giving silent cheers just for Adam. He was our starting quarterback, and his stellar performance won the game 24–7. I waited for him outside the locker room after the game, like he had asked me to. I was thankful for the mixed crowd of girls and boys waiting for the players to emerge; I hated to be one of "those girls" waiting for her jock boyfriend. "Those girls" that Mo and I usually mocked for their made-up-from-head-to-toe appearance and the way they shamelessly wore their boyfriends' letterman jackets, despite the obvious size issues. I wasn't much for clichés. Mo insisted on waiting with me. I think she really just wanted to see Rick. Whatever her reason, I was glad that she was there.

As Mo and I talked over our plans for the rest of the weekend, I heard cheering and looked up to see that the football team was starting to make their way out of the locker room. Adam walked out, searching the crowd, his mouth spreading into a huge grin when he spotted me. Walking over, he gave a few high-fives to friends as the cheering continued, but he kept his eyes locked on me. I held my breath as I took in the sight of him. His dark hair was wet and more wavy than usual; he was wearing loose jeans hanging low on his hips, a white linen shirt tucked in, sleeves rolled to the elbows. His eyes were shining under the outside lights of the gym, and his smile almost sent me over the edge.

I heard Mo mumble under her breath, "Someone's

gettin' some tonight!" and then pranced away in the direction of Rick's car. If I felt that I could turn from Adam's stare, I would have rolled my eyes at her, but he had me in a trance.

He approached me and unexpectedly put his arms around me, lifted me up in the air and twirled me around. I breathed in his clean scent and felt a little dizzy. I manage to tell him, "Great game," though he was squeezing me so tight it felt as if I couldn't breathe. Either that or his presence and smell alone had left me breathless. He set me down, mumbled, "Thanks," and led me to his car by the hand.

"So did you enjoy the game?" he asked once we were in his BMW.

"Yeah. You were amazing," I said, nervously running my fingers through my windblown hair.

"Thanks. The guys were all on fire tonight." He placed his warm hand on my leg and looked directly into my eyes. "Honestly, though, I couldn't wait for it to be over so that I could see you."

"Really?" I asked, surprised by his honesty, knowing that I had been counting the minutes until I could be alone with him as well.

"Really," he repeated softly as he turned toward me, gently placing his hand on the back of my neck, pulling my face closer to his. My breath quickened at his touch and the sudden realization that he was about to kiss me. He gently pressed his lips to mine and pulled back slightly, grinning, waiting for my reaction. I was frozen in place, except for my heart, which was beating quick and heavy, giving me away. *Traitor.* He brushed his thumb across my cheek, and I felt his lips against mine again but much firmer this time as he separated my lips with his own. I closed my eyes and began to kiss him back as I felt his tongue slide in and gently stroke the inside of my mouth. And just when I felt I could kiss him like this forever, he pulled back, kissing me softly on the cheek.

Turning his attention to starting the car, he smiled and asked if we should head to my house. I mumbled some kind of response as he reached into the backseat and grabbed three movies, which he placed in my lap. I was still trying to catch my breath as he explained that he wasn't sure what kind of movie I liked, so he had rented a chick flick, a comedy and an action thriller. On the short drive to my house, we decided on the comedy, as it would require the least of our attention.

Mo's earlier comment flashed through my mind as I wondered what his intentions were tonight. I suddenly felt nervous. I'd had my fair share of make-out sessions, sometimes taking things a little too close for my comfort, but I had never actually gone all the way. I had never dated anyone who I felt that close to.

I knew that Adam was definitely not a virgin. I remember the infamous relationship he had had with Summer Jenkins during his freshman year. It had been a hot topic, because she was a senior. She had graduated in my older sister's class. Adam was a starter on the varsity boys' basketball team as a freshman, and that had got Summer's attention. She wasn't exactly a prude, if you know what I mean. Adam had dated two other girls that I knew of. I wasn't sure what he had heard about me, but I definitely wasn't Summer Jenkins.

My house was dark when we arrived, except for the light over the kitchen sink which was always on. I turned on the overhead lights in the kitchen and living room and spotted a note on the counter from my mother. "Well, it looks like we have the house to ourselves for a while. My mom and Scott are at the Tyson's playing cards," I said, immediately regretting it. He raised his eyebrows at me suggestively, and I rolled my eyes back at him trying to diffuse the sexual vibe in the air.

I gave him a quick tour of my house. The kitchen, living room, family room and the upstairs bedrooms—more importantly, my bedroom. He stood in my room looking at the wall of pictures of my friends and family that were displayed, laughing at the ridiculous pictures of Mo and me ranging from the age of eight until now. He walked over to my CD collection and looked through it, noting all the ones we had in common. He then walked back over to where I was standing in the center of the room watching him, pulled me into a hug and whispered into my ear, "I like your room."

Feeling his warm breath on my ear, I reached up and clasped my hands around the back of his neck. He was so tall that I had to arch my neck to look up at him, but he saw my intent and lowered his face to mine, as our lips pressed together again. I kissed him slowly at first, gently opening my mouth and accepting his tongue. I stroked his tongue with mine, and he pulled me closer to him. My heart was beating so fast. I felt his hands resting on my lower back, his thumbs drawing circles on my skin under my shirt. I ran my fingers through his hair, and I heard him moan softly. He started to walk me backward toward my bed, our lips still exploring.

I didn't want to stop kissing him, but, knowing that I didn't want this to go any further, I pulled back and mumbled, barely able to speak, "We should probably start the movie. It's getting late." He cleared his throat and released me only to grab my hand and lead me downstairs. As I started the movie, Adam slipped off his shoes and leaned back on the couch, as if he had been to my house a hundred times before. I liked that he felt so comfortable with me.

He reached out for me and pulled me down to sit between his legs. With my back against him, I laid my head on his shoulder. We sat like this in silence for a while, watching the movie. I couldn't concentrate on anything, only the rise and fall of his chest, and the feel of his breath against my neck. I don't think that he was really watching the movie either, because he suddenly asked me about my dad, motioning toward a family portrait on a table next to us.

I usually didn't like to talk about that subject, but I felt comfortable with him in that moment, and I sensed I could trust him. So I told him about my dad's affairs, his drinking and my parents' divorce. I told him that I only saw my dad once every few years, whenever he decided to grace us with his presence. How he had moved around from place to place: Seattle, San Francisco, Las Vegas and finally Corpus Christi, Texas.

In return Adam told me about what it was like to grow up with three brothers and loyal parents. How he loved to play sports, especially basketball—his favorite—but how sometimes the pressure that his dad put on him to win was overwhelming. He told me that his family was very involved in their church, and they attended several times a week. Adam didn't go to parties usually, because he didn't drink. He wasn't even supposed to start dating until he turned seventeen, which was a few months ago. He kept most things from his parents, because they were really strict and their church didn't allow it.

I was intrigued learning so much about him for the first time, even though I have grown up alongside him in this small town. I talked about Mo and our crazy adventures over the years. He laughed as I told him about the time Mo and I made a video of ourselves and sent it in to a contest, trying to win a meet-and-greet with one of our favorite rock bands. We had tried to appear like we were in college, the video taking on more of a comical effect than an attempt to win a serious contest. We hadn't won, unsurprisingly.

We had made friends with the local radio station DJs —more likely we annoyed them to the point that they knew exactly who we were—who granted us access into the station to help select the song line-ups, awarding us with backstage passes to most of the concerts we attended and always giving us the bands itinerary, complete with hotel locations. Adam found this fascinating. We talked like this for what seemed like hours, until he looked at his watch and realized that he was going to be late getting home by his curfew. I walked him to the door, and he gave me a sweet, gentle kiss on the lips. Whispering good-bye in my ear and giving my hand a firm squeeze, he turned and headed out into the dark.

I was beaming as I closed the door and walked upstairs to my room. Adam was so sexy and yet sweet at the same time. I fell asleep dreaming of his face.

Firsts

In the weeks leading up to homecoming, Adam and I found every minute possible in our crazy schedules to see each other. Weekdays we rarely went to bed without talking on the phone, and we spent plenty of time during school writing each other notes. Adam usually wrote me letters filled with compliments and words to describe how much he was thinking of me. He could be really sweet. Lunch seemed to end each day with a make-out session in his car, leaving me breathless and flustered while I rushed to English class. The weekends we spent going to the movies or hanging out at my house. My mother adored Adam. He had won her over by playing a very complex classical piece on our piano. My mother, an accomplished pianist herself, could appreciate his talent. I listened in amazement, wondering if there was anything that he didn't excel at.

It was a Saturday evening, the first time he had invited me to his house for dinner. I had not officially met his parents, although I knew them from a distance. It was impossible to live in this town and not know everyone. His mom was an excellent cook and clearly enjoyed pleasing her family with her culinary skills, as she graciously accepted our compliments.

His mother was sweet but a little intense; his father was funny and lovable, much like Adam. Adam resembled his father. They were both tall and muscular with the same deep blue eyes and thick wavy hair, although his father's hair was handsomely gray. Adam's three brothers were there too. His two older brothers lived nearby and were visiting for the weekend. One had just graduated from college and the other was a junior at WSU.

His younger brother, Josh, was a freshman at our school, and I was getting to know him pretty well. He was friendly and very innocent, unlike Adam. He stood an inch taller than Adam and looked more like their mother. He had her straight light-colored hair—that he wore a bit long and shaggy—and her hazel eyes. After dinner I helped his mom with the dishes while we chatted about my family, hobbies and what I wanted to do after high school.

We ended the evening playing cards at the dinner table. They taught me how to play hearts, and I was the constant focus of their laughter as I fumbled my way through the game. On the drive home, Adam told me how much his family loved me but complained that he was having a hard time keeping his hands off me. He didn't touch me the entire time we were there, but he made up for that when we were in the car.

Our football team won the homecoming game, and Adam was ecstatic. The team went out to celebrate, and I went to Mo's house with a few of our friends to eat pizza and watch music videos. We spent the evening planning out our attire for the dance the following night. It was informal this year. The theme was Fishing in the Dark, and we had all decided on wearing blue jeans and boots. I chose my favorite pair of jeans that sat low on my hips, a black flowing top that showed off my cleavage and my black-heeled boots.

The night of the dance Mo and I were getting ready at her house, singing along to our favorite grunge band. She had hot rollers in my long hair and was carefully applying my eye makeup. "I hate you for looking so good in those jeans, you skinny bitch," Mo complained as she recapped a tube of black mascara.

"Oh, please. You look totally hot tonight. Your hair is amazing," I said, feeling a hint of jealously for her perfect blond tresses. She had decided to wear a short denim skirt with her worn brown cowboy boots. She looked perfect.

"Well, when I'm done with you, your hair will look amazing too!" She removed the rollers from my hair, combing through it with her fingers as she coated it with hair spray. When she was done, she stood back to admire her masterpiece. "Adam is going to go nuts over you tonight."

I stood and looked at my reflection in Mo's full-length mirror. I looked tall and thin—my heeled boots giving me just enough height—while my skin was still deeply tan from the long summer, even though fall was upon us, threatening to bring snow by Halloween. My green eyes stood out with the colors that Mo had used on my lids, my full lips brushed with a subtle pink gloss, and my hair was shiny and long with full perfect curls. I felt beautiful.

"Wow, nice work, Mo!" Standing next to her, we both glanced in the mirror; I put my arm around her and gave her a quick hug. "Thank you. I love it."

When the boys arrived, we ran to the car giggling like the two giddy schoolgirls that we were.

~

From the moment we stepped out of the car, Adam had his

hands on me, and they stayed there for the duration of the dance. He was either holding my hand or had his arm wrapped around my waist, as if he had some claim on me. I didn't mind; I felt proud to be his date. With each slow song, Adam pulled me into his arms and held me close as we swayed to the music.

"You look beautiful tonight," Adam whispered against my ear as we danced. His hands were gripping my hips, holding me close. Our bodies were molded against each other from the chest down, my hands wrapped around his neck as I twirled his dark hair in my fingers.

"Thanks. You don't look so bad yourself," I said, burying my face against his chest to hide my burning cheeks. He leaned in and kissed me on the neck, setting fire to my insides. I couldn't remember ever having been this affected by someone before. Adam had gotten under my skin, and I feared for my heart and where it all might lead.

We left the dance early and drove to our friend Jeff's house. His parents were out of town, so he had invited most of the junior and senior class to a party. When we arrived, we were immediately assaulted by the smell of booze and cigarette smoke. Jeff handed each of us a beer as he shouted a loud welcome over the blaring music. Adam looked uncomfortable, and I remembered that he didn't drink.

I set down our full beers on the table and grabbed his hand. "Hey, come with me," I said, leading him into Jeff's bedroom. I closed and locked the door, muting the loud music and rising voices. "I'm sorry. I forgot that you don't do parties or drinking. Is it okay that we're here?"

"Yeah, I'm fine," he assured me. "Rick really wanted to come, and I told him that I would drive."

"Well, we can hang out in here until he's ready to go," I said, standing with my back pressed against the door.

"Are you okay with that?" he asked hesitantly.

"Of course. I just want to spend time with you

anyway," I said as I reached for his hands, interlacing our fingers.

And with that said, he pulled me into his arms. I felt so small and fragile wrapped up in his long limbs. He was wearing a black shirt that clung to his chest, and I could feel his strong physique underneath it. I wrapped my arms around his waist and buried my head in his chest. He pulled up my chin so that our gazes met. "You look so good tonight. I was getting jealous watching every guy in the room check you out while we were dancing. You have no idea the effect you have on me—and every other guy, for that matter."

"You're so crazy, Adam," I said, shaking my head as I felt a blush spread across my cheeks. I had never been good at accepting compliments.

"Only because you make me that way, Kendi." He suddenly picked me up and threw me over his shoulder, softly spanking me on the bottom. I screamed and started laughing hysterically. He threw me down in the middle of Jeff's queen-size bed, straddled me and started to tickle my sides. He knew that it drove me mad. I tried to wiggle free, but he had me pinned. I pleaded for him to stop through my uncontrolled laughter, and he finally gave in.

Placing a hand on either side of my head, he leaned down and kissed me. First on the lips and then my chin, my neck, trailing his tongue up to my ear. It sent shivers down my spine. He gently nibbled on my earlobe as I reached underneath his shirt and ran my hands up his back. He sat up and pulled his shirt over his head, throwing it to the floor. I admired his chiseled chest and abs as he rolled onto his side facing me, his head propped up in his hand.

Looking into my eyes, he trailed his other hand slowly up underneath my black top, leaving fire in its wake. I felt his hand cup my breast through my bra, as he leaned down to kiss me. My body burned at his touch, and I could almost hear my own heartbeat. I tried to slow my breath while I concentrated on his tongue exploring the inside of my mouth. I felt his thumb graze my nipple underneath the lace of my bra. He rolled onto his back, pulling me on top of him, his tongue stroking the roof of my mouth.

I rose up and straddled him so that I could pull my top off over my head, and then I lay down on top of him. The feel of Adam's bare skin against mine alerted every one of my senses, and I wanted to feel more of him. Adam ran his hands along my back and unclasped my bra, taking it down over my arms as he kissed my shoulder. He pulled me up higher and took my nipple into his mouth. Not able to contain the pleasure that Adam unleashed, I moaned. He flipped me onto my back again and rolled slightly toward me, placing his leg between mine. I could feel his hip digging into my flesh through our jeans; his hand ran along my side, his lips urgently pressed against mine. I sensed a raw hunger rising in me. I had never wanted or needed anything as much as I did him in that moment. His own need for me pressed against my side.

As if reading my mind, he started to unbutton my jeans. My breath caught in my throat, and he pulled his mouth from mine to look into my eyes. I knew that he needed to know if this was what I wanted. I nodded, and pulled his mouth back to mine, running my hands through his hair. He finished with the buttons on my jeans and pulled them down past my hips. Softly caressing my most sensitive flesh through the sheer fabric of my panties, he rolled on top of me. He pressed his hips down on me, his own hard flesh replacing his hand, and I gasped at the sudden ache building inside me.

I reached down to work on his jeans, suddenly feeling too much fabric between us. He kicked off his shoes, and I helped him pull his pants and boxers down his legs, his lips never leaving mine. I could feel the smooth skin of his erection against me, and nerves pooled in my gut. He pulled away, kneeling at my feet as he removed my boots and finished removing my jeans from my body. He reached into the pocket of his jeans and pulled out a condom before shucking them over his feet and to the floor. He pulled a blanket over the top of us as he lay down next to me. His lips met mine more gently this time as he brushed my hair away from my face.

"Are you sure you want to do this?" he whispered in my ear.

"Yes," I said between breaths. He reached down and fumbled with the condom, and I heard the party going on outside the room for the first time. Until this moment I had forgotten where we were, caught up in the intensity of his touch. "Adam, this is my first time."

"I know. Don't worry. I won't hurt you." He rolled over, spreading my legs open with his so that he could lie between them. He hovered above me, kissing me intensely, his mouth moving to graze his teeth along my neck and shoulder. I moaned and arched my hips up toward him. He brought his lips back to my mouth, lightly biting my lower lip, and I ached for him. He slowly lowered his hips and gently placed himself inside of me. I cried out softly from the relief and from the pain.

"Oh, God, Kendi," he moaned. He moved slowly, circling his hips and then deepening himself inside me gently, sweetly, keeping his promise. It felt incredible, a battle between pleasure and pain. I closed my eyes and took in every sensation. Adam's breathing heavy at my ear, on my neck. The dew rising on our skin as we moved against each other. I ran my hands along his back, feeling his hard body under my fingers. Adam's hands were everywhere, caressing my breast, my side, my hip, as he continued to move inside of me. He started moving harder, faster, and I could feel his breath quicken. He moaned my name against my ear, and then he thrust himself deep inside me until he collapsed on top of me, trying to catch his breath.

After a few minutes, he pulled his weight off me and brushed the hair back from my face again, wiping the beads of sweat from my brow. "Are you okay?" he asked sincerely.

"Yeah, I'm great," I breathed, barely a whisper.

"Your skin is so soft, like silk," he said as he trailed his hand over my flat stomach. "I already want more of you, and I was just inside you a few minutes ago." He groaned and buried his head into the sensitive space between my neck and shoulder. I ran my hands through his curls as he placed gentle kisses on my neck. But knowing that the party was in full swing and that we couldn't hide forever, Adam reluctantly got up and handed me my clothes. I felt a little sore as I moved around to get dressed. I knew tomorrow would be worse.

Fully dressed I pulled my long locks back into a ponytail in an attempt to tame my wild hair. Adam finished getting dressed and pulled me into a hug. "You're incredible, Kendi. And I'm not talking about what we just did, although that was incredible too." He brushed his lips against mine. I wrapped my arms around his waist as we held each other, holding on to the moment for a little bit longer before we joined the party to find Rick and Morgan.

"Are you guys ready to go?" I asked Mo as I approached a table where she was playing a drunken game of quarters with Rick and a few others.

"Yeah, sure, right after I sink this last shot." She smiled as I heard the quarter *clink*, landing in the shot glass. "Score," she yelled, raising her arms in the air as the guys at the table all guzzled down their beers.

We said our good-byes and headed out to the car. I shivered as the cold air hit my face.

I slid into the backseat next to Mo, and the boys sat up front. I sat quietly staring out the window, lost in my own thoughts, as the other voices in the car faded into the background. Replaying in my head the intimate moments that I had just shared with Adam, I felt myself blush and brought my hand to my mouth to conceal the elation splayed across my face.

When Adam pulled up in front of my house, the boys both jumped out and opened the back doors for us, abruptly pulling me from my thoughts. As Adam and I walked to my front door, I saw Rick push Mo back against the car and kiss her on the mouth. I was thinking about how excited Mo must be when my thoughts were interrupted by Adam pulling me into his chest, his arms wrapped around me, holding both of my hands behind my back. "Everything okay?" he asked, genuinely concerned. "You were awfully quiet in the car." He leaned down and kissed me delicately on the lips before I could respond.

"Mmm, I'm fine. I wish that you didn't have to go," I managed to mumble.

"Me too," he moaned against my lips. "I'll call you tomorrow?" he said with a questioning tone. With that he released me and walked toward the car, yelling out, "Hey, Rick, keep it in your pants, we're late!" By the way that Mo was stumbling up the porch, I was relieved that she was staying at my house and not the other way around.

"Soooo," Mo questioned while we were putting on our pajamas in my room a few minutes later. "Where were you guys, and what were you doing?"

"Nowhere and nothing," I deflected, wanting to keep my amazing night to myself just a little bit longer. Turning the attention to her, I asked what was going on with her and Rick. She beamed and told me about her night. How he had told her how much he liked her, how much fun they had together and of course his dramatic kiss good-night. I was relieved that she was happy doing all the talking. When she had finished with her recap, I wished her good-night and rolled away from her. There was no way that I could sleep with visions of Adam's naked body replaying in my mind.

Just when I thought that Morgan had dozed off, she asked bluntly, "Kendi, did you sleep with him?"

"Yes," I said, then sighed after several seconds had passed. "And it was so incredible. He was really sweet, and he has the most amazing body."

"Do you love him?"

"I don't know. I'm not sure what that feels like, but I have definitely never felt like this before, ever."

"Sounds like love." Mo yawned as she drifted off to sleep.

Love

The fall flew by, and, before I knew it, winter was upon us and with it the cold and snow. And of course basketball. Adam's schedule was even more intense with late practices and multiple games each week. I was his biggest cheerleader. I couldn't get enough of watching him play. He was the top scorer in nearly every game, and it didn't hurt that he looked incredibly sexy in his uniform. Watching him rip his warm-up pants from his body—the snaps along the outer seams breaking open simultaneously to reveal his bare muscular legs—was worth attending each and every game alone.

We had to get very creative with our schedules, carving out time in the day to see each other. We still had lunch every day, but we also skipped our sixth period Independent Studies class to spend time together. We usually parked his car on a deserted road and had sex in the backseat. Since homecoming we couldn't seem to keep our hands off each other. Although many times we would just sit in his car with the heat blasting and talk. We talked about how much he enjoyed farming. His family owned and operated a large successful wheat farm, which was a common way of life where we lived.

My great grandparents had been wheat farmers as well, and, while most of the family were happy to take over the family business, my grandfather had had other plans. He had gone to college and earned a business degree, starting a small car dealership in hopes to do something different with his life. So while my immediate family was not earning a living from a local crop, most everyone who lived here was. Adam loved the lifestyle and was prepared to return to run the family business after completing college. I wasn't surprised but could not share in his enthusiasm about coming back here after college. I couldn't wait to escape the limits of this small town. I was ready for something else entirely.

We talked about how much I enjoyed writing poetry and short stories. How I would love to pursue a degree in English, but my true passion was medicine. I was a humanitarian at heart, even at a young age. My mother often teased me, reminding me that I couldn't save everyone, when I had the overwhelming desire to cure world hunger or cancer after watching the nightly news or an ad about starving children in Ethiopia.

This desire, combined with my ambitious need to do something better—to be better than what I had known, successful enough to escape small-town life—led me to the idea of medicine. My first experience with the medical field in my freshman year sealed the deal for me. I had blown out my knee during a soccer game—probably due to my lack of coordination again. It had been a pretty severe injury, which required multiple X-rays, MRIs and eventually surgery. I became fascinated with orthopedics and radiology, and thus became my dream of becoming a doctor one day.

Adam wanted to pursue a degree in agriculture or

business, but he really wanted to play basketball and was hoping for a scholarship. He had applied to several schools in and out of the state. I was selfishly hoping that he landed a scholarship somewhere close by. I didn't want to think about Adam leaving for college or what would happen next year when he did, regardless of how much distance would separate us.

~

The crowd around me was cheering loudly, but I stood silently still, nervous for Adam as the tied score glared red from the scoreboard, the clock ticking, leaving only minutes in the game. Adam received another foul and was pulled out of the game, his younger brother, Josh, taking his place. I knew this would only add to his frustration. Josh was a freshman but was getting plenty of playing time on the varsity team. Although Adam never talked about it with me, I could tell that he was more than a little bothered by it.

Josh was an asset to the team, but, when they were playing side by side, it was hard not to notice the tension. The brotherly competition often elevated to the point that they appeared to be playing against each other rather than on the same team. On a rebound Josh sunk the ball, and the crowd went wild. The other team scored as well, tying the game once again. With seconds left on the clock, Josh banked a three-point shot. And that ended the game. The buzzer was barely audible over the roaring crowd.

As the two teams shook hands, the crowd rushed the court to congratulate the boys. Mo and I followed the stream of people inching toward the players as they made their way in the direction of the locker room. Adam always waited for me before retreating to the showers, but, tonight, for the first time, he wasn't there. I shrugged and followed Mo over to the rest of the guys. After telling Rick what an incredible game he had played, I walked over to congratulate Josh on his winning shot.

"Hey, great game!"

He thanked me, wrapping me up in a big sweaty hug.

"Ew, gross, Josh, you're all sweaty."

"Sorry." He laughed, rubbing his forehead with his hand and purposely wiping more sweat on the back of my shirt.

I instinctively punched him in the arm, as I would with my own brother, and called out, "See ya later," as I made my way through the crowd to find Mo.

Twenty minutes later Mo and I were sitting among a much smaller crowd, clearly the last to leave the gym, as we waited for Adam.

"Can't you just call him later?" Mo whined, not wanting to wait around the gym when we had better places to be. "You know that he is going home after this."

She was right, but I couldn't leave without seeing him first. I knew that Adam would have to head home so that his dad could go over the game with him while it was still fresh in his mind. Adam was always so bothered by this. His dad caught the whole game on video so that he could critique Adam's performance afterward. And after watching Adam gain four personal fouls, I knew that his dad would have plenty to say.

Adam finally emerged from the locker room, looking awfully sexy in his faded jeans and wet hair, but I could see in his eyes that he was upset. He was so hard on himself. They had just won the game, and he was the top scorer by far, but he still wasn't happy.

He walked over to me, and I threw my arms around him while I congratulated him on a great game. He just stood there with his gym bag slung over his shoulder, arms at his sides. He seemed distant and cold.

"Hey, what's wrong?" I asked quietly.

He pulled my arms away from his body and led me around the corner where we had more privacy. "Nothing. I have to head home. I'm sure that my dad is waiting for me."

He was avoiding looking me in the eyes, so I reached up and cupped his cheek until his blue gaze met mine. "Adam, clearly something is wrong. Why didn't you wait for me tonight?"

He pulled my hand away from his face and shrugged. "I was just frustrated with the way I played tonight. We may have won, but it was not my best game." His face tensed as he continued. "And as if I didn't have enough on my mind, I see you cozying up with my brother. What the hell was that all about?" he asked with an accusatory tone.

"Are you serious?" I asked, stunned at what he was insinuating. "He's like a little brother to me, Adam. I was congratulating him on his winning shot."

"Just because he banked a few shots doesn't mean he won the game. I scored most of those points," he quickly pointed out, practically jumping down my throat.

I was taken aback by his obvious resentment of his brother, and the jealous and hurtful tone that he was directing toward me. It was infuriating, and I could feel the heat spreading over my face from my anger. "Yes, I know, Adam. You're being a little ridiculous right now," I said, practically shooting daggers at him with my eyes. "I'm gonna go. Mo's waiting for me. I'll talk to you tomorrow. Hopefully you'll be in a better mood then." I started to walk away, but he grabbed my arm, pulling me against him.

"I'm sorry, Kendi. I shouldn't take my frustration out on you," he whispered in my ear, stroking my hair down my back with his hand. "I just can't stand to see you touching anyone else, especially my brother."

I pulled away from him. "Well, you should have a little more faith in me," I replied with an edge in my voice, clearly still upset by his remarks.

"Where are you girls headed anyway?" he asked, blatantly ignoring my comment.

"We're going to Amber's house for a bit and then home. Mo's staying over." I folded my arms across my chest, defiantly.

"Kendi, please don't drink tonight. You know I hate it when you go to parties."

"Have faith, remember? I can take care of myself." I kissed him on the cheek and walked away. I was feeling irritable from our conversation and couldn't get out of there fast enough. I knew I could be stubborn and overly independent—as my mother pointed out repeatedly—but he could also be very jealous and controlling. This was not always the best mix of personality flaws. I cared about him though, and I didn't want to say anything hurtful that I would regret, so walking away was clearly the best option.

And just to spite him, I drank four wine coolers at Amber's house before Mo and I went home. If I was lucky, he would be in a "Don't ask, don't tell" mood when I talked to him the following day.

~

Adam and I recovered from our little feud quickly. It wasn't the first, and I was sure that it wouldn't be the last either. We couldn't seem to stay mad at each other for long. It took just one touch of his hand or a quick brush of his lips to ignite the fire that burned in me, leaving behind any trace of frustration that I may have felt. Our relationship was passionate, meaning that the highs and lows were extreme, but I couldn't imagine it any other way.

A few weeks later I was sitting in a chair outside the guidance counselor's office waiting to see about next quarter's registration, when Josh came bounding up and sat beside me.

"Hey," he whispered.

"Hey yourself," I whispered back.

"You waiting to see Mr. Shelby?" he asked as he fidgeted with a piece of paper in his hand.

"Yep. I have to go over my schedule for next quarter, trying to make the best of my pre-reqs. What about you?"

"I don't know. I got a note that he wanted to see me. Probably about the game this weekend." He held up the paper in his hand, and I nodded. Mr. Shelby was also the boys' basketball coach.

"How's everything going with Adam?"

"Great, why do you ask?"

"I was just curious. He's been really moody lately, and I thought maybe you two were having issues."

"No, everything's fine. I mean, we definitely have our fair share of disagreements but nothing serious. Adam was pretty bent out of shape a few weeks ago when you and I were chatting after one of the games. He doesn't seem to like us hanging out," I added, instantly feeling guilty as the words left my lips. Adam would probably feel a sense of betrayal from this conversation that I was having with his brother.

"Really? That's weird. You're like the sister that I never had! And besides he knows I'm seeing someone."

"What? Since when? I thought that you weren't supposed to date for another year or so?" I asked, totally shocked that I had not known about this and happy that I could redirect the conversation.

"We're keeping it quiet, because my parents would kill me if they knew. But I've been seeing Katie Brewster since basketball started."

I let this information seep in as I tried to picture Katie with Josh. She was cute but in a very simple athletic way. She was a senior and could be nice when she wanted to be. I thought that she was nice anyway; Mo thought otherwise. Mo had it out for Katie, some kind of rivalry over a guy. Mo couldn't understand why anyone would be interested in Katie when she "looked like a dog," as Mo so bluntly put it. She even went as far as placing a can of Alpo dog food in Katie's locker once a week for several months. Of course Katie still to this day had no idea who the culprit was. I tried to stifle a laugh as I thought about how crazy Mo could be sometimes.

"What's so funny?" Josh asked, pulling my thoughts back to our conversation.

"Nothing. I just can't believe that I didn't know. It's nearly impossible to have a secret around here."

"Well..." He was about to say something but was interrupted by Mr. Shelby calling my name. "Don't say anything," he quickly whispered as I waved good-bye and followed Mr. Shelby into the office.

I couldn't help myself though. That afternoon Adam and I were sitting on the couch at my house, and I asked him why he didn't tell me about Josh and Katie.

"I didn't think anything of it. It's really just an innocent fling. It's not like they're sleeping together or anything." He shrugged, feigning indifference.

"Well, it's kind of exciting. It's Josh's first girlfriend," I said while I stroked Adam's fingers with mine. In one quick move he had me on my back on the couch, his body pressing against mine.

"Can we not talk about my brother right now? I have practice in an hour," he said in a sultry voice, warming my insides.

"What would you like to talk about?" I whispered while nibbling on his earlobe.

"I happen to have a few things that I'd like to... discuss." He smiled at me, his dimples melting me in place as he rocked his pelvis against mine. I giggled at what he implied as he kissed my neck seductively. We spent the hour like this, playfully kissing and touching on the couch.

"You're killing me, Kendi," he teased, as he stood up

and adjusted his obvious arousal. "I have to go to practice now and burn off some sexual frustration." He leaned down to kiss me, and I pulled him back on top of me, kissing him more intensely. He felt so good against my body, warm and comfortable. I hated to see him leave.

"I. Have. To. Go," he tried to say with his lips pressed against mine, as I held his head firmly in my hands.

"Please stay," I begged. "I'll make it worth your while," I added, moving my hands to the clasp of his jeans, the tips of my fingers just barely grazing the skin under the waistband of his boxers.

"I can't be late for practice," he groaned, clearly torn with his decision. He gently removed himself from my grip and sat on the couch next to me, pulling me up into his lap. He drew me into his arms and kissed me tenderly on the mouth, stroking my hair softly with his hand. "I wish I could stay with you, believe me," he whispered, pulling back slightly to look into my eyes. "But I really have to go."

"I know, but it was worth a try," I sulked, as he set me on my feet. I walked him to the door and paused to kiss him again, reluctant to say good-bye.

~

After placing second in the state championships, Adam was offered a basketball scholarship at Gonzaga University, which was only an hour away. He was so excited to have the opportunity to play basketball in a program with such integrity and yet still be close to me. I was so proud of him but secretly was nervous about next year. I tried to push away any negative thoughts that I had about him leaving for school. He would only be an hour away, but we were heading in two different directions next year, and I had watched many other couples grow apart in similar circumstances.

I was starting to look at colleges for the following

year, and none of them were close. I had always planned on getting as far away as possible from this town, without having to pay out-of-state tuition. I wasn't sure about my future or our future together, but I was sure that I was in love with Adam McCoy, and I couldn't imagine my life without him.

It was a weekday; a snowstorm the night before had left the school no choice but to declare a "snow day." Adam drove his dad's truck, armed with snow chains, to my house so that we could take full advantage of a whole day together while my mom was at work. I was alone in the house except for my brother, Scott, who was glued to the television armed with enough junk food to last the entire day. When I answered the door, Adam lured me outside and then pummeled me with one snowball after another. I screamed in surprise from his attack.

I jumped off the porch, determined to get him back. It wasn't long before our clothes were damp and our fingers numb from handling the snow without gloves. We ran inside, breathless, seeking an escape from the cold. We ended up in the shower, together, our wet clothes left in a pile on the bathroom floor. It was the most intimate I had ever been with someone, yet I felt so relaxed and comfortable with him. We took turns washing each other's hair and running soap over our bodies, eventually fulfilling our need for one another when we could no longer deny it.

Pressing my back against the cold tile, he wrapped my legs around his hips, burying himself inside me until we both found our release, Adam pulling away at the last second. When the water started to run cold, we dried ourselves off and went in search of dry clothes. An hour later, Adam and I were lying on the floor in my living room in front of a blazing fire, trying to thaw our hands and feet, still cold after our snowball fight despite the heat from the shower.

We were on our backs looking up at the ceiling, our

fingers laced together on top of my chest, talking quietly. He rolled onto his stomach, propped up on his elbows, looking intently into my eyes. I felt him tuck a strand of my still damp hair behind my ear, his finger lingering on my cheek, as he traced the outline of my jaw.

"Kendi, I just want you to know that I love you. I truly and honestly love you. I've never felt this way about anyone before," he said softly, his deep blue eyes searching mine for a response.

"I love you too, Adam."

He rolled on top of me, kissing me on the mouth, as I ran my hands through his hair.

Nothing else seemed to exist as I lost myself in him.

I felt so happy, confident that, whatever our plans, we would always be like this, as we were in that one moment. Just us against the world.

Reality

I heard his voice, and it wasn't just in my head. He was here, welcoming everyone and leading us in prayer. The robe he wore bore truth to what he was, the choices that he had made. And seeing him in the flesh, standing in front of me with our memories fresh in my mind, brought back the truth of what I had done and the choices that I had made. And in this moment I felt the deep loss of many things, not just my grandfather. I began to cry softly, tears running down my cheeks. Marie handed me a tissue, and I gently wiped my eyes, but the tears continued to flow. I could hardly follow what Adam was saying while he spoke about my grandfather's life and death, but Adam's voice filled my ears and my mournful heart.

It was time for me to speak, and I tried to calm myself, so that I could get through it with a little bit of grace. I approached the altar, avoiding eye contact with him as he sat down. He was so close, I felt my knees shake. In deep concentration I fought against all thoughts of him and focused on the sheet of paper in front of me. In a shaky voice I began to read aloud the words that I had written. I could feel Adam's eyes on me while I read the beautiful reflection of my grandfather and his life as I knew it. I held back tears as I thought about all the wonderful memories that I had of my gramps and how much I would miss him.

I felt regret for the years that I had stayed away, wrapped up in my own life's tragedies. The last time that I had seen him was a year ago, at my grandmother's funeral, and, before that, I had only visited a handful of times during college, my visits getting less frequent after my move to California. I always blamed it on my busy schedule. I was, after all, an overworked and underpaid radiology resident, which left very little time for family and friends. I knew that wasn't the entire reason that I stayed away, but those reasons were buried deep inside my heart, and I couldn't think of them now. I knew that my grandpa was proud of me. My mother said that he spoke of me often, always sure to mention that I was a "doctor," though I had a few years to go before I practiced within my specialty. I wonder if he would still be proud of me if he knew all the choices that I had made.

As I finished speaking and made my way back to my seat, I looked across the room. It was large with wooden beams stretched across the length of the cathedral ceilings; carefully etched stained-glass windows cast a rainbow of colors across the space from the light of the sun shining through. I felt an ache in my heart as I remembered a hot summer day that I had spent in this very room nearly twelve years ago and the agonizing year that followed.

Crash

The summer after Adam's graduation brought us closer together. I think that we both felt the approaching doom that his departure for college was going to bring to our relationship. We made every minute count. I was busy waiting tables at the restaurant where I had worked every summer since starting high school. It was easy money, and I enjoyed the customers, which varied from our regulars that came in every day to the summer travelers who were just passing through. I was saving every penny I earned for college.

Adam was working for his parents, gearing up for the annual harvest in midsummer, which was the busiest time of year in our little town. His shifts usually started at dawn, keeping him busy until late in the evening. Between his long workdays and my late dinner shifts, it was hard to find time to spend together. Adam often stopped by the restaurant after the dinner rush and sat at the counter sipping a soda, hoping to spend a few minutes with me between customers.

When I had the occasional weekend off, we would drive to the city for dinner and a movie, sometimes with Rick and Mo in tow. They had been dating off and on since homecoming. I couldn't keep up with all the drama in their relationship, but the four of us always had a great time together. Mo and I went out almost every night after I closed the restaurant. She was getting excited about starting our senior year. I would probably be more excited if I wasn't so worried about Adam and me spending the year apart.

It was early August. Mo and I had convinced our parents to let us drive to Seattle to stay with our friend Shelly, who was starting her junior year at Seattle University. We had planned to tour Seattle U and the University of Washington—Udub—while we were there. We spent most of the three-hour drive singing along to our favorite bands. We knew we were getting close when the endless golden fields were replaced by dense green forest. Seattle looked like another world. I had been there many times before, but driving there on my own gave me a new sense of freedom.

Shelly gave us a tour of her college campus when we arrived. Seattle U was a great school, but I knew that it didn't offer everything that I was looking for. After the tour, we grabbed a bite to eat before driving to a party in Fremont, a hip neighborhood within Seattle.

It was a warm, balmy night, and the heat in the small house drove the party to the backyard. An eclectic array of music was blaring from the house speakers; small twinkling lights hung from the fence, wrapping around its posts like vines; and a large crowd was gathered around a beer keg, drinking from red plastic cups. We followed Shelly over to the keg, trying to blend in as she stopped to say hello to people she knew along the way. A tall guy with thick blond hair and warm brown eyes offered to fill our cups. He held a cup up to the spout with one hand, as he pumped the keg with the other. He handed me a frothy beer with a grin on his face, and I thanked him, feeling a little shy.

He offered a full cup to Mo and Shelly, and then turned to me with his now free hand extended. "Hey, I'm Jason."

"Hi. Kendi," I replied, shaking his hand. He had a firm grip, strong arms, and, when our gazes met, I realized that he was really quite dreamy. I felt Mo nudge my arm, and I released his hand and introduced her. The three of us chatted easily while Shelly mingled about the party, obviously very popular among the crowd. We talked about how we knew Shelly and what our plans were in Seattle. He seemed surprised that we were still in high school but excited for us to tour the Udub campus. He was starting his junior year there in the fall, working toward an engineering degree. Jason refilled our cups, and Mo and I went in search of Shelly.

"Hey, there you guys are," she said as we walked toward her. "So I see that you met Jason. He seems kinda into you, Kendi, and, believe me, he never pays much attention to anyone."

"First of all, I don't know what you're talking about, and, second, I have Adam, so it really doesn't matter what Jason is into," I said playfully.

I heard Shelly mutter under her breath, "Well, that sure wouldn't stop Adam."

"What does that mean?" I asked, instantly defensive. She seemed surprised that I had heard her and shrugged, mumbling, "Nothing," as she walked away. I felt a knot in my stomach at her comment. Shelly may live in Seattle, but she kept in touch with a number of people back home, and she visited quite often. I couldn't shake the feeling that I was missing something. I gulped down the nearly full cup of beer in my hand and headed back toward the keg for a refill. I needed something to drown out the little voice in my head that was telling me that something was wrong.

"Hey, wait up, Kendi," Mo yelled as she scrambled after me. "Don't listen to Shelly. Adam would never do anything to hurt you. He loves you," she said, placing her hand on my shoulder from behind as we weaved through a group of people dancing on the patio.

I stopped to face her. I didn't want to ruin the night. "Yeah, I know. I'm fine. Let's just have a good time tonight, okay?"

Mo smiled as her eyes scanned over the crowd. "Sounds good to me. There are some really hot college guys here!"

I laughed and rolled my eyes at her. "You're crazy, but I love you anyway."

"Yeah, well, right back at ya," she said as she looped her arm in mine and pulled me toward the keg.

$\sim$

The next morning we woke up early so Shelly could drive us back to Fremont to get Mo's car. Shelly's roommate had given us a ride home from the party after the three of us had consumed more alcohol than I cared to remember. We exchanged hugs with Shelly before driving to the University of Washington campus, our last stop before heading home.

From the moment we stepped foot on the Udub campus, I was in awe at its sheer size and beauty. The long fields of grass, bright-colored flowers, wooded paths leading everywhere filled with people jogging or taking a leisurely stroll, and the massive brick buildings that housed the classrooms where I could potentially be sitting one day. I knew that this was where I wanted to be. It was hard to contain my excitement as we walked through campus on our guided tour. I knew that the University of Washington had one of the best medical schools in the country, and, with a little sweat and hard work, maybe I could get in.

We ate lunch at a little Mexican café on Lake Union and then started our long drive home.

As we drove over the mountains, watching the evergreens and crystal blue lake passing by, I was quiet and deep in thought. I was imagining my future in Seattle, wondering where my relationship with Adam would be in a year when I graduated. And then my thoughts drifted to Shelly's comment again. I went over every moment in my head that Adam and I had spent together over the summer, trying to find something that felt off. Before I drove myself crazy, I pushed aside these thoughts and turned my attention to Morgan.

We talked about the college tours and where we saw ourselves in a year. We had always planned on going to the same school, but we would settle for living in the same city. I couldn't imagine not seeing Mo every day. We had been practically joined at the hip for as long as I could remember.

I asked what the latest was with Rick, and she shrugged. I was curious since she had been really flirty at the party and had even kissed someone good-night.

"We both know that our relationship isn't going anywhere since he is leaving for Arizona next month for school. So we're spending the rest of the summer together, just having fun."

"Kinda like good friends with benefits," I teased. We both laughed, and, as I looked over at her to make another smart remark, a horrifying image caught my eye. A large semitruck was barreling through the intersection, and, before my mind had time to process what was happening, I heard a deafening crash.

*L*oss

I woke up completely disoriented, trying to make out my surroundings. I decided that this must be a hospital room by the incessant beeping I heard. My body hurt everywhere, and my throat was so dry I could hardly swallow. I heard my mom softly repeating my name and looked up to see her tear-stained face searching my eyes for a response.

"Hi, Mom," I croaked, barely able to say the words through my parched lips. "So thirsty," I tried to say. She held out a spoon containing ice chips and helped me swallow it. It barely quenched the thirst, and I asked for more with my expression. She continued to feed me until I was satisfied. I closed my eyes for a moment, and my last conscious vision flashed through my mind.

I suddenly tried to sit up calling for Mo. The crushing pain in my head brought me back down to the pillow, and I searched my mother's face for answers. Tears flowed down her cheeks, and I could see the pain in her eyes. My heart broke. I knew that she was struggling for words and that could only mean that Mo's injuries were far worse than mine.

I braced myself for the worst as my mom whispered, "She didn't make it, sweetie. I am so sorry. There was nothing they could do. She was already gone when the paramedics arrived."

I tried to process what my mom was saying. I imagined Morgan lying next to me, needing me, calling for me…dying. And I had been unconscious, unable to help her.

As if reading my mind, my mother said, "She didn't suffer. She was killed instantly by the impact. There was nothing that you could have done, Kendall." All at once the severity and finality of the situation hit me, and a loud sob escaped my lips. Tears started to flow down my cheeks, and my mom leaned over and hugged me gently. I cried for what seemed like hours.

I finally took a deep breath and asked, "What happened?"

She wiped my eyes with a tissue. "A truck ran a red light. The driver saw your car passing through the intersection, but he wasn't able to stop in time. He hit the driver's side of the car. Morgan's injuries to her neck were fatal." She wiped her own eyes, struggling with the details that she knew I needed to hear. "You had a bleed in your brain, a subdural hematoma, I think the doctor called it. They were able to stop it with surgery, but you were unconscious for quite a while. You broke your collarbone and a few ribs, but you're going to be okay, sweetie." She sighed loudly, holding her hand to her heart. "Thank goodness. We were all so worried." She brushed back the hair from my face, pulling at the strands that were stuck to my dry, cracked lips.

I turned my head away. I felt relieved that I was okay, that I was alive and in one piece. But it felt wrong to feel this way. Mo was gone. Another sob burst out of my chest, and I cringed from the physical pain that I felt. My mom called for the nurse, and, through my tears, I watched a short blond woman dressed in pink scrubs administer something into the tube in my arm.

My vision started to blur as I tried desperately to hold on to an image of Morgan. Anything to keep the reality of this nightmare from taking her from me. In the end, I lost the battle and drifted into unconsciousness.

When I awoke again, I felt nauseous, and my head still throbbed. I scanned the room, looking to see if anyone was here with me. I could see my mom asleep in a chair next to my bed. She looked uncomfortable, her skin pale under the fluorescent lights of the room. I tried to call for her, barely able to make a sound. She instantly woke at the sound of my hoarse whisper.

"Hey there. How are you feeling?" she asked quietly.

"Okay. My throat is still dry, and my body aches everywhere." I brought my free hand up to my collarbone, the source of a throbbing pain which I could not ignore. I looked at my mom, confused by the bandage that was covering my chest.

"When your collarbone broke, it punctured your skin. The doctor set the bone and stitched you up. He said that it should heal just fine."

I cringed at her words, as she gently stroked my hand in understanding.

"Are you up for some visitors? Marie, Scott and Adam have been in the waiting room for hours to see if you're okay."

"Marie is here?" I asked, tears already forming in my eyes.

"Yes, she came as soon as she heard. She's so worried about you. We all are."

"Have you talked to Mo's parents?"

"Yes, we spoke here at the hospital when they brought you both in. They're not taking the news very well, as you can imagine."

I nodded, wondering how they would ever get through this. How *I* was ever going to get through this. "Can I see Marie and Scott first? And then I want to be alone with Adam for a while."

"Sure, Kendall," she said, stroking my face. My mother stepped out of the room, returning a moment later with my sister and brother in tow. I immediately broke down at the sight of them. We all four hugged, huddled close together, crying. I felt their strength and support as they wrapped me up in their arms. We didn't say much. What was there to say?

After a while we said our good-byes, and I wiped the tears from my eyes, preparing to see Adam. He looked tired when he walked in, like he hadn't slept in days. The moment we locked gazes, he crushed himself against me. I could feel his overwhelming relief from the way his body sagged into mine. I winced from the pain in my chest, a combination of the broken ribs and my breaking heart.

"Oh, God, Kendi. I'm so glad that you're okay. This is so terrible. I'm so sorry. I'm so sorry." He continued to tell me how sorry he was through his own sobs as we held each other, unrelenting tears streaming down our faces.

~

I was released from the hospital a few days later with careful instructions regarding my head injury, along with a printout listing all my follow-up appointments. My head was wrapped in a bandage. I tried not to think about the small shaved area underneath. My mom assured me that my hair would grow back in no time. My right arm was in a sling, my chest wrapped tightly to brace my broken ribs. I was quite a sight, but it was a small price to pay to walk away from the accident with my life.

54

Once in the car I told my mom to take me to Morgan's house. I needed to see her parents. I was nervous, not sure how they would feel about seeing me; while I was alive and breathing, their daughter was not. But they embraced me when I walked into their home. From the way they clung to me, I felt like they needed me as if I were their only link to their daughter. And the truth was, I needed them too.

The next few days were a blur. I spent most of my time with Mo's family as we prepared for her funeral. I still couldn't believe that she was gone. Her presence lingered everywhere. I was waiting for her to pull her car into the driveway any moment and bound into the house, yelling, "Surprise," with her infectious smile, as if this was all a very bad joke. Our favorite CD still sat in my stereo where she had left it; her prized blue sundress still hung in my closet where she had placed it before our trip; and her sketch of a tiny wizard drawing stars with his wand was still stuck to my bulletin board, as a reminder of the matching tattoos we were going to get when we turned eighteen.

Adam came by to see me each afternoon after work, holding me, not really sure what to say. His silent presence was exactly what I needed. I could see that he was hurting too but trying to stay strong for my benefit. I held on to him tightly, fully aware that I didn't know how many more moments I would have with him. Life was suddenly so precious and unpredictable. I didn't know what to believe in, what was real and what was just an illusion that could disintegrate at any moment.

The funeral felt like a really bad dream. I wasn't ready to say good-bye. I hadn't slept much since the accident. Every time I closed my eyes, I could hear the roar from the collision. I dreamed of Morgan, lying bloody and beaten, helpless, calling my name, and I would wake up screaming, drenched in sweat. My mother was always there to comfort me until I was able to fall back asleep. I sat in the front of the church, exhausted and heartbroken.

It was a hot summer day, and the bright sun was streaming through the stained-glass windows, warming everything it touched. I didn't feel the sun's warmth or anything for that matter. I felt numb as I watched Adam, Rick and several other close friends carry her casket out of the church. It was a beautiful ivory hue with pink roses—her favorite—etched around the edges. At the cemetery, I watched through tear-filled eyes as they lowered her in the ground. I still was not ready to say good-bye as I dropped a single pink rose on top of her casket and walked away.

Time passed slowly. I couldn't work because of my injuries, so I tried to keep busy reading the stack of books that my mother bought me or playing video games with Scott, but it was hard to even get myself out of bed. I just wanted to sleep. The nights were too dark and quiet, bringing back painful memories from the accident and the moments leading up to it. During the day I was too exhausted to stay awake.

Marie stayed home for nearly two weeks after the funeral to keep a close eye on me while my mom was at work. It was a huge comfort to have my sister there. I had missed having her around. She helped me with my baths, drying and combing my hair for me—simple tasks that were nearly impossible with my dominant arm in a sling. She forced me to eat and curled up on the couch with me while we watched old movies.

She tried desperately to bring a smile to my face, but everything seemed to remind me of Mo, and I struggled with the unfairness of it all. Morgan would never smile again. I replayed the last moments of her life in my head, over and over again. Could I have done anything differently? Why didn't I see the truck sooner? I wished that I would have told her I loved her one more time. I punished myself every day trying to understand why she was gone, and I was still here.

Adam came by to see me as often as he could, but I saw him less and less as the summer came to an end. He would be leaving for school in three weeks. I registered for my classes, but I couldn't imagine going back to school...not without Mo.

Life

My sister had gone back to college. Scott was spending more time with his friends, happy to get out of the house. I found myself alone while everyone continued about their life as if nothing was different. I was trying desperately to carry on a somewhat normal existence.

Adam came over early one afternoon, taking time off work so that he could see me. In an attempt to cheer me up, he turned on some music and lifted me up from the couch. He pulled me into his arms, and we began to dance to a slow ballad. He had his arms around me, his hands resting on my lower back. My right arm, still in my sling, lay awkwardly between us, as I wrapped my other arm around the back of his neck, lightly brushing my fingers along his hairline. We danced like this for a few minutes, and, then to lighten the mood, Adam started singing loudly, twirling me around the room. I couldn't help but smile, and he beamed at me, knowing that his plan was working.

"I've missed that smile," he said in my ear. Feeling his breath on my neck awakened something in me, and I pulled his face to mine, pressing our lips together. It had been weeks since we had been intimate. I had been lost in a thick cloud of grief, but kissing Adam in that moment felt like watching the sun break through the fog. I clung to him as if letting go would cause me to lose my way, falling victim to the darkness once again.

Responding to my sudden need for him, he pulled me up into his arms without breaking our kiss and carried me upstairs to my room. Taking our time, our lips exploring each other's bodies, we slowly undressed each other one layer at a time. Adam was gentle with me, worried that he would hurt my still broken body. He rolled on top of me, hovering, attempting to keep his weight off me, and slowly lowered himself inside me. My need for him was overwhelming. I moaned loudly, unable to contain my pleasure as I found my release, every deep emotion that I had been harboring escaping me with it. I crashed back to earth as Adam found his own release, calling my name through clenched teeth. We held each other tightly, trying to catch our breath. Wrapped up in Adam's arms, I felt for the first time since the accident that I was going to be okay. That my life, though forever changed, would continue on, and I knew that I should embrace it.

~

I finally received the "all clear" from my doctor, and he removed my bandages and my sling. I was starting to feel like myself again, physically at least. I succumbed to my friends' persistence to get me out of the house and went to a party to celebrate my clean bill of health. It felt strange to be laughing and having fun after everything that had happened. I tried to enjoy myself, but, in the end, I called Adam to come pick me up and take me home.

I started my senior year of high school the following Monday. It was a hard day, and I spent more time in the bathroom sobbing than in my classes. The faculty members were very understanding and gave me my space. It was harder than I thought to be in those familiar halls without Mo and without Adam. Adam insisted on driving me to school every morning and taking me home at the end of the day. At least until he left for college.

That day came all too soon. We planned to spend the evening together to say our good-byes. Adam's parents were moving him into the dorms the following day. Adam and I drove out of town to one of his fields, and he pulled a blanket from the trunk. We walked into the darkness several yards from the road with the guidance of a flashlight, and he spread out the blanket on the recently cut field. I could hear crickets chirping all around us in the stillness of the night. We were on our backs gazing up at the incredibly lit sky, every star clearly visible from this secluded place.

I felt so small, just the two of us in this enormous world. And just for a moment, it felt like our problems were so small in comparison to the millions of others who looked upon this same sky. And I thought of Mo out there somewhere, and I quietly made a wish that Mo was at peace —and hoping that someday soon I would feel complete again. I sighed and snuggled in closer to Adam.

"Thank you," I said, breaking the comfortable silence.

"For what?" he asked, pulling me even closer to his side.

"For this, for bringing me here and for being so supportive lately. I love you so much."

"I love you too, Kendi," he said, placing a soft kiss on my forehead. "I'm going to miss not seeing you every day. But I'll call you as much as I can. And we'll see each other on the weekends."

"I know. It won't be the same though." I sighed.

"No, it won't," he whispered and slowly rolled on his side, placing his knee between mine, his arm over the top of me. Propped up on one elbow, he bent down and gently pressed his lips against mine, pulling back slightly and whispering, "I won't be able to do this every day," and he kissed me again. Moving his lips to my ear, he whispered, "Or this," sending chills down my body as he caressed my ear with his tongue. "And I won't be able to do this either," he whispered, as he trailed his tongue down my neck. I gently stroked his back with my fingers completely aware of every part of my body as it came alive under his delicate touch.

Continuing his erotic assault, he brought his hand up under my shirt and moved aside my bra as he brushed his thumb across my erect nipple. "And I definitely won't be able to do this," he breathed into my ear.

I pulled him on top of me, forcing his lips against mine while I ran my fingers through his hair, pulling it tightly into my clenched fists. He groaned in response to my sudden frenzied attack. I was unable to contain the desire burning inside of me. I'm not sure what came over me, but his slow and delicate movements were not what I wanted. I wanted him right now, and I did not want to be gentle about it. I started to pull up his shirt, and he finished pulling it over his head, tossing it aside. I ran my hands all over his smooth, hard back, digging my nails into his skin. He groaned even louder.

I held him closer to me, kissing him hungrily, trying to feel every inch of him against me. Not feeling satisfied, I prompted him to roll on his back, and I moved on top of him. I sat up and pulled my shirt off over my head. I unbuttoned his pants and quickly discarded them before straddling his lap. I leaned down to press my breasts against the warm skin of his chest as I kissed him with an urgent need, grinding myself against his bare flesh.

He ran his hands up the back of my legs, under my skirt, grabbing my backside with both hands. He wrapped his fingers in the thin lace of my panties and tugged hard, ripping them from my body in one swift move and slipping his fingers inside me from behind. I gasped at the instant pleasure, feeling like I might combust at his touch. With trembling hands, I managed to slip a condom in place. My breath was almost a pant as I took him in my hand and placed him inside me. Feeling in complete control, I rocked against him hard and fast. He matched my movements with his own. I could feel my need building quickly. I rocked harder, sitting up and pressing my hands against his chest for leverage.

"Oh, God, Adam," I cried out as I felt his length deep in my core. He moaned my name in a husky voice along with other words that I couldn't focus on as I felt my entire body tense. Just when I felt like I couldn't hold back another moment, Adam grabbed my hips and buried himself deeper inside me, sending me over the edge as we both finished together. Breathless I melted against his chest, feeling the thud of his racing heart on my cheek. We stayed like this, neither one of us wanting to move, as our breathing slowed.

"Wow," Adam said. "What was that all about?" he asked with a huge grin on his face.

I blushed and looked away, suddenly aware of how out of control I had been.

"Hey, nothing to be embarrassed about. That was amazing."

"Yeah, it…was. I don't know what happened. I think that the thought of not seeing you every day got the best of me."

"I should leave you more often," Adam said smiling, brushing my hair from my face. We both laughed. Feeling a chill, I shivered, and Adam held me against him.

"I can't believe that I'm going to say this, but we

better get some clothes on you before you freeze to death." I playfully hit him on the shoulder and sat up trying to find my shirt in the dark. I slipped my shirt on over my head and threw Adam's clothes at him.

"Hey, what was that for?" Adam asked when his clothes hit him in the face.

"That was for ruining my favorite pair of underwear," I smirked as I crawled up his legs until I was looking him in the eye. I pushed Adam down on his back again and kissed him tenderly. Adam reached under my skirt and slapped my bare ass. "Hey, watch it, mister," I warned, pulling my lips from his.

"You're going to drive me crazy the rest of the night knowing that you aren't wearing any underwear under this skirt."

"That's too bad," I said, kissing him again before he could get up to dress.

We packed up our love nest and slowly made our way back to the car. The chill of fall was in the air. September was usually a warm month but the evenings were already getting colder. I wasn't ready for the cold weather yet. I wasn't ready for anything that life was throwing at me these days.

We sat in Adam's car for hours, just talking, not wanting the night to end. He wasn't concerned about his curfew since this was technically his last night at home. Adam told me how excited he was to start basketball practice next week and about his roommate that he would meet for the first time tomorrow. His name was Brock, and he was also from a small town but from the other side of the state. Adam had talked to him on the phone, and he seemed like a nice guy. They would both be freshman on the team.

Adam had registered for English literature, a psychology class and statistics. He had early morning classes so that his afternoons were free for basketball practice. It sounded like a busy schedule to me, and I was wondering where I would fit into it. Adam cupped my chin in his hand and brought up my face to meet his.

"Hey, don't worry. We'll have plenty of time for each other. It's only an hour drive."

I gave him a small smile and leaned into his hand as he stroked my cheek. "And what happens when you meet someone, a gorgeous college girl that you can't resist?" I asked. Adam was so incredibly good-looking; I knew that he would have the attention of every girl he met. And he was very friendly—too friendly for my taste—with everyone. To say that I was worried about Adam meeting someone else was an understatement. I was terrified.

"Kendi, I only want you. I can't imagine my life without you in it. And how do I know that you won't find one of your classmates irresistible? The guys in school are waiting for me to leave so they can have a shot with you, trust me. I know what they're saying."

"Yeah, right. And I have known them all since kindergarten and have never been interested in any one of them. Well not since the fourth grade anyway." I giggled at the thought.

It was really late, and I didn't want my mom to worry, so I sadly asked Adam to take me home.

He walked me to the porch, and, before I could kiss him good-night, he pulled something out of his pocket. "Kendi, I have something for you. I want you to have this ring to wear to remind you of me and how much I will always love you." He reached for my right hand and slipped it on my ring finger. It was a perfect fit. I gasped and held my hand up to the porch light to admire the beautiful sapphire stone set inside a ring of small diamonds.

"It's beautiful, Adam. It's too much though. You shouldn't have, really."

"You're worth it, and I had the inside engraved, so you have to accept it."

I looked at him in awe. I couldn't possibly love him any more than I did at that moment. I pulled off the ring to look at the inscription on the inside of the white gold band. *Always*. I slipped the ring back on my finger and threw my arms around his neck, pulling his mouth to mine. Without breaking our kiss, he picked me up off the ground and twirled me around.

"I love you so much, Adam. Thank you."

"I love you too. I'm glad that you like it."

"That reminds me. I have something for you also. Wait here." I left him standing on the porch for a moment while I slipped inside the front door and grabbed a wrapped gift off the entry hall table. "This is for you. Open it tomorrow after you get settled."

"Okay," he said, shooting me a curious look.

I had put together a small book with all of my favorite pictures of us and several poems that I had written for him. I wanted him to have something of me that he could keep at school. I suddenly felt vulnerable as he took it out of my hands. The words that I had written on those pages were a direct window to my soul, and I usually didn't share my poetry with anyone, not even Adam. I silently hoped that he would like my gift.

"Good luck tomorrow. Call me…if you want," I added, trying not to sound too needy.

"Of course I'll call you. I miss you already." He pulled me into one last embrace. "I love you," he whispered before walking to his car. He stopped and glanced back at me several times, his sad expression matching my own. I waved good-bye as he drove away.

$Bliss$

Adam did call me the next day after his parents left his dorm. He told me that his room was a decent size for a dorm room, and his roommate was cool. He thanked me endlessly for the book that I had made for him. He hadn't read through all the entries yet, but he loved what he had read so far. I could sense the sincerity in his voice, and I was relieved to hear it. He was headed out for dinner with some of his teammates, so we only spoke for a few minutes.

After that I settled into a nice routine. I went to school, studied hard and made a point of reconnecting with people that I had not spent much time with over my tragic summer. I went out to lunch with my friends Tracy and Liz, whom I had known since kindergarten, like most of my classmates. The overwhelming despair that I felt from Morgan's death lessened with each passing day, and I no longer was consumed by thoughts of her. I still thought of her daily, missing her like crazy, but I could smile and laugh without the added guilt. Adam called nearly every night before he fell asleep. I kept the phone near my bed so that I never missed one, even when it was late and I had already turned in for the night. He would drive down to see me most weekends, and I even drove to see him at school a few times.

The first time I went to see him, he gave me a tour of the campus and took me out to lunch. I met his roommate and was a little surprised that he was on the basketball team. He was really nice but seemed like more of a partier than an athlete. I could have sworn that he had been smoking pot right before I met him. I asked Adam about this at lunch, and he confirmed my suspicions. He didn't think that Brock would be on the team for much longer once they started routine drug testing. I thought that this was hysterical, but Adam didn't see the humor in it.

"Come on, admit it. It is kinda funny that my straitlaced boyfriend has the biggest stoner on the basketball team for a roommate."

"Whatever." Adam shrugged, throwing a fry at my face. I giggled and threw it right back.

A few weeks later Adam called to tell me that Brock had been expelled from school and sent home. It was hard to miss the excitement in his voice. "Don't you feel bad for him at all, Adam?" I asked, confused by his enthusiasm.

"Of course I do, but now I have the entire room to myself. They aren't moving anyone else in. So we have total privacy when you come to visit, and I can study in peace. This is going to be so much better."

The thought of having his room all to ourselves did sound pretty nice.

"In fact, what are you doing right now? Why don't you come see me?"

"Right now? Adam, it's a school night." I glanced at the clock, considering his invitation.

"You could be here by five. I had early practice today,

and I'm done studying. Come on, I miss you," he pleaded with me.

That was all it took to convince me.

"Okay, I'll think of something to tell my mom. See you in an hour." I hung up the phone and changed my clothes, replacing my sweatpants with my favorite pair of jeans. I convinced my mother that I was going to Liz's house to study, and she reluctantly handed over her car keys, reminding me not to be home too late. I hated to lie to her, but my need to see Adam outweighed the risk of her discovering my dishonesty. I thought of Adam the entire drive, blaring my favorite songs on the car stereo. When I got to his building, I slipped in through the open door as someone was leaving and knocked on the door to his room a moment later. Completely surprised that I was standing outside his door already, Adam pulled me into an enormous hug and kissed me tenderly on the lips.

When he pulled away, he swept his arm across the room and asked, "What do you think of the place?"

I glanced around the room and took in all the changes he had made. He had pushed the twin beds together to form a huge bed off to one side of the small room. On the other side of the room sat the ugliest orange chair that I had ever seen, positioned in front of a small television. His dorm-issued desk sat beside the door.

"Wow, you didn't waste any time did you? Nice chair," I said with a smirk as I set my car keys down on the desk.

"Hey, not bad for a few hours' work, huh? Come here." He pulled me back into his arms and kissed my hair, inhaling deeply. "You smell so good. I missed you so much," he whispered as he kicked the door closed with his foot. He lowered his face to mine and kissed me gently. Moments later I felt his tongue in my mouth as he lifted me in his arms, my feet leaving the ground until he laid me down across the new makeshift king-size bed. I was lost in his arms for hours. It was the first time that we could be together without watching the clock or worrying about who might find us. It was just Adam and me, alone, in our own blissful world.

Eventually reality settled in, and I realized how late it was. "Adam, I have to go. My mom will be furious if I'm home too late. It's already nine o'clock, and I have an hour's drive ahead of me." Each time I attempted to get out of bed to get dressed, he pulled me back down in his arms again. I didn't want to leave him. It took all the strength I had to step away from him long enough to put my clothes back on.

"I wish you could stay the night with me," he pouted while pulling on a pair of faded Levi's. His hair was a complete mess, curls spiked in every direction, the top two buttons of his jeans were undone, the muscles of his chest and abdomen flexed in the dim light as he pulled a T-shirt over his head. He looked completely and utterly edible in this moment. The thought of sleeping in his arms the entire night, my head resting on *that* chest, my fingers brushing through *that* hair, was tempting, but I knew that tonight was not the night.

"I can't tonight, but I think that we can definitely plan something soon."

His mouth turned up on one side into a seductive grin as his mind processed this idea. "Promise?"

"I promise."

Satisfied, he finally walked me out to my car and kissed me good-bye with one hand grabbing me behind the leg, inching it up around his hip and the other hand gripping my backside. I pushed him away before he got too carried away and drove off into the night. His kiss lingered on my lips the entire trip home.

I kept my promise. The following weekend I packed an overnight bag and headed to Gonzaga. I told my mom that I was staying the night with Liz. She was so happy to see me spending time with friends that she didn't ask many questions. I told Liz my plan just in case my mom decided to check up on me. Adam and I spent the entire night wrapped up in each other in his dark room with a Counting Crows CD playing on Repeat in the background. We had ripped off each other's clothes in the first few minutes after I had arrived, not wasting any time at expressing our need for each other.

Hours later we did it again, slowly this round, savoring every moment, every touch. We talked about how natural it felt to be together. Adam told me that he could see me in his future and could imagine spending his life with me by his side. He told me how hard it was for him to go days without seeing me. I told him that I felt the same way and that I couldn't imagine my life without him in it. We talked about all the things that young couples talk about. How many kids we wanted to have—I said two, he said four—what we would name them—we both liked the name Zachary for a boy and Madeline for a girl—and what kind of wedding we would have. We talked until the sun's rays began to filter in through the curtains, and then we drifted off to sleep, exhausted from the sleepless night.

It felt amazing to spend the entire night in Adam's arms. I fabricated sleepovers at Liz's or Tracy's house as often as I could to have them instead with Adam whenever possible. I felt a sliver of guilt lying to my mother, knowing that I would eventually get caught in my lies, but I didn't care. I couldn't stay away from Adam. I wanted to be with him every minute, and I ached for him when we were apart.

Lies

It was our first day back to school following Thanksgiving break, and Josh came looking for me in the parking lot after our final class of the day was let out. He clearly looked upset, and my first thought was that something had happened to Adam. He assured me that Adam was fine, but that we needed to talk. I told him to meet me at my house in ten minutes. I had to drive Scott home from school. A million things were flashing through my mind. What on earth did Josh need to talk to me about, and why was he so upset?

I met Josh at the front door a few minutes after I got home. He looked tired and impatient to talk about whatever it was that was bothering him. It had just started snowing outside, and his dark jacket was already wet and speckled white with snowflakes.

"Come in, Josh, it's getting cold outside." I gestured him to the living room.

"Kendi, I have to tell you something, and you're not

going to like it." He ran his hand through his hair, reminding me of Adam and the way he seemed to do that subconsciously when he was upset or nervous. "I was talking to Katie last night on the phone, and she told me something that you should know."

"Okay. I wasn't aware that you guys still kept in touch since she left for college."

"We still talk once in a while, but that's not the point. We were talking about what happened between us and why we drifted apart over the summer, and she confessed to me that she slept with Adam. She said that it was an ongoing thing, lasting all spring and summer. They were sleeping together behind my back…behind *our* backs."

I just stood there, staring at his face, trying to process the words that he had just blurted out of his mouth. "What are you talking about?" I could feel bile rising in my throat as images started to fill my mind.

"I know that it's a lot to take in, believe me, but I wanted you to hear it from me first. I am so sick over this. Not so much that Katie lied to me for five months, but that my own brother did this to me…and to you. I'm sorry that my brother is such a fucking prick, Kendi."

He started to reach for me, to console me, as my eyes filled with tears. I shook my head and held out my hand to hold him back.

"Josh, I can't do this right now. I can't…" I was trying my best to hold it together, but I was fighting with too many emotions at once. I turned and ran up the stairs to my room.

"I'm sorry, Kendi. Call me later, okay?" I heard him yell up the stairs, followed by the front door closing.

Call it denial but I couldn't believe what Josh had just told me. Katie Brewster just wasn't Adam's type; it didn't make sense. But deep down inside, where the sick feeling was festering, I knew this was possible. And every moment where things seemed out of place before now plainly screamed at me.

Without thinking, I picked up the phone and called Adam. The phone rang in my ear a few times before I heard his voice.

"Hello."

I didn't bother with the usual greetings. "Tell me that you didn't sleep with Katie Brewster, Adam." I tried to keep my voice from breaking.

I heard him sigh, then silence. I took his silence as a confession, and I felt the dam break inside of me. The tears that I had been keeping at bay spilled down my cheeks.

"What the fuck is going on, Adam?"

"Who told you, Kendi?"

"Really, Adam? Is that even relevant right now? How could you? Are you still sleeping with her? I just don't understand…" My voice trailed off, my mind so cluttered with questions that words dissolved into tears.

"Kendi, let's not do this over the phone. I need to see you. Let's talk about this tomorrow in person."

"Fuck you, Adam." Frustrated at his lack of response, I slammed the phone back on the receiver. I collapsed on my bed sobbing into my hands. I cried for what seemed like hours, but eventually the questions were eating away at me, and I knew that I had to see him. I headed downstairs, grabbed my coat and car keys, and headed for the door.

"Where are you going, Kendall?" my mom called out to me.

"Out," was all I managed to say as I slammed the door closed. I stepped outside into the cold. It was already dark, and the ground was dusted with white snow, heavy snowflakes still falling. It was probably not the best driving conditions, but I didn't care. As I drove east on the freeway, with the windshield wipers swiping away the heavy snow and tears spilling from my eyes, I felt the anger brewing inside me.

I arrived at the university and was able to slip into his building and walk straight to his room. I pounded on his door, and he opened it with surprise. As soon as I saw him, I melted, and the tears started to flow once again. He pulled me inside the room, into his arms, and stroked my hair as I rested my cheek on his chest.

"I love you, Kendi," he whispered into my hair. Hearing his words, unsure of what was real and what was a lie, the anger that had built up inside me during the drive here exploded, and I pushed him back, hard.

"How could you do that to me, to us? You ruined us. Do I not mean anything to you, Adam? Was it all lies?"

He stepped toward me with his arms outstretched, wanting to pull me back into them. "Kendi, I'm sorry. It wasn't what you think." His words angered me even more.

"Really? What was it then? You slept with her for months. You lied to me for months," I screamed at him while pounding my fists into his chest. "I trusted you, Adam. I love you so much. Why?" I asked, desperately wanting to understand his actions.

He grabbed my wrists and held them tight to keep me from hitting him.

"Why?" I asked again as I looked up at him through wet lashes. I could see tears in his eyes, and I caved as he pulled me back into his arms.

"I'm so sorry, Kendi. I never meant to hurt you. It's been over for months. I'm so sorry. I love you so much," he said, resting his chin on my head.

I collapsed against him, suddenly exhausted from my emotional outburst. I sobbed against his chest. He reached down and pulled me up into his arms, carrying me over to the ugly orange chair and sat down holding me in his lap. He held me while I cried. The truth was, he was my best friend, and I needed his comfort even though he was the cause of my pain.

A part of me had died with Mo, and Adam was the only thing keeping the rest of me in one piece. He was my shelter, my rock. When the sobs subsided and I could catch my breath, I pulled away to look at him. He looked different to me, and I realized that I didn't really know him anymore. Would we ever be able to go back to what we had before? Would I ever see him in the same way again?

With a broken voice, I said, "Tell me everything from the beginning and don't leave anything out. You owe me that much. You owe me the truth." I pulled myself out of his arms and sat on top of his desk across from him, hugging myself tightly to fight the internal chill that was invading me.

I sat quietly, letting him talk without interruption, absorbing his every word.

He told me that it had started at a basketball game toward the end of the season. He was upset because Coach had just told him that he was starting Josh for their game instead of Adam. Katie had walked by him outside the locker room, and he had just grabbed her and kissed her without thinking, wanting to take something from Josh. Much to his surprise, she had kissed him back. It hadn't taken long for that kiss to evolve to more, physically.

They had skipped classes often, meeting at her house, and, during the summer months, they had spent many evenings together while I was working. He told me that it didn't mean anything to him, that he did not have feelings for her and that he loved me. He assured me that everything between us was real and that he had stopped seeing her after the accident. Mo's death and my near brush with death had made him realize how precious life was and how lost he would be without me. He had wanted to tell me so many times, but he had been afraid of losing me.

I suddenly felt sick. I had heard enough. I stood up and turned toward the door.

"Kendi." Adam stood and stepped closer to me. "Don't leave. Say something," he said.

I turned back to see fear in his eyes. "What do you want me to say, Adam? I'm hurt and confused. I need to go."

"Please, Kendi, stay with me. We can work this out. I don't want to lose you."

He tried to put his arms around me, but I pushed him away. "Don't, Adam. Don't touch me. I feel sick just looking at you. I need some time to think." I held my hand out to keep him away from me. Before turning again toward the door, I pulled the ring that he had given me from my finger and slammed it down on the desk. "Good-bye, Adam." I walked out the door, shaking from the anger that consumed me. I drove home slowly in the falling snow, trying for the life of me to understand what had gone wrong. Why I wasn't enough for him. When I finally walked in the door to my house, my mother was waiting for me.

"Kendall, Adam called to see if you got home safely. What were you thinking driving there in this weather?"

"Sorry, Mom. We got in a big fight, and I just had to see him. Don't worry, I drove carefully," I said, setting the car keys on the kitchen counter.

"Is everything okay? You look really upset," she said, her face etched with worry.

"Can we talk about this later? I just want to go to bed." I was too exhausted to have this conversation with my mother.

"Sure, honey, get some sleep. I love you." She gave me a hug, and I slowly walked up the stairs, mumbling that I loved her too.

The phone was ringing by the time I crawled into bed. I ignored it. I heard my mom answer it, telling someone, most likely Adam, that I was home but I had already gone to bed. I couldn't sleep. I opened the drawer of my nightstand, and pulled out handfuls of letters and notes that Adam had written me over the past year and a half. I read through every single one and obsessed over every lie that he had written, questioning every moment that we had shared. I felt lost and longed for Mo to help me through the mess that my life had become. Sleep finally took me, and I dreamed of Morgan for the first time in months.

Run

"Kendi, are you ready?" Marie's voice brought me back to the present, and I looked up at her with a blank expression. I glanced around to find that people were starting to file out of the church. Marie and I were sitting alone in the pew. The rest of my family was most likely standing in the foyer thanking everyone for coming as they left the funeral. "You looked like you needed a minute, so I told everyone to go ahead and that we would be right behind them." Marie smiled at me knowingly.

I could see the questions in her eyes, so much that she wanted to say to me, struggling with the promises that she had made long ago. Adam's presence brought back all the pain from the past, pain that Marie had witnessed firsthand. I stared ahead to the front of the church and thought of Mo and how much I missed her, how much I had needed her over the years. I thought about Adam, how much time had passed and yet he still pulled at my heart as if he owned it even after a decade. I suddenly felt like I had been running, running for years without rest, and I was tired. All the years pushing myself forward, burying myself in school and work, never looking back. Overwhelmed with memories, grief and exhaustion, I buried my face in my hands and sobbed.

"Oh, Kendi," my sister said as she put her arms around me, fighting back her own tears.

I finally pulled myself together. Marie grabbed my coat and handbag, as we started to walk down the center aisle to the front entrance. The church was completely empty, and I wondered how long I had been lost in my own thoughts. We were halfway down the aisle when Adam appeared from a side door and started to walk toward us. I stopped walking, unable to move. He was wearing jeans now and a light blue button-down shirt, untucked, resembling the young boy that I remembered more than the man—a pastor of all things—that he had become.

"Are you okay?" I heard Marie ask, her voice sounding distant, drowned out by the pounding of my heart. Realizing that I wasn't going to answer, she told me that she would wait for me in the car. She handed me my coat and walked away. Adam approached me. He looked the same. He was still adorable with his wavy hair and huge deep blue eyes. He had filled out more, and I could see the lines around his eyes that were not there in his youth.

"Kendall, I'm so sorry about your grandfather." The formality in his voice as he said my full name shocked me. I wasn't sure what to expect, but the truth stung; we had become strangers, and I was to blame.

"Thank you. It was a beautiful service, Adam." My voice was barely a whisper. "I wasn't expecting to see you today."

"I fill in for Pastor Phillips every now and then. I offered to cover the service today, given my personal connection to your family. I'm surprised that your mom didn't tell you."

"I flew in late last night. I'm sure that she didn't think of it." I tucked a loose strand of hair behind my ear as a wave of silence filled the space between us. "Well, it was good to see you. Thank you for today." I glanced toward the foyer— my only escape. "I better go. Marie's waiting for me." I felt weighted down from the dense awkwardness that hung in the air. I wanted to run out of the church, to flee from that moment. Ignoring the urge to sprint to the car, I turned from him slowly, taking one step at a time as I neared the exit.

"Kendi…"

I closed my eyes, bracing myself against the pain and desperation in his voice. "Yeah," I said, as I turned to face him.

He took a few steps toward me, closing the distance that I had started to put between us. "We should talk. Before you leave again. There are things that need to be said."

"Adam…" I started to protest but he stopped me. I was going to say that it had been years, that there was nothing left to say. It was all so far behind us now, what good was it to bring it all up again? Of course the ache in my heart told me otherwise.

"Here's my address. I'll be home later today and tomorrow. Please just think about it."

He placed a slip of paper in my hand, and the sudden brush of his skin against mine sent chills through my body. The words were caught in my throat, and I said nothing. I clenched the paper tightly in my hand and walked quickly out of the church, not bothering to put on my coat. The cold air burned my lungs as I stepped outside and inhaled deeply. I hadn't realized until that moment that I had been holding my breath. Tears stung my eyes as I ran to the car where Marie was waiting. I slammed the car door closed.

"Just drive," I blurted out before Marie had a chance to say anything.

She pulled the car away from the curb in silence, but once we reached a good distance from the church, the words that she had been holding back for years surfaced. "I know that I took a vow never to discuss this, but I have to say something now. Kendi, it's been ten years. You need to tell him. He deserves to know, and maybe it will be good for you. You could move on. I mean *really* move on."

I exhaled loudly through my mouth, trying to calm myself. "I can't, Marie. It's been too long. He'll hate me, and I'm not sure that I can deal with that."

"Is that worse than you hating yourself? I want you to be happy, and keeping this from him is eating away at you. I can't sit back and watch you destroy yourself over this anymore. Tell him. Please."

She was right; he deserved to know. But I had buried the truth for so long, hidden behind my shame and guilt. How could I tell him now? And I had so many others to consider as well. My mother for one and my boyfriend, Derek.

Derek and I had been seeing each other for two years. I was introduced to him almost immediately after moving to Southern California. He was smart, funny and completely gorgeous. We met at a party that my attending physician held shortly after I started my residency. Derek had gone to school with Dr. Watson at UCLA, although Derek went into finance and was now an investment banker.

He was a few years older than me, already settling into his career at the time, and I was just starting a four-year residency. We spent the evening talking outside on the large deck overlooking the ocean. He asked me out to dinner at the end of the night, and we exchanged numbers. My residency left me little time for a personal life, but he was patient, and somehow a few dates blossomed into something more, and now I couldn't imagine my daily life without him.

He had wanted to be here with me today, but he was in New York for a very important public launch of a new company. I wanted to come alone anyway. I guess part of me kept him at arm's length when it came to my past. I hadn't realized until now—seeing Adam for the first time in years—that I hadn't completely given myself to Derek.

That explained my hesitation when he had asked me to move in with him, and the anxiety I felt every time that he talked about the future. I was not ready for the future or any big steps until I finished my residency; at least that was what I told myself. But now I knew that maybe it was more than that.

Although, in my defense, I had no idea where I would end up when my residency was completed. The lucky ones were offered jobs where they wanted to be, but nothing was certain in this field, and sometimes people had to go where the job took them. Of course, Derek insisted that he would move wherever he had to so that we could start a life together. Marriage, kids—he wanted it all. I could hardly speak of those things, but he seemed so sure. How could I marry him or have his children when there was so much about me that he didn't know? I finally realized how unfair I had been to Derek…and to Adam.

"He wants to talk. He gave me his address." I remembered the crumpled paper that I held in my clenched fist and opened it up to look at it. And there written on a torn piece of notebook paper was his neat and perfect script staring back at me. *I need to see you, Kendi. Address is 705 Elm Drive. I'll be home over the next few days. ~A*

Seeing my name written in his familiar handwriting brought back so many memories from that time, a time when I thought life was so complicated. Looking back, life was actually quite simple then; well, at least in comparison to where it had all led.

Better Days

Days turned into weeks, and I had not seen or heard Adam since that night, although not for his lack of trying. He tried calling almost every day, and I refused to take his calls. He stopped by my house, and my mother would tell him the same thing each time: that she was sorry, but I didn't want to see him. He even came to a few of Josh's basketball games, in hopes to see me, but I blatantly ignored him. He finally resorted to mailing me letters, which I placed in my drawer, unopened. It was killing me not to have him in my life, but his lies and deceit were irrevocable. I knew that I could never trust him again, and I was still dealing with the pain and humiliation that his choices had left me with.

Josh and I had become close friends through it all. He was hurt too, although I often told him that he couldn't avoid Adam forever. They were family, and sooner or later they had to deal with what happened. In the meantime, I was happy to have Josh to vent to. We often criticized Adam and Katie, pointing out their flaws and annoying behaviors, finding solace in the idea that they were both heartless, selfish human beings, and that we were better off without them.

We also revisited the past, noting certain events that should have raised red flags for both of us, but neither one of us had suspected anything. I think sometimes that is the worst part, the feeling of being blindsided. The smoke screen was so thick that I couldn't possibly have seen the truth. The lies definitely hurt the most. I could see why my mother was always so adamant about telling the truth. The pain she must have felt from my father's own lies, I now understood all too well.

I had confided in my mother about what had happened between Adam and me. Of course, this led to a conversation that I had successfully avoided having with my mother until then. The sex talk. She asked me the obvious question, had Adam and I been having a sexual relationship as well? Avoiding the look in her eyes, I had answered her honestly. She was amazingly understanding but wanted to make sure that we had been "safe," especially since I was not the only person that he had slept with. I assured her that we always used a condom. Leaving out the few times that Adam had simply "pulled out" before anything happened. She had been extremely supportive while I tried to recover from my heartache, and it had brought us closer together. Her eyes told me that she struggled with seeing her youngest daughter in so much pain. My grief over losing Morgan had nearly crushed the both of us and now this. It had been a hard year.

I spent countless hours on the phone with Marie. She offered a more realistic perspective than my mother, having gone through a difficult breakup in high school as well. She was furious over the situation and threatened to come home several times to "kick Adam's ass." The visual alone brought a smile to my face, reminding me of the time that she had punched Tyler Stevens in the face after he had bullied me for months in the fourth grade. He never bothered me again, and the fact that he had been beat up on by a girl was never forgotten.

It was comforting to know that Marie had my back, but causing Adam physical harm wouldn't have changed anything. I clung to her every word, the wisdom that only an older sister could provide, like when she promised me that this was just a bump in the long road ahead of me, that I would learn from this life experience, thankful that it had occurred to prepare me for something bigger and better that awaited in the wings. That she knew it was hard to see past the hurt now, but eventually I would get over Adam, and this would all be a piece of my past, nothing but a story to tell. I hoped that she was right.

Other than Josh and my family, I didn't talk about Adam with anyone. I told Liz and Tracy that Adam and I had simply broken up, but I didn't tell them about Katie. I was too humiliated.

I focused on my schoolwork, completing the endless college applications that I had requested and applying for the local scholarships suggested by Mr. Shelby. I couldn't wait to break free from the painful reminders my small hometown represented. College would be a fresh start, and I was looking forward to it. I had originally picked up several applications for colleges near Adam, but I needed to be as far away as possible from him. So I concentrated on the ones in the Seattle area, as far north as Bellingham.

~

It was Valentine's Day. I treated it like any other day, ignoring the vases full of roses and obscenely large balloon bouquets that arrived throughout the day to the school's front office. I would not be receiving anything this year, and I was okay with that, but I didn't need the constant reminder that Adam and I were through. I had survived Christmas and New Year's without him, finding solace in my sister's company while she was home from college and spending time with Mo's family. I could survive this.

I went home from school early. I just wanted to be alone. I set down my backpack in the entry hall and headed upstairs to my room. I opened the door and was shocked to see vases full of white and red roses strategically placed on every flat surface that my room had to offer. A white envelope with my name on it was on my bed among a colorful array of rose petals. This could only be the work of one person. I immediately grabbed the envelope and decided to finally read what Adam had to say.

> *Kendi,*
>
> *I hope that you don't mind me invading your private space like this, but I need to get your attention, somehow, so that you will hear me out.*
>
> *Let me start by saying that I am completely lost without you. I love you so much. I know that I cannot take away the hurt that I have caused you and that nothing could ever justify my actions. If I could go back in time, I would make different choices. But I can't. I am begging you to forgive me. I have learned a lot from this. I guess that is part of life, learning from your mistakes so that you don't make them again. I just wish that I had not made such a costly mistake with someone I care about so deeply.*
>
> *Please, Kendi, can we talk about this? Is there any part of you that might be able to forgive me and let me back into your life? You are my best friend, and I miss you terribly. I know that my actions are making you question everything now, but, in my heart, there*

has only ever been you.
    For what it's worth, Happy Valentine's Day!
    Always,
    Adam

I couldn't stop the tears that ran down my face as I read his letter over and over again. I wanted to forgive him. I wanted things to go back to what they were before, but I knew in my heart that I could never stop questioning him. I still loved him. I had been waiting for those strong emotions to fade over time, but they were just as strong as ever. I wasn't sure what to do now. I wasn't ready to face him, so I crawled into my bed and hugged my knees to my chest until I fell asleep.

~

I never called Adam or responded to his desperate and over-the-top Valentine's display. The dozens of roses he left in my room had wilted, losing their beauty and velourlike appearance. I had thrown them out with the trash. He never tried to call me again or stop by to see me. I guess that I had finally succeeded in pushing him away. My emotions were so torn. The part of me that wanted to move on was relieved by his absence, but the other part of me was afraid for him to move on. I feared that he was seeing someone else, and the thought of him with another girl was pure torture. So when Chase Roberts asked me to the Spring Fling, I halfheartedly said yes. I needed a distraction and maybe I would even have fun.

Chase had moved here from Phoenix at the beginning of the school year. He was a junior, and I had been listening to the girls talk about him for months. He was a mystery that every young female wanted to solve, the newest and latest thriller, and it didn't hurt that he was a tall, blue-eyed, blond-haired dream. I hadn't taken much notice before, but, now that I knew he must be somewhat interested in me to ask me to a dance, I couldn't help but feel flattered. I definitely was noticing him now. In one day I had learned that he was in a few of my classes, was pitcher for our baseball team, and had moved here with his mother and younger sister to be closer to his grandparents.

The night of the dance I spent extra time applying my makeup and curling my hair. I had not looked my best at school for the past few months, and I wanted to be sure that Chase saw my full physical potential. I chose a pair of fitted dark jeans with a flirty bright pink top. Satisfied with my reflection in the mirror, I went downstairs to wait for Chase to arrive. He rang the bell, and I shooed my mother away to avoid any embarrassment.

I opened the door and felt a huge grin spread across my face at the sight of him. I couldn't remember the last time that I had felt like smiling. His golden hair was messy but in a purposeful way and slightly hanging over one eye. He wore distressed light-colored jeans and a snug black T-shirt that showed off a hint of muscle underneath. His simple attire made him look sweet and dangerous all at the same time. I watched his soft blue eyes as he drank me in from head to toe.

"Wow, you look great, Kendi!"

I felt myself blush. "Thank you. Are you ready to go?" I pulled the door closed behind me as I joined him on the porch. I suddenly felt nervous. I had never been on a date with someone I didn't already know. One of the many curses of growing up in a small town. He seemed completely relaxed though as he casually took my hand in his and led me to his car. He helped me into his faded red old-school Chevy Blazer and then walked around the front to get in the driver's seat. I smiled at the thought of how much my gramps would approve of Chase's car. Owning a dealership that exclusively sold American-made vehicles, my grandfather loathed foreign cars. He ridiculed Adam constantly for driving a BMW. A sudden pain stabbed my chest at the thought of Adam, so I pushed him to the back of my mind and vowed to not think of him for the remainder of the night.

Chase looked over at me and asked, "Ready?"

"Yep," I replied as he started the Blazer with a thunderous roar, Pearl Jam blaring on the stereo.

"Sorry about that," he cringed as he turned the volume down.

"That's fine, I love that song."

"You have good taste in music. That's a relief," he teased, lightening the mood. We drove to the dance listening to music rather than making small talk, and I felt a little less nervous by the time we pulled up to the high school gymnasium. He held my hand again as we walked into the dance. There were bright-colored paper flowers draped over everything and white twinkling lights wrapped around large potted trees that bordered the gym floor. The room had been transformed into a bright and "springy" scene, and I sighed at the unfamiliarity of it, hopeful that tonight I would not be haunted by memories. As my girlfriends began to notice our entrance, they approached us excitedly. I know that they were all dying to know how my night with the "new hot guy" was going. We stood in a tight group, talking loudly over the thumping bass of the music.

When the music slowed, Chase asked me if I wanted to dance and, as I nodded in reply, led me to the dance floor. He pulled me into his arms gently, swaying to the music. I put my arms around his neck and watched my friends dancing around me. I felt his lips near my ear as he said, "I've had my eye on you for a while now but wasn't really sure if you were available or not. I asked around to get the scoop on you. I hope that you don't mind. Anyway I'm really glad that you're here with me."

I slid my hands from his neck down to his arms so that I could see his face. "I'm glad that I'm here with you too. So tell me something about yourself, since I don't have the luxury of getting any town gossip on you."

He smiled at me and asked what I wanted to know.

"Well, did you break some poor girl's heart back in Phoenix when you moved here?"

He laughed at my flirtatious question and replied, matching my tone. "How do you know that some girl didn't break my heart before I left?"

"I can't imagine any girl wanting to let you go." I smiled at my boldness and bit my lower lip as I anticipated his response.

He brushed his thumb across my lips and smoothed them away from my teeth, smiling. Pulling me back into his arms, he picked up the pace as we finished dancing to the song.

His quiet confidence was completely hot, and my body was acutely aware of every place he touched me. The night flew by as Liz, Tracy and I danced up a storm while our dates watched from nearby. I felt myself let go, and I was having fun for the first time in months.

Chase walked me out to the car as the dance was coming to an end. It was a relatively warm night, considering that it was not officially spring yet. We leaned back against the front of the Chevy, listening to the music drifting out from the gym. Chase reached over, tucking a strand of my hair behind my ear, and I turned to look at him. I suddenly felt uncomfortable sharing such a quiet, intimate moment with him. He sensed my tension and pulled his hand away.

"Listen, Kendi. I know how much you've been through this past year, and I'm not here to put any pressure on you. I like you, a lot. I think that you're gorgeous and funny…and incredibly strong."

I cringed at what he was referring to; he really had

asked around about me.

"I had so much fun with you tonight. We can leave it at that…or not. Whatever you want."

The soulful harmony of Boys II Men was playing in the quiet of the parking lot, and he pulled me close to him, swaying to the music for one more dance. When I looked up at him, he held my chin in his hand and very sweetly pressed his lips to mine. I kissed him back just as softly for a moment but then quickly pulled away, burying my head against his defined chest as we danced.

The mood was lightened on our drive home as we teased one another, laughing the entire time. Chase was so easy to talk to, and my earlier nerves had been replaced with a sense of comfort and ease. Chase brought the car to a stop in front of my house, and I immediately tensed when I saw the black BMW parked in my driveway. I decided to end my night right there in the car to avoid any kind of confrontation.

"Thank you, Chase, I had such a great time tonight, really. See you on Monday at school?" I asked with one hand on the door handle.

"Let me walk you in," he insisted.

"That's okay. It's late." I waved him off.

"Can I call you this weekend?"

"Sure, that would be great. Bye, Chase." I tried to open the door before he could sense my sudden anxiety, but he grabbed my arm, and I turned to face him. He pulled me toward his side of the car, his hand holding the back of my head as he kissed me again. This time he parted my lips and slipped his tongue into my mouth. It was easy to get caught up in his kiss; he was new and exciting and so, so hot.

When he pulled away, I was breathless and disoriented.

He whispered, "Good-bye," and I fumbled to get the door open and climb out. I walked slowly up the sidewalk trying to clear my head of Chase's kiss and grasp the idea that Adam was in my house. I hadn't seen him in so long, I was nervous.

I found Adam sitting in the family room watching TV with Scott.

"Hi," I said quietly as he looked up at me with intense blue eyes.

"Hi," he said back. Scott cleared his throat and excused himself to go to bed. I had forgotten how attractive Adam was. I stared at him for several minutes, neither of us saying anything. My heart ached for him. I wanted to go to him and feel his arms around me. But I was afraid to let my guard down; the hurt was still so raw.

"What are you doing here, Adam?" I asked, breaking the silence.

"I need to talk to you. Scott invited me to wait for you. Spring Fling, huh?"

I could see the hurt in his eyes, knowing that I was at a dance with someone else. "Adam, there is nothing to talk about it. You shouldn't be here." My voice cracked as I tried to keep my emotions under control.

"Actually there is something that I need to tell you. Come sit with me." He motioned toward the couch where he was sitting. I sat down, but as far away from him as possible. He turned his body to face me and leaned forward, his elbows resting on his knees.

"Kendi, I know that you've moved on and that our relationship is over. I've been trying to accept that. I'm a complete mess without you, and I'm torn up inside over the pain I've caused you." He ran his hands through his thick curls, taking a deep breath. "I guess that I've been lost, really, these past few months. I've missed you so much, and Josh has been hostile toward me. I don't know how to make things right. I've been confiding in my pastor, not sure who to turn to after you wouldn't take my calls or answer my letters. He involved my parents, worried about the choices that I had made. It has been humiliating to say the least." He let out a long sigh and continued.

I wasn't sure what he was trying to tell me.

"Kendi, I'm going to Africa soon to do some missionary work for my church. The people really need me, and I'll be able to focus on my faith without distraction. I haven't made very good choices lately, and I need to make amends. My parents feel very strongly about this, and I don't really have much of a choice."

I was hanging on his every word, trying to follow his incessant rambling. "Adam, what are you saying?" I asked, confused.

"I'm leaving for Africa in a few months."

"For how long?"

"Two years most likely. I'm so torn about this decision. I know how important it is to my parents and my church. But I can't imagine not seeing you or talking to you for that long."

"We can't talk?"

"No, I can't have any distractions, and I won't really be near a phone every day. But we can write. It was easier to accept this once I realized that you weren't going to forgive me. I need to do this so that maybe I can forgive myself…for hurting you and for hurting Josh too."

I was trying to keep up with what he was saying, but it was all coming at me too fast. I brought my fingers to my temples, trying to ease the headache that was fast approaching from Adam's news. "Adam, this is crazy. I admit that I've been upset, and we haven't even talked about what happened or how we're feeling, but I guess I thought that I would have more time. Whether I can ever forgive you or not doesn't matter anymore—you're leaving. I mean, Africa, really?"

"I know that it's a lot to process, but I wanted you to know before you heard it from someone else."

"What about school?" I hugged my knees into my chest in an effort to keep myself from his touch.

"I'll take two years off and then go back. I spent most of the season on the bench, so I don't think that I'll be missing out on some big opportunity by leaving," he said with a smirk. His voice grew quieter as he continued. He reached out, resting his hand on my knee. "School will be here when I get back. The question is, will you? That's my biggest fear, losing you for good."

I pulled his hand from my leg and practically threw it off of me. "I can't answer that, Adam. Two years is a long time, and I don't even know where I'm going to school yet."

He clasped his hands in front of him and looked at me intently, his eyes full of sympathy. "I know."

I was overwhelmed by his presence and this news. As much as I wanted to move on, I guess that I always knew that he would be in my life somehow, given that we both shared this town as our home. The thought of him not being here surprised me. "I don't know what to say," I whispered. I buried my face in my hands.

Adam moved closer and pulled me into his lap, wrapping his arms around me. I let him comfort me. It felt too good, and I was too tired to fight him. I missed him so much. I breathed him in. His scent, the feel of his arms around me, the warmth of his breath on my neck. I still loved him. He had broken my heart, and I was still hopelessly in love with him. I let him hold me for what seemed like forever. He didn't say anything else to me, I sensed that he was content to have me in his arms and did not want to ruin the moment.

I finally pulled away and told him that he should go. It was late, and I was exhausted.

"I don't want to let you go," he whispered against my ear.

"You don't really have a choice, do you?" I said

quietly, my voice devoid of emotion.

He reluctantly released me, and we both stood to leave the room. Facing me, he cupped my cheek in his hand, "Can I see you again, Kendi?" he asked hopefully.

"I don't know, Adam. I don't know if this changes anything." I shrugged. I looked down at my feet as he pulled his hand away. I was afraid of giving in to him. I wasn't ready to hand him my shattered heart. I heard him take in a deep breath through his nose and let out a loud sigh, raking his fingers through his hair. Looking up at him when his silence continued, I met his smoldering eyes.

"Did you kiss him, Kendi? Do you like him?"

His questions caught me off guard, and I realized that he must have wanted to ask me this all night. I had completely forgotten about Chase, caught up in so many mixed emotions that Adam's presence alone had invoked. I closed my eyes briefly, breaking away from his intense stare. "Adam…don't ask me that."

His hands were resting on his head, and he began running them through his hair frantically, pacing side to side. The muscles in his jaw were taut. "Kendi, it makes me crazy to think of you with someone else."

His comment brought up the anger that I had worked so hard to move past over the last few months. "Don't do this. You know that *you're* the reason that we're here right now even having this conversation. You ruined us. You broke my heart," I yelled at him, the despair that I felt unmistakable in my voice. I shook my head in disbelief at his possessiveness. "Go home, Adam."

Moving in my direction, he pleaded with me, "I'm sorry, Kendi. I don't want to upset you. I still love you so much." He groaned when I stepped out of his reach. "This is killing me," he said through clenched teeth.

I walked to the door and opened it, stepping aside so that he clearly got the message that it was time for him to go.

Shaking his head, he walked past me but stopped and turned around in the doorway. "I'm not giving up, Kendi. I'll call you every day until I leave. I'll never stop trying to make this right."

"Good night, Adam." I was fighting against the tears that threatened to spill from my eyes. I didn't want him to see me cry. I had shed too many tears for him. He turned and walked out the door. I locked the door behind him, turned out the lights and trudged up the stairs. I was exhausted. My mind was whirling from the past few hours. My great night with Chase, Adam's news, being in his arms…that would all have to wait. I slipped into my pajamas and surprisingly fell into a deep sleep.

~

I awoke to the phone ringing endlessly. I had no idea what time it was, but it didn't seem like anyone else was home to answer it. I picked up the receiver. "Hello."

"Did I wake you up?" I heard a male voice, and it took me a moment to realize that it was Chase.

Sleepily I replied, "Yeah, what time is it?" I rubbed my eyes and took notice of the sun streaming in around my closed blinds.

"It's eleven o'clock, sleepyhead," he teased.

I couldn't remember the last time I had slept so much. "I guess I was really tired. What are you doing?" I yawned.

"I was just thinking about you. Some of us are going hiking around the gorge. Do you wanna go? It's a beautiful day finally."

"Hiking? When are you leaving?" Hiking did sound appealing, perfect for clearing my head.

"Dale, Travis, Liz and I are heading out in about half an hour. I'm driving. Should I pick you up?"

"Sure. I'm going to jump in the shower. Pick me up

last, okay?"

"Sounds good."

"Chase?"

"Yeah?"

"I had a great time last night, but I'm not really ready for…"

"I know, Kendi," he said cutting me off. "I'm cool with just hanging out. For now."

"Thanks."

"Don't thank me yet, Kendi," he said, laughing. "See you soon."

"Bye." Smiling, I hung up the phone and bolted out of bed. I quickly took a hot shower and pulled my hair back in a high ponytail. I threw on some cutoff jean shorts, an old UCLA T-shirt and a soft gray pullover sweater. I grabbed my hiking boots and a baseball cap and headed downstairs. I was just finishing a glass of orange juice when I heard the doorbell ring. After throwing a water bottle and a granola bar into my backpack, I met Chase at the door. He looked cute in khaki cargo shorts and a powder-blue T-shirt. He was wearing a dark baseball cap, turned backward, his crazy blond hair poking out from behind the strap that stretched across his forehead.

"Hey, stranger," he teased as he leaned in and gave me a peck on the cheek.

"Hey," I said shyly, my cheeks ablaze.

"Ready?"

I nodded.

"Everyone's in the car waiting. Travis insisted on riding shotgun, so I hope you don't mind sitting in the back."

"Of course not."

As we walked out to the Chevy, Liz threw open the door and bounded out to give me a hug. "I'm so glad that you're going with us. There is way too much testosterone in here." She laughed as I hugged her in return and climbed into the middle of the backseat.

Liz was one of those people that everybody loved. She was petite, just a dainty little thing, with thick dark hair that she wore in a pixie cut. She was very outgoing and always smiling. She had been a godsend this past year, making sure that I focused on the important aspects of being a high school senior.

I needed the constant reminder that I was young and that I should be having fun. The events of the past year had unfairly forced me to grow up, showing me how cruel life could be. But I wasn't going to dwell on the past anymore. I wanted to let my hair down, relax and have fun. I focused on the laughter around me, the sunshine on my face and the music that Chase had just turned up on the car stereo as we all sang along. I couldn't help but smile each time that I caught Chase glancing at me in the rearview mirror. He seemed genuinely pleased to see me look so happy.

It was a perfect day, the best combination of mindless fun and thought-provoking activity. It was hard not to contemplate your life while staring out at the breathtaking landscape of the gorge from several thousand feet above with the crystal blue Columbia River dividing it down the middle. Our chatty group grew silent as we took in the view, feeling small and insignificant among such an enormous natural wonder.

We could hardly contain our laughter when Chase cupped his hands around his mouth and shouted, "Holy shit," into the vast space surrounding us, his echo so clear that it seemed as if someone was shouting "shit" right back at us. There was a part of me that was worried about Chase's expectations, but he kept it platonic and light. Besides the peck on the cheek on my doorstep and the occasional squeeze of my hand while we were hiking, it was obvious that he was just being my friend, and that was exactly what I needed.

Mending Fences

As the days grew longer, spring bearing its gifts of warm sun and colorful bloom, I slowly let Adam back into my life. He kept to his word, calling every night, and I finally surrendered and began to accept his calls. It had started with awkward silence and small chitchat about our day but had slowly evolved into our familiar banter leaving us both laughing and feeling like friends once again. And eventually our conversations drifted into dangerous territory about the past and our future. Not so much our future together but our individual paths that were slowly being laid out before us. The past still brought up too many emotions for both of us: hurt, guilt, anger. But we were making progress.

He was waiting to get his orders for his mission, which would tell him where he was going exactly and when he would leave. I was waiting to receive my college acceptance letters so that I could decide where I wanted to go. I had been accepted to a few small schools already, but I was holding out for Udub or Western. Our fates had been sealed, each of us embarking on our differing versions of life's next step. I wasn't sure where that would lead, nor was I sure if Adam would ever be part of my life again once we both took that next step, but I knew that I didn't want to waste the time that we had together, even if it was just to have my best friend beside me. I had already lost Morgan. I wasn't ready to lose Adam, not yet anyway.

I eagerly checked the mailbox every afternoon, waiting to hear back from the last few schools that I had applied to when I finally received a large, thick envelope from the University of Washington. I closed my eyes tight, hoping that my suspicions were correct while I tore open the envelope. Peeking at the letter I held in my hand, I read "Congratulations" and exhaled the breath that I had been holding. Scott was standing next to me anxiously awaiting the results. "I got in," I screamed. "Oh, my God, I got in." I hugged Scott while I jumped up and down, throwing off his balance, nearly dragging us both to the ground.

"That's amazing. You have to call Mom and tell her."

"I will." I ruffled his short dark hair and wondered when he had grown taller than me. I still thought of him as a little boy, even though there were only a few years between us. I sat down to read the entire letter, and then called my mother at work to share my good news. She was ecstatic, her voice full of pride as she told me that she knew I could do it. After my mom hung up, I immediately called Adam to tell him. He knew how much I wanted this, and I had been agonizing over whether or not I would get in for weeks.

He answered on the first ring. "Adam, I got in," I squealed at the sound of his voice.

"Jeez, Kendi, calm down. You got in where?"

"Udub. I got my letter today. I can't believe it!"

"Kendi, that's great! I'm so excited for you."

"Thanks."

"Well I guess this helps you plan out the next few years of your life."

"I guess so," I replied, the excitement draining from my voice knowing that these plans would not include Adam. Hearing my solemn response, he tried to encourage me.

"Hey, Kendi, this is a good thing. You deserve this, and you should be celebrating."

"I know, and I'm excited obviously. But I already miss you, and you're not even gone yet."

"I already miss you too."

~

There was an undeniable sense of exuberance in the air as the year trudged on, bringing us closer to graduation and freedom. My friends and I embraced the final weeks of high school, planning our senior trip, senior prank, the classic senior skip day and our graduation parties. I was experiencing an assortment of emotions as we approached the school year's end. I had always assumed that finishing high school would only bring excitement and happiness, but I was starting to feel a sense of sadness with the thought of saying good-bye to friends that I had known for twelve years, and of course the uncertainty of what the future held for Adam and I was disheartening.

Still I focused on the fun events unfolding as graduation drew closer and of the precious time that I had with my friends. Chase and I had developed a friendship that had flirted with the possibility of becoming more, but I had explained to him that I was leaving for college soon, and we were better off as friends. That didn't stop his obvious advances and pleas to give him a chance. He had become a strong figure in our little group, so I dodged his advances playfully to avoid any awkwardness among our friends. In all honesty, I enjoyed having him around. He made me feel happy and fun, his presence refreshing, representing nothing from my past. Despite what he might feel for me though, my heart belonged to Adam, and I feared that it always would.

Adam had been asking me for weeks to spend a Saturday with him. I had been avoiding it at all costs, always coming up with some excuse. I had a study group, or I already had plans with the girls—anything to not spend a great length of time with him. It was so hard to be near him and keep up with this "We're just friends" charade. I was afraid to let him back into my life on any other terms. Especially with his imminent departure looming in the air. He finally succeeded in convincing me to meet him at Gonzaga so that we could toddle around town, go shopping or catch a movie.

We had just finished lunch at our favorite gourmet pizza restaurant and decided to take a stroll through Riverfront Park to enjoy the fresh air and sunshine. Summer was just around the corner, the temperature rising as it drew near. Adam reached for my hand as we walked along the trail. I thought about pulling it away, but it seemed innocent enough.

"Have you heard anything more on your mission?" I asked, interrupting the comfortable silence that had fallen over us.

"Yeah, actually I got a call yesterday."

"And?" I asked when he didn't volunteer any more information.

"And they're sending me to Ghana first and then South Africa. I may move around a bit, depending on where the need is. I'm going to help with an agricultural project that teaches basic farming skills to the youth and will provide crops to feed the community. Given my background, they thought it would be a good fit."

"That sounds exciting, Adam. You're going to be making an extraordinary difference in these people's lives.

I'm so proud of you." I nudged him with my elbow as we continued to walk through the park hand in hand.

"It is exciting, but honestly I'm a little scared. I'm not sure what the living conditions will be like or the language barriers, and what if I get sick or something?"

These were all things that I had wondered about myself, and I prayed that Adam would be safe when my mind wandered to the darkest of places.

I tried to encourage him. "You're not going to be alone there, and I'm sure you're not the first to have these concerns. Do you know when you're leaving?"

He hung his head sadly and said, "The first week of September. September 7th to be exact."

"I can't believe that you've been keeping this information from me all day."

"I didn't want to ruin our day. I'm having the best time with you today. It feels like old times."

It did feel like old times. We were comfortable with each other, laughing easily, but his comment hung heavy in the warm air. It wasn't like before; everything had changed, and everything was about to change even more.

As if reading my mind, Adam sensed the shift in the air and pulled me to the side of the path. We stood in the shade of a large maple tree, Adam facing me. "Hey," he said as he lifted my chin with his hand until our eyes met. "We have the whole summer to spend together." His finger stroked my cheek, his touch igniting sparks through my body, and I couldn't help but watch his lips as he spoke to me.

"That's not it, Adam. I just wish that we weren't here in this place, that things were different. And then I think of all the reasons that brought us here, and I just feel sad."

"I'm sorry, Kendi. I will never stop apologizing, but I can't change the past."

"I know, but sometimes I wish you could change the future." I knew that I sounded like a whiny little girl, but it was an honest expression of my feelings. He released my chin, and I looked down at my feet as I kicked the grass around with my shoe.

"We don't know what the future holds, Kendi. We can't change what hasn't happened yet. Maybe this time away will heal our wounds, and we can pick up where we left off when I get back."

"Not likely." I sulked. With a hand on the small of my back, he pulled me closer to him and cupped my chin with his other hand, drawing my eyes to meet the intense blue of his once again.

"Why not?" he whispered, his breath on my face from his close proximity.

I shrugged, not knowing what to say.

He glanced down at my lips and leaned in to kiss me.

I looked down, subtly avoiding his intention, and he rested his forehead against mine instead, letting out a heavy sigh. We stood like that for several minutes, both his hands now resting on my lower back, mine dangling at his sides with fingers gripping the belt loops of his jeans. I closed my eyes. My breath quickened as I fought against my desire to kiss him, to lose myself in him. I could feel his rapid heartbeat and his breath on my face. I wanted him so badly, but I didn't want to complicate things between us. I didn't want to wonder where he was or who he was with. I didn't want to doubt everything that he told me. I felt like I had more control over my heart this way, that I was guarding it somehow.

"Why not?" he whispered again with his own desire evident in his voice.

I didn't have a response. I couldn't articulate a sentence right now if I tried. All my focus was on fighting this pull I felt between us. Backing away from him, I reached for his hand as we continued down the path, once again in silence.

~

Graduation was just around the corner, and the party circuit had begun. I was definitely in the mood to let loose after working so hard all year academically. Saturday night was no exception. My mother and Scott had gone to Seattle to help Marie move into a new apartment. She had just graduated from college a few weeks ago and was starting an amazing advertising job for a cellular phone company. I stayed behind to spend time with friends knowing that I would be in Seattle soon enough myself. I was really looking forward to having Marie close by. Her new apartment was only a few minutes' drive from campus.

I had the house to myself for the night, which meant the girls were staying at my place. Tracy, Liz and I spent the afternoon lounging around, eating junk food and watching 90210 episodes that I had recorded. When the sun began to make its descent, we showered, primped and poured back a celebratory shot of my mother's finest tequila while dancing to our favorite song at an ear-shattering volume. It wasn't long before Chase, Travis and Dale came by to pick us up. Rick was home from Arizona for the summer and was throwing a party at his house. We were all going.

Upon arrival at his house, Rick approached me and wrapped me in a huge hug. "Hey, Kendi. It's so good to see you. How are you?"

It was so good to see him too. I had avoided him during Christmas break, knowing that his presence would have evoked painful memories of Morgan and Adam. "I missed you, Rick. I'm actually doing pretty good. How about you, college boy? How's life?"

"Great, it's good to be home though. Come on, let's get you a drink." With his arm around my shoulders, Rick led me to the kitchen where an endless supply of liquor and beer awaited. "Pick your poison." Liz and Tracy were already in the kitchen pouring tequila into several shot glasses that were lined up along the counter. "Tequila it is," Rick declared. We all raised a shot glass, toasting to friends and slamming the amber liquid to the back of our throats.

After my third shot for the evening, I decided to stick to beer. My mind was already in a haze, my body relaxed, and I was having way too much fun. I was thankful that Adam didn't attend parties. I was able to let my guard down, to take a break from the exhausting game of defense that my heart had been playing when in Adam's presence.

Liz turned up the music, and the crowd erupted in screams, bodies moving to the beat. I felt warm arms around my waist, as Chase pressed his body against my back, moving with me to the music. For once I didn't care. I pressed into him and continued dancing. The night wore on, and Chase continued to step over boundaries that I had placed between us months before. Maybe it was the alcohol or the sense of freedom I was feeling, but I let myself enjoy the feel of Chase's hands all over me. Although when he drew me in close and kissed me on the lips, it suddenly felt wrong. I knew in that moment that, every time Chase had touched me, I had been thinking of Adam. And now, with Chase's tongue rammed down my throat, my mind was fully aware that this was definitely not Adam. I pushed him away. "Chase, stop. I'm sorry, I can't do this."

"Come on, Kendi. We're just having a little fun tonight." He pressed me to him again. I put my hand against his chest to hold him back.

"Not anymore, Chase. I'm sorry. I think that I had too much to drink." I turned to walk away, but I didn't get very far in the sea of bodies dancing around us. I felt him grab my arm and pull me back.

"Kendi, come on, loosen up. Just admit it. You're enjoying this as much as I am."

"Let go, Chase. I didn't mean to give you the wrong idea." I tried to pull my arm away, but he held on tighter. Suddenly Rick was there, asking if there was a problem.

"Everything is fine, Rick," I assured him. Chase released my arm, shaking his head as he stormed off. *Great, he was mad.* This was what I'd tried to avoid from the beginning, but I'd let myself get carried away.

"I need another drink," I said to Rick as he followed me to the kitchen. Two more tequila shots helped me forget about my encounter with Chase. I was officially drunk, and, like an overprotective brother, Rick didn't leave my side. Sitting on a bar stool at the kitchen counter with him standing next to me, feeling completely uninhibited from the alcohol, I began to talk openly to Rick about Adam. "Did you know that Adam was sleeping with Katie that whole fucking time?"

"No, Kendi. I didn't know. I was his best friend, and I had no idea. Honestly, I don't know what he was thinking. You couldn't pay me to tap that."

"I know, right? What did he see in her? It still hurts so much to think about it."

"I'm sorry that he hurt you, Kendi. Honestly, you're so beautiful and smart and so much fun, I can't understand why he'd risk losing you for her. But, Kendi, Adam does love you. I do know that much."

"Yeah, well he should have thought of that before acting like such a selfish asshole." A tear slipped down my cheek as I reached for the nearly empty tequila bottle.

"Hey, slow down. I think you've had enough."

"Are you my daddy now? Lighten up, Rick, it's a party." He smiled and I filled two shot glasses, handing him one. With a clink of our glasses, I felt the tequila warm my insides once again.

Rick took the shot glass from my hand and blurted out, "I miss Morgan." Just hearing her name made my heart stop in my chest.

"I miss her too…every day." Another tear fell down my face; Rick reached up and wiped it away.

"Come on, party girl, let's dance." As we danced among our friends, I started to feel light-headed. The alcohol was getting the best of me. Rick must have noticed and led me down the hall to his room. "Are you feeling okay, Kendi?"

"Yeah, just a little drunk," I slurred.

"Why don't you lie down for a little while? I'll be back to check on you." He took my shoes off and tucked me in, dimming the lights. I heard him set a trash can next to the bed and close the door behind him as he left. He was so sweet to take care of me.

The next thing I knew, Adam was sitting beside me, stroking my hair. I must have dozed off for a while. I glanced at the alarm clock next to the bed displaying 12:10 a.m. in glowing red numbers. "Adam, what are you doing here?" I asked quietly.

"Rick called me and said that you might need a ride home. Are you okay? He said that you had a lot to drink."

"Yeah, I'm fine. Can you take me home? Chase drove, and we kind of got into a fight. He can bring the girls home later."

"Yeah, come on. Let's get you home." Adam picked me up and cradled me in his arms with my shoes in hand. I wrapped my arms around his neck, snuggling in close, welcoming the comfort. He stopped to whisper something to Rick on our way out, and then we left. I slipped my shoes on in the car while Adam drove. We rode in silence, my eyes watching everything that passed by outside my window. My head was still swimming from the alcohol, and all I could think about was how much I wanted to be with Adam. He walked me to the door and unlocked it for me with my key.

"Are you going to be all right by yourself?"

"Yeah, I'll be fine. Thank you for bringing me home,"

I whispered. He pulled me against him, wrapping me up in a friendly hug, and I rested my cheek against his chest. His familiar smell melted me. It felt so good to be in his arms. I instinctively looked up at him, and, with my hands in his hair, I slowly brought his mouth to mine. I kissed him gently. He hesitated briefly but began to surrender to my lips with his own. His lips felt so good. God, I had missed this.

Maybe it was the alcohol or my conversation with Rick, but I was at a point of retreat. I was tired of denying my feelings for Adam. I ran my fingers through his thick hair as I pulled him closer to me, devouring his mouth with my own. With his arms around my waist, he lifted me up slightly, my feet inches from the ground and carried me into the house. We made it only to the kitchen as he hoisted me up, settling me down on the kitchen counter.

Standing between my legs, he continued to kiss me, holding me close, stroking my hair down my back. My hands were everywhere. In his hair, digging into the strong cuts of his back, gripping his backside. I tugged at his T-shirt, and he raised his arms as I lifted it up over his head. He slowly unbuttoned my shirt and pulled it from my arms as I crushed my bare skin against him. The smooth skin of his toned chest against me warmed my insides more than the tequila had. I ran my hands up and down his bare back as his tongue pushed its way into my mouth.

I reached down and started to unbutton his jeans. He grabbed my hand and held it in place, denying me access to what my body craved. This was not like him. I ached for him, and I needed this more than ever.

"Adam, please," I whimpered.

"Not like this, Kendi," he said quietly against my mouth. Resting his forehead against mine with his eyes closed, he sighed. "You're drunk. Believe me, I want this more than I have ever wanted anything but not like this."

I knew he was right, but I couldn't help but feel hurt

by his rejection. Adam never refused sex. I turned my face away from his, embarrassed that I had let myself get carried away. He softly kissed my cheek and reached for his shirt, pulling it back on over his head.

He picked up my shirt and said, "Let's get you to bed." I let him lead me by the hand up the stairs to my room. He grabbed a T-shirt from my closet and after unclasping my bra, he slid it on over my head. It felt cool against the heat of my skin. He laid me back and pulled off my shoes and shorts. I quietly let him take care of me as he pulled my blanket over me, tucking me in. He leaned down and kissed me on the lips, so sweetly. I flung my arms around his neck and kissed him back.

"Stay with me, Adam," I begged. "Just hold me, nothing more. Please." I had torn down the wall that I had built between us, and now I couldn't stand the thought of being apart from him.

"All right," he said on a breath. He slipped off his shoes and shirt and crawled under the blanket, pulling me tight against him. With the heat from his skin and the steady beat of his heart drumming against my cheek, it wasn't long before I fell asleep.

~

I woke in the morning, alone, thirsty, with my heart pounding in my head. I groaned at the thought of the amount of tequila I had consumed last night. I remembered being in Adam's arms and wondered if it was just a dream. I rolled onto my side where I remembered him lying when I was last conscious. In his place, a note sat on my pillow.

> *Kendi,*
> *I could have held you in my arms forever, but I*
> *was afraid of how you might feel when you woke up*

*and the alcohol had worn off. I hope that you are not
full of regret. Whatever you are feeling now, thank
you for letting me be with you last night. I have
missed you so much. I love you, Kendi, more than you
know.*

> *Call me when you wake up.*
> *Always,*
> *Adam*

How was I feeling? I didn't feel regret but a longing
for Adam. I still loved him, and I feared how that love would
grow over the next few months with my guard down. I feared
how lost I would feel again without him when he left. *Weak.* I
had fought so hard for the small amount of strength that I had
built up over the past few months, and, now in one night, I
felt depleted. At the same time, I felt free of the tension that
had been nearly suffocating me lately. I stretched my stiff
muscles and slowly sat up in bed. The room swayed around
me as I struggled to ward off the waves of nausea slamming
into me. I pulled on a pair of sweatpants and made my way
downstairs for a glass of water and aspirin.

Loud snoring drifted up the stairs as I made my
descent. Sprawled out on the family room floor and couch
were Chase, Travis and Dale. Blankets, pillows and clothing
were strewn all over. I cringed at the memory of Chase from
last night. I gulped down a glass of cold water, swallowing
three aspirin and crawling back into bed. My clock read 8:20.
I picked up the phone and called Adam. At the sound of his
voice, a warmth spread through my body, a smile exploding
across my face.

"Hey," I said.

"Hey, how are you feeling?"

"Not great, but it was worth it."

"Whatever you say."

Silence.

"Thank you for bringing me home last night and staying with me. I wish that you were here with me right now." I heard a loud sigh on the other end.

"Really?"

"Really."

"I'm so relieved to hear you say that. I thought for sure that you were going to tell me that last night was a mistake."

"Adam, I love you, that hasn't changed. And I want to spend the summer with you before we both leave, but, please, I am begging you, please, don't break my heart again. I need you to be honest with me always, and even then it will be hard to trust you. I don't want any regrets. I just want to enjoy these last few months."

"Kendi, I promise I will never make the same mistakes again. I know that I need to earn back your trust. I miss…us. I will do anything to make this right."

"You sure about that?"

"Yeah."

"Then get over here, now!"

"Well, almost anything. You have a few houseguests that it would be better if I didn't run into. I can't stand the thought of anyone else wanting you, Kendi. And I know what he wants!"

"Adam! You have nothing to worry about. But I understand."

"I'll call you later, Kendi. I love you."

"I love you too."

After talking to Adam, I drifted back into unconsciousness. Hours later, I awoke to Tracy and Liz pouncing on my bed. They demanded to know what had happened with Adam. I told them everything, and then I told them what had happened with Chase.

"So you and Adam are back together?" Liz asked.

"Yeah, I guess so," I answered, sounding unsure.

"Even though he is leaving in September?" she reiterated.

"*Because* he is leaving," I said matter-of-factly.

"Just be careful," Liz warned. She knew about what had happened with Katie. It was hard to keep anything quiet in this town.

"So back to Chase," Tracy chimed in. "He really got mad at you last night?"

"Yeah, is he still here?" I asked, dreading the inevitable conversation that Chase and I were going to have.

"Yep, the guys are still crashed out downstairs," Tracy answered.

"Well, we better go wake them up. My mom and Scott are going to be home soon." We cranked the music up in the family room for their wake-up call. It was not received well. After the moaning and groaning subsided, Chase pulled me down on the floor next to him.

"Hey," he said with a shameful look in his eyes.

"Hey yourself," I replied back. In the same moment, we both blurted out, "I'm sorry," followed by our light laughter and sighs of relief.

"Chase, I don't want things to be awkward between us, and I'm sorry if I gave you the wrong idea last night. We were just having fun, but I never meant for it to amount to anything physically. Things are complicated for me right now."

"I know. I saw you leave with Adam. I'm sorry for pushing you last night. I just wanted you to see how much fun we are together, and how great you and I could be, if you would just let down your guard. But I understand now why you have your guard up. It's because of him, isn't it?" I rolled onto my back beside him and gazed up at the ceiling, relieved at how easy it was to talk to him, even after what had unfolded.

"Yeah, it's because of him, Chase. I love him."

"I care about you, and I just want you to be happy, even if it is with him." He nudged my side with his elbow.

"You're a good guy, Chase," I said as I rolled back onto my stomach, propped up on my elbows so that I could see his face. "Thank you for being so understanding." If Adam didn't own my heart, I would be lucky to be with Chase. He was caring and considerate, which says a lot for someone who looks the way he does. He was gorgeous. Even looking completely disheveled first thing in the morning, he still took my breath away. I roughed up his hair with my hand. "Now go brush your teeth. I can't stand your morning breath any longer," I teased. He pulled me into a friendly headlock, and, bringing his face close to mine, he began to pant in my face. His breath smelled like tequila and cigarettes. "Gross, Chase. Cut it out." I tried to push him away from me.

He let go, laughing hysterically. "Fine, you win," he said before standing up and pulling me to my feet by the hand.

I sent everyone on their way and cleaned up the house before my mother returned from Seattle. As I loaded the breakfast dishes into the dishwasher and wiped down the kitchen counters, I couldn't stop smiling. My heart was filled with what can only be described as pure joy. I was so grateful for great friends, even Chase. And opening my heart to Adam again filled me with an indescribable feeling of completeness. I tried not to think about September. I was excited to start school in Seattle, to finally be away from this small town. I just wasn't sure how I was going to say good-bye to Adam. We had the summer, and that would have to be enough for now.

Falling

Graduation day brought mixed emotions, and I tried to focus on the celebration. My thoughts drifted to the people who should have shared this day with me. Their absence was hard to ignore. My dad was missing another big milestone in my life. I had stopped expecting him to show up since my third-grade dance recital, but I couldn't help but be hopeful that one day he would surprise me. And Morgan should have been standing here with me, smiling in her cap and gown. Her chair on the stage was left empty and in her place laid a blue graduation cap and a single pink rose.

I could see my family seated a few rows from the front with Adam sitting among them. My gramps and grams were smiling proudly from their seats, reminding me of the envelope that my grandfather had presented me with the night before. He had given me a check for a surprising amount, and, on the memo he had written *For my Kendi, for med school.*

The check would hardly put a dent in the heavy build-up of expenses that a lifetime of school would amount to, but I knew that it was a considerable amount for him with his modest income. I was moved beyond words at his generosity and the sheer fact that he believed in me. My family was so important to me; I wanted to achieve big things. I wanted to make them proud. I could hear their loud cheers when my name was called, and I walked up to receive my diploma.

Once each of my classmates had received their diplomas, I picked up the rose on Mo's seat and walked down the stairs to where her parents were seated in the front row. I handed them the rose, hugging them fiercely before returning to my seat as I heard the auditorium explode in applause. Mr. Stuart, our superintendent, announced the graduating class of 1995. I threw my cap into the air with the rest of my classmates as we cheered for the success of our past and the possibilities of our future.

Adam finished his last semester of school and moved back home. We both started our summer jobs. I was working at the restaurant again, and Adam was working for his parents. I had much better hours this year and spent every spare minute with him. On my days off, I usually met Adam in the fields, and he taught me how to drive a tractor or a combine. I could tell how much he enjoyed the solitude of farming. Driving a tractor seemed like a tedious job to me, but Adam had a huge grin on his face, happy to be sharing such a big part of his life with me.

I also started attending church with him on Sunday mornings. My family was religious. My grandparents could be found every Sunday morning sitting in the pews of our church, where they had been parishioners for years. My mother, sister, brother and I attended only for Christmas and Easter and a few other days of the year. I had a strong faith in God but never felt the need to put it on display by sitting in church every week. Church was a big part of Adam's life and he wanted me to share that with him as well. I had never felt closer to Adam, and, yet at the same time, I felt our differences erupting like a volcano, separating us with insurmountable terrain and smoldering lava.

~

We spent many evenings lying in the dark gazing at the stars and talking about our future. Tonight was no exception. We were sprawled out on a blanket in the middle of the high school football field. Everything was so quiet and still. I wondered if I would miss these quiet moments when I was living in the city surrounded by hundreds of college students.

"What are you thinking about?" Adam asked, pulling me from my thoughts.

"Just wondering if I'll miss the little things about living here. As much as I can't wait to be in a new city living among swarms of new people, this is all I've ever known."

"I hope that you'll miss me," he admitted.

"Of course I will. You're not one of the 'little things' in my life that I was referring to. You're a huge part of my life." He rolled onto his stomach and looked into my eyes intently.

"Kendi, I want to always be a big part of your life. I can't imagine my life without you in it. I need to know what you see happening over the next few years, honestly."

"Adam, I can't tell you that. Everything is changing in my life and in yours. There's too much uncertainty that comes with change."

"I don't want a vague answer, Kendi. I want to know what you *want* to happen."

"I know that I *want* to be with you. I don't *want* you to go to Africa. At the same time, I *want* to go to college, and I *want* to go to med school. Beyond that, I don't know. I want a lot of things, Adam, but that doesn't change the course that we're on."

"I want to be with you too. I want to marry you, Kendi. I can see us living our life together, having kids. I want that. I don't want to leave you either, but I want to go to Africa. I feel like this mission is calling to me. I can't explain it, but I know that I need to do this. Will you wait for me?"

I didn't know what to say. Two years was a long time when you were eighteen years old. That was two Christmases, two New Year's, two birthdays…so much can change in that amount of time. I wanted to promise him that I could do it, but deep down inside I knew that he was asking for too much. College was supposed to be fun. College was parties, new friends, new boys, new experiences. College was where you made mistakes and you learned from them.

I tried to imagine that he was going to be at Gonzaga for the next two years rather than oceans away without any modern means of communication. How would I answer his question then? If I could see him on weekends and holidays and know that we could spend the summers together, would I be more certain of our future? In that scenario, I felt like I would have more of him to hold on to, that our relationship would be worth fighting for. I chose my words carefully.

"I can't answer that. I want you in my life. I'll write to you as much as I can. I'll want to share all the details of college life with you. Anytime that something exciting happens or if I'm upset about something, you're the first person that I want to talk to. I can't see that changing, despite the miles that will separate us. If I'm being honest, I have to tell you that I won't let opportunities pass me by waiting for you to come home. If the accident taught me anything, it's that life's too short, and we never know how much time we have left. I will always have a place for you in my life, Adam. I won't know what that place is until we get there. Only time will tell, I guess. That's the most I can promise you right now."

I could see the sadness in his eyes as he traced the contours of my face with his finger.

"You're amazing, Kendi. You're so beautiful and smart, and you have the kindest heart of anyone I know. I want you to be happy. I hope that you're always as honest with me as you are now. I love you for that." He leaned down and kissed me. I pulled him into my arms, holding on to what we were in that moment as if my life depended on it. He parted my lips with his own as our kiss became more urgent, our bodies pressed together. The passion in our kiss continued on into the night until he finally pulled away, leaving us both breathless.

"We can't do this, Kendi." It wasn't the first time he had pulled away in recent weeks. We had not been together in that way since we had reconciled. One of us always seemed to hesitate for our own personal reasons, and we left it at that. I wanted to take things slow. I feared the vulnerability that came with opening myself up fully to him. Although it had been getting harder and harder to say no. In that moment, I was saying yes. My body ached for him. But his words were loud and clear.

"Adam, it's okay. I can't wait any longer," I assured him.

He collapsed onto his back next to me, distancing himself from me. "No. I can't go down that road again. This mission means so much to me, and I vowed to choose a more honest and moral path this time. I know how hard this is, trust me, but I can't be with you like that. I'm sorry."

I let out a long sigh, trying to slow my breathing. "I get it, Adam. Wow, this is going to be hard though," I said as I stretched my arms out above my head, feeling the cool grass under my fingers.

"I know. We can still mess around, Kendi. We just can't let things get too far. I could never say no to holding you like this. I love you too much." He pulled me back into his arms, kissing my neck tenderly.

Warmth spread through my body, desire consuming me once again. "Adam," I protested, pushing him away. "I need a minute."

He laughed at me. "Look at you, all hot and bothered."

"Very funny," I smirked, hitting him in the arm with my fist. And with that he straddled me, pinning my arms above my head, and kissed me endlessly in all the right places. It was pure torture, exactly what he had been hoping for.

~

I tried to find a balance between spending time with Adam and the rest of my life. Between my hours at the restaurant, shopping with my mom for college necessities, parties with Liz and Tracy, and the precious hours spent with Adam, I was more than busy, and the summer was flying by too fast. My fears were all coming true as I completely opened myself up to Adam. I fell in love with him more and more each day. The very idea of spending my life with him was blossoming inside my heart like a bud at springtime.

Our long and heartfelt conversations seemed to revolve around our future, and I found myself sharing Adam's certainty that our relationship could withstand a two-year separation living on different continents. We talked about all the possibilities. When he returned from Africa, he could finish school at Udub or another school in Seattle. We could get married and rent an apartment in Seattle while I finished med school.

What we didn't talk about was what happened after that. Where would we live or what if I had to attend med school out of state? What about Adam's agricultural aspirations? These were all questions that I held in the deep crevices of my mind, afraid to speak them aloud, afraid to burst the safe and colorful bubble that we were floating in. What I did know was that I loved him with every cell in my body, and that had to be enough for now. So I floated along, playing my part of the lovesick teenager that I was.

I couldn't seem to keep my hands off Adam. The fact that I couldn't have him the way I wanted, physically, made me want him even more. I could sense that Adam was having a difficult time living up to the promises that he had made, and I tried not to press the issue. I respected his decision, and I supported his faith and commitment to his church, even if I could not relate. On numerous occasions he had voiced his opinion about the way that I lived my life, and hoped that one day I would convert to his church and share his faith with him. I tried to be understanding but I could not make any promises. I was comfortable with my faith and my own religious beliefs, and I knew that this was yet another barrier that would inevitably stand between us.

So for now we held each other, devouring one another with our mouths and hands until one of us, usually Adam, pulled away before we lost all sense to stop. Removing the physical acts from our relationship left us with additional time to talk and explore our hearts rather than our bodies, and I felt our relationship grow on an emotional level. I felt connected to Adam in a way that I hadn't before, and this made me feel more exposed and vulnerable than ever.

Despite my best intentions, I was falling in deep all over again—completely lost in him.

Good-byes

It was the one-year anniversary of the accident, the day that I lost Mo. I woke early in the morning with a new sense of loss, like I was losing her all over again. I went for a run before the summer heat rose to an unbearable temperature. I was trying to clear my head, but, with each stride, images of her smiling face filled my mind. I found myself at the cemetery near the edge of town. It was easy to find her headstone. I had been there countless times over the past year. I looked down at her name etched in gray slate with her birthdate and the last day that she had smiled beneath it. I ran my fingers across my collarbone, feeling the long, jagged scar that would always be with me to remind me of that cruel day.

"I miss you, Mo," I whispered into the wind. When I felt the tears slide down my cheeks, I started to run again. I ran faster, harder, as if I could outrun the pain that threatened to bring me to my knees. I reached my house and stood on the porch, bent over with my hands on my thighs, trying to catch my breath. My lungs burned from the overexertion. I welcomed this physical pain, a reminder that I was still alive, and, although the guilt from this simple fact overwhelmed me at times, I was grateful.

With a heavy heart I made my way upstairs to take a shower. I needed to be with Adam. He was the only one who understood the crushing emotions that I dealt with when it came to Morgan. The guilt, the loss, the pain, the traumatic memories that still occasionally haunted my dreams. I threw on a navy sundress, dried my long hair and drove to his house unannounced. His parents were out of town, and we were supposed to meet later in the day, but I couldn't wait.

He answered the door looking adorable in khaki shorts and a blue Gonzaga T-shirt. His dark wavy locks were in complete disarray. He instantly smiled, his dimples bigger than ever and calling to me.

"Hey," he said empathetically as he noticed the state that I was in.

"Hey," I replied as my tears fought their way to the surface. He drew me into his chest and held me tight as I melted against him. He eventually lifted me into his arms and carried me inside to his bedroom. I had never been in his bedroom in his parents' house. They were always home, and we were not allowed to hang out in there. He sat me on his bed, which was covered with a blue-and-green flannel comforter. His walls were adorned with shelves displaying dozens of trophies from various sporting events. Posters of professional basketball players covered the walls and a small crucifix hung above his bed. The room was surprisingly clean.

Adam lay down on the bed next to me, pulling me back into his arms. "Tough day, huh?" he asked as he absentmindedly played with my hair. I could only nod in response, and he squeezed me tighter. I felt so safe in his arms with my face buried in his chest. He pulled up my chin with his hand until I was looking him in the eye.

"Just breathe, Kendi. We'll get through today just like any other day." He kissed me softly on the lips. When he kissed me with more intensity, I responded by running my hands through his hair. I surrendered my thoughts and let my body take over as I focused on the feel of his hand running up the bare skin of my leg, electricity coursing through my body. I lost myself in his kiss, and it wasn't long before he was pulling my dress off my body and running his hands along my breasts, the smooth planes of my stomach, down to my most sensitive flesh. My desire was unbearable, and I instinctively pushed him away.

"Adam, stop. It's too much," I whispered. Ignoring my plea, he kissed each place where his hands had been until I felt his warm lips on my flesh. I jerked at the intense ripple of pleasure that shot through my body. He spread his hand firmly against my lower abdomen, holding me in place. He had never taken things this far before, well at least not in recent months. I could feel my release building, unrecognizable moans escaping my lips. I was just about to fall over the edge when he stopped and slowly kissed his way back to my lips.

"Adam, you're killing me," I groaned. He looked at me then, his sultry eyes burning right through me as I sensed something shift in his mind.

"You are so beautiful," he said as he ran his hand down my naked body, caressing every curve along the way. I was on fire, nearly ready to explode as he kissed me again, his intentions undeniable. I pulled his shirt over his head and ran my hands along the muscles of his back, bringing him closer to me. I kept waiting for him to pull away but he never did. I reached for the clasp on his shorts and removed the remaining clothing from his body.

"Are you sure?" I asked hesitantly, afraid that he

would change his mind.

"I need to be with you like this, Kendi. Just this once. God, I love you." He buried his face in my neck, his lips seducing me as he delicately brushed them across my skin from my ear down to my shoulder. He lowered himself inside me as he called out my name. I fell over the edge, hard, crying out loudly, as my body exploded around him. Adam took his time, not wanting it to end, loving every inch of me while my body responded to him time and time again. When his desire finally got the best of him, I felt Adam thrust deeper inside of me, moaning my name against my ear, as shudders raked his body. He collapsed on top of me, burying his face in the crook of my neck. We stayed wrapped up in each other, completely spent, until his weight was crushing me, and I tried to wriggle out from underneath him.

He rolled to the side of me and propped himself up on one elbow, brushing my hair behind my ear with his free hand.

"I've missed this. Being this close to you." He leaned down and kissed me lightly on the nose and then kissed my lips, lingering for just a moment. "I love you so much."

I ran my fingertips through his hair, pulling his face closer to mine as I kissed him more firmly on the mouth. "I love you too," I whispered. I loved him so much in that moment that my chest hurt. We spent the rest of the day holding each other, our legs tangled together under his sheets, our clothes left untouched on the floor.

~

Before we knew it, it was September, and Adam was preparing for his trip to Africa. I had a lot on my mind and had been feeling distracted all week. Adam was scheduled to leave in two days, and I was moving to Seattle to start school a week later. Most of our friends had left for colleges at the end of August, and I had already said my good-byes with promises to stay in touch. Adam's church had held a farewell ceremony, and I had sat back and sadly watched how excited Adam was about the selfless, life-changing experience that he was about to embark on. I was happy for him and extremely proud of him, but I couldn't help but selfishly sulk about how much I was going to miss him.

Adam had brought me his favorite Gonzaga sweatshirt that he practically lived in. He said that he wanted me to have it to keep me warm while he was away. I was sitting on my bed holding his sweatshirt up to my face, inhaling his scent, as he handed me a small velvet box.

"What's this?" I asked, as I slowly opened the box, feeling nervous until I saw my sapphire ring shimmering in the sunlight that streamed in through the gaps in my blinds. "My ring," I said solemnly.

"I want you to have this back. I gave it to you almost a year ago, and I meant what I said. "I will always love you."

I slipped it back on my finger where it belonged. "Thank you," I said, letting the waves of sadness wash over me as I looked down at my hand, admiring the beautiful ring that I had completely forgotten about. A ring that represented a happier time, a less complicated time—or so I thought.

"Is everything all right?" he asked, leaning in to meet my downcast eyes. "You've been acting so strange lately, like you're a million miles away."

I bit down on my lip as I thought about what to say.

"Okay, now you have me worried. You're biting your lip."

He knew me so well. How could I keep this from him? "Adam, I'm late." I blurted out. I wanted to take it back as soon the words escaped my lips.

"Late for what?" he asked, completely clueless to the bomb that I was about to throw into our world.

"My period, it's late. It's never late."

"Whoa, hold on. Are you trying to tell me that you're pregnant?" And it finally sank in. Hearing the **P** word roll off his tongue brought the reality of the situation to the surface.

"I don't know, maybe." I bit down on my lip harder, cringing at his words.

"What do you mean, you don't know? Did you take a test?"

"Not yet."

He rubbed his hand over his face in frustration. "Let's not have this conversation until we know for sure. There must be some other explanation."

"Okay," I said quietly. We sat in silence as my mind wandered back to that unbelievable night in his room. We hadn't used a condom; we had been careless, caught up in our emotions. I searched his eyes, and I knew that he was thinking about the same thing.

"Oh, my God, this can't be happening. Fuck," he said, running his hands through his hair. "My parents will probably disown me and everything that I've been working toward will be over, just like that." He swept his arm across the space in front of him to emphasize his words.

"Adam, you're freaking me out." I was scared enough as it was; his anger was more than I could take.

"I'm sorry. I'm not mad at you. I just can't believe that I was so stupid. Let's find out right now. I can't get on that plane until I know for sure." He held his hand out for me. "Come on."

We endured the hour drive to the nearest city in silence. We agreed that we could not purchase a pregnancy test at the local drugstore. Rumors spread quickly in a small town, and this was one of those things that needed to be handled discreetly.

Adam took charge and purchased the first pregnancy test that he spotted on the shelf. I felt like a child unable to say or do anything.

On our drive home Adam let out a loud sigh and spoke to me calmly for the first time since I had told him that I might be pregnant. "Kendi, if you really are…pregnant, I'll stay home and support you. We could get married. This doesn't have to be a bad thing." He rested his hand on my leg as he glanced over at me for my reaction. I didn't know what to say. Part of me loved the idea of him staying and not leaving me to go to Africa, but the rest was hard to imagine. I didn't want to stay; I wanted to go to college. Getting married? Baby? We were way too young. What about my dreams, what about med school? What would our parents think? To say that I was terrified was an understatement.

"Adam…I don't know what to say. Let's just wait and see what the test says." We arrived at my house, and I slowly made my way inside with Adam trailing behind me.

In the bathroom I read the directions on the box twice before following them step by step. I waited the three minutes alone, the longest three minutes of my life, silently praying for only one pink line.

When I finally walked out of the bathroom and told Adam that the test was negative, that I wasn't pregnant, I could see the overwhelming relief in his eyes. He held me close as he whispered, "Oh, thank God." I was still shaken up over the events of the day, unable to share his relief.

~

Two days later I found myself in the airport with Adam and his family, saying good-bye. We had said our real, heartfelt, tear-jerking, stab-to-the-heart good-byes the night before when we were alone at my house. We had held each other for hours, kissing and touching, nothing more. Adam had more than once promised to love me forever, and swore that he was going to come home and marry me, if I still wanted him. I had told him how much he meant to me and how I couldn't

133

imagine ever loving someone as much as I loved him. In a moment of weakness, I had promised to wait for him. Tears had welled up in his eyes as he kissed me deeply. He had to pry my hands from his body when it was time for him to leave. I had cried myself to sleep once he was gone.

Now I was in his arms once again but with his family as an audience, I did my best to hold myself together. I wanted to be strong for Adam; I knew this was harder on him. He was saying good-bye to everyone that he loved and traveling far away to the unknown. When a voice came from the overhead speaker announcing his flight's last boarding call, he gave final hugs to his family, and they stepped away to give us our privacy. I swiped at the tears falling down my cheeks as Adam pulled me into his arms.

"I promise to write you as soon as I get settled. Don't forget how much I love you." He swiped away his own tears. I wanted to beg him to stay; I wanted to tell him things that would change his mind; I wanted to hold on to him just a little bit longer. But I knew that I had to let him go. This is what he wanted, and I had to accept that. I clung to him tightly.

"I love you, Adam. Please be safe."

"I love you too. Good-bye, Kendi." He pulled out of my arms and turned to go, the airline assistant patiently waiting by the gate for his approach.

"Bye, Adam," I whispered as he walked away from me. The second he was out of sight, I collapsed into the nearest chair and sobbed into my hands, unable to keep up my composure any longer. When I was able to, I stood and walked to the window and watched until his plane was pulling away from the gate. I spread my palm against the warm glass, imagining him doing the same from his small window on the airplane. I felt an arm around my shoulders, and glanced to my side to find Josh there. I leaned my head against him, welcoming his comfort. I watched until Adam's plane ascended into the sky, whispering good-bye, suddenly aware that the only part of him that I had to hold on to were the promises that we had made to each other.

Stay

The sun had begun to cast a bright stream of light into my mother's kitchen as I absentmindedly traced my finger over the letters of my grandfather's initials that were skillfully etched into the dark wood of the kitchen table. My grandfather had built the table with his own hands—a sentimental reminder of his love for woodworking in which he had mastered over the years. I replayed the funeral in my mind on a continuous loop, unable to shake the overwhelming nostalgia that had consumed me from the moment that I had seen Adam in the church.

I stirred cream and sugar into my steaming cup of coffee, hoping that a good dose of caffeine would lift the heavy fog that my mind had seemed to be lost in. I hadn't slept well, too many memories weighing down on my heart. Adam had stirred something in me that I hadn't felt in a long time, and I was trying to sort through the jumble of feelings that surrounded me. The day before had proved to be an emotional day, mourning the loss of my grandfather and seeing Adam after all those years.

I had spent the evening with my entire family, drinking and laughing as we reminisced about growing up with Gramps. My uncle had even brought out my grandfather's old slides, and we had watched our lives pass by on the big white screen set up in the family room. Images from my childhood had flashed by: so many precious memories of my father that I had forgotten, as well as all the treasured moments that I had shared with Gramps.

I had clutched my chest, fighting against the familiar ache, when images of Adam and me illuminated the screen. Pictures from my junior year prom when my grandfather had loaned us his LeMans-blue '69 Corvette convertible for the night. I had smiled at the look on Adam's face in the photo of my gramps handing him the keys; the picture had captured more than just memories. The pictures from my high school graduation had revealed just how inseparable Adam and I had been; his body was within inches of mine in nearly every photograph. I had stared at the girl that I had been, unable to ignore the look of youth and innocence, the naïveté that I had lost so shortly after. The trip down memory lane had been bittersweet.

I heard the shuffle of my mother's slippers on the hardwood floor, pulling me from my quiet thoughts as she walked into the kitchen.

"You're up early." She yawned as she poured herself a cup of coffee.

"I couldn't sleep."

"Are you okay? You were so quiet yesterday."

"Mom, why didn't you tell me that Adam was going to be officiating Grandpa's funeral?"

"Honestly, Kendall, I didn't think that it was a big deal." She sat down next to me at the table, wrapping her hands around her coffee cup. "You've barely mentioned him since high school. Every time that I tried to ask you about him after he left, you shut me down. I thought that he was just a blip from your past…until I saw your reaction to him yesterday."

She waited for me to explain, but I wasn't ready to talk to her about how I felt about Adam, not until I sorted it out for myself. Instead I wanted to know more about him. "Why was he there yesterday? He said that he 'fills in for Pastor Phillips.' What does that mean?"

"Well, Adam was the pastor at his church for a few years, but he unexpectedly resigned. Since then he's been focusing on the family business. I heard he even purchased some of his own land recently. He's still technically a minister, so he helps out with weddings and funerals at a few of the churches in town. Aunt Margaret actually requested him for your grandfather's funeral, knowing that he would put a personal touch on the service, which he did so beautifully."

"So he came back here when he returned from Africa?" I asked as we both took a sip of coffee.

"Yeah, pretty much. He never went back to school, although I heard that he's been taking online courses from WSU to finish his business degree."

"Huh." I paused, my mind processing this new information. I had never asked about him before. I had tried to push him completely out of my mind and my heart, scolding myself in moments of weakness when I allowed myself to wonder about him. "So why did he resign?"

"I'm not sure. There was a lot of talk around town, but I never believe anything I hear."

"Talk about what?"

"That he was involved with someone, you know… physically, which went against his beliefs, because he wasn't married," she said, waving off the information as if it was useless gossip.

"Oh, who was he involved with?" I asked, my curiosity piqued.

"I don't know, Kendall, probably no one. It was just talk."

I could tell that my sudden inquiry was grating on her nerves. "Sorry, I was just curious. I guess seeing him yesterday brought up a lot of memories."

"That's understandable. You two were so close once upon a time. I was surprised that you didn't stay in touch, but I know how hard it is when you're young."

"I moved on, Mom," I said flatly, feeling defensive for reasons unknown to my mother.

"You certainly did." She reached over and placed her hand on top of mine. "I'm so proud of everything that you've accomplished, Kendall, but honestly sometimes I wish that you would slow down and smell the roses."

"Mom, it's nearly impossible to slow down as a resident."

"I know. I just miss you."

"I miss you too," I replied as she stood up and kissed me on the head.

"I'm gonna take a shower before your sister and brother wake up," she said while making her way upstairs.

As I finished my coffee, I decided that I needed to see Adam. My flight back to Los Angeles was the following afternoon, so I couldn't put it off any longer. I took a hot shower, dried my long hair and carefully applied my makeup. I pulled a pair of tight dark jeans over my toned legs and chose an ivory sweater that hung low across my chest. I don't know why I felt the need to impress him. I helped my mother prepare brunch for everyone, and we sat around the table, eating and talking like old times. I nonchalantly mentioned that I was going to visit an old friend, and Marie gave me a reassuring nod, knowing exactly who I was going to see. The afternoon had crept by slowly but I had stalled long enough.

I didn't need to look at his address, I knew where he lived. It was a small house on the edge of town that had been in his family for years. I drove my rental car slowly through town, listening to the snow crunching under the tires. Small fluffy snowflakes were falling against the windshield, melting away instantly, but sticking to the ground. I had forgotten how beautiful the snow could be, how peaceful it made everything feel. I parked in his driveway next to a black Chevy Tahoe and slowly made my way up the sidewalk.

Before I could knock on the front door, a dog began to bark inside, and Adam threw open the door, startling me. A large yellow Labrador sprung out the door, jumping up and down, nearly knocking me to the ground.

"Cooper, get down," Adam said with an authoritative tone. The dog retreated back inside, leaving Adam and me staring at one another in an awkward silence.

"Kendi, you're here," he said quietly, never breaking eye contact with me.

"I just wanted to say good-bye. I'm flying back to L.A. tomorrow." I couldn't tell him why I was really there, not yet anyway.

"Oh. Well, come in. It's freezing out there." He stood back, holding the door and motioning for me to come inside. The house was warm and cozy, a fire burning dimly in the brick fireplace. I glanced around the room to see the framed pictures of his brothers with their families on the mantel, a beige couch facing the fireplace with an old dark leather chair nearby. A black vintage upright piano sat against the far wall, littered with sheet music. An eating area off the living room led into the kitchen. From where I stood, I could see dark marble countertops, distressed white cabinets and stainless steel appliances—the kitchen had definitely been renovated recently. Straight ahead was a wide hallway that led to the bedrooms and bathroom.

"This is nice, Adam."

"Thanks. I've slowly been updating, one room at a time. Can I get you anything to drink?"

"No thanks, I'm fine." I moved closer to the fireplace, reaching out to warm my hands in the heat radiating from the flames. I removed my coat and laid it over the back of the couch. His home felt comfortable—familiar—although I had only been in this house once that I could recall. But Adam's warmth was etched into every detail of its interior.

Adam was barefoot, wearing dark jeans that hung low on his hips, a wrinkled blue T-shirt clung to his chest, his hair the usual mess of dark curls that I remembered. He was still beautiful, and I had to look away before my eyes revealed the attraction that I still felt toward him.

"You look amazing, Kendi," he said, drinking me in from across the room.

I could feel the blush set in across my cheeks as I quietly thanked him. He walked over and sat down on the couch near where I stood, sinking into the depth of its comfort. I sat down next to him, perched on the edge of the cushion, slightly turned toward him.

"So yesterday was…awkward." He smiled, melting away the tension in the room with his honesty and charm.

I let out a sigh. "Yeah, I wasn't expecting to see you at my grandfather's funeral of all places."

"I've envisioned running into you for years, and that wasn't exactly the circumstances that I'd hoped for."

"What circumstances do you usually envision?" I asked, my curiosity getting the best of me.

"You know the kind where we run into each other in town, one that warrants big hugs, followed by dinner to catch up and reminisce about old times." He laughed but I could tell that he had honestly thought about it before.

"Do you think a reunion under any circumstance would be like that?" My tone was casual but his smile faded;

his expression became serious in a matter of seconds. He reached over and pulled at a loose strand of my hair, tucking it behind my ear. His gesture triggered so many memories that I was suddenly too aware of his close proximity. I could smell his all-too-familiar scent, feel every breath that he took. My heart rate had spiked, and I tried to focus on taking slow, even breaths.

"No, I guess not. When something is taken from you unexpectedly, without so much as an explanation, and years pass without any kind of closure whatsoever, I guess that leads to an awkward situation under any circumstance."

I could sense his sad but resentful tone, and I wasn't sure what to say to that. I stared into the fire, focusing on its warmth to avoid the sudden chill that passed between us.

"I'm sorry, Kendi, that wasn't fair."

I turned to look at him, incredulously. "Is that why you asked me to come here, Adam? So you could play the blame game? So you could get all this off your chest, this *stuff* that you've obviously been carrying around with you all these years?"

He reached over and held my hand in his with a pleading look in his eyes. "No, of course not. I'm sorry. I didn't mean for it to come out like that. I don't know why I asked you to come here. I needed to see you, alone." He was quiet for a minute, obviously wanting to say more but not sure how to say it. "I need to know why?"

"Does it matter? That was years ago, Adam. Let it go."

"The thing is, I can't...just let it go. I wanted to call you so many times when I got back, but I think that I was afraid of what would happen, afraid of just how much you had moved on."

I pulled my hand away from him. "That's just it. I moved on, and you should too." I started to stand up, knowing that it was time for me to go. I shouldn't have come.

I wasn't comfortable with the direction the conversation was heading. Too many emotions were already unveiled, and I hadn't even told him the truth about why I was here.

He pulled me back down beside him. "I don't want you to think that I've been pining for you all these years, because I haven't. I moved on too, but, seeing you yesterday, well, it brought up so many things that have been left unsaid for far too long." He brought his hand to my face, softly stroking my cheek with his thumb. "Don't you think we need to say them?"

I looked at his deep blue eyes, so intense, so full of questions, questions that I couldn't answer. I knew that it was cowardly, but I couldn't tell him. His hand on my face sent chills rippling through me. The silence was building, but neither of us could turn away. He leaned his face closer to mine, his thumb brushing across my lips, and I suddenly couldn't breathe. I bolted from my seat, grabbing my coat on the way as I ran out the front door. I could hear the dog barking, the sound muted over the loud pounding of my heart in my ears. I heard the door close, shutting out the dog's deep bark completely and then footsteps on the porch.

I stopped and turned back at the sound of his voice, powerful in the stillness that surrounded us.

"For the record, I never stopped loving you. Seeing you here, having you here now, I can honestly say that I still love you. I wanted a life with you, Kendi. How could you walk away from me without even saying good-bye?"

"Adam, you don't know me. I'm not the same person that I was back then." I shook my head, unable to believe that he could still love me.

"People don't change that much, Kendi."

"There was too much hurt between us. I knew that I wanted more from life, and I was worried that I would never be able to trust you again." As soon as the words left my mouth, a sob escaped me. I was the one who could not be trusted. What Adam did was hurtful. But I had done things that were unforgivable. If he only knew. The guilt washed over me and I fought back with anger. "I couldn't stay in this town any longer. I couldn't breathe here. I still can't breathe here. This is not the life that I wanted," I yelled, raising my arms, gesturing toward the wheat field behind him and the farm equipment parked on the other side of the driveway. "Besides, you left me first, remember?" I knew these words hurt him deeply, but I said them anyway. I needed him to back off. I just couldn't think about the lie that was wedged between us. I couldn't let him see the guilt that was haunting my soul.

"We could have talked about it. We could have made other plans, together."

"No, Adam. It was always about you and what you wanted. Don't you see? I had dreams too. I needed to move on with my life."

"And now, have you…moved on? I can see it in your eyes, Kendi. You feel it too, this…pull."

"Please, don't do this, Adam," I pleaded. "Just let me go." I could not endure the pain in his eyes any longer as he just stood there looking at me from the porch. Tears made their way down his cheeks, and he hung his head in defeat. I turned to walk away. The snow was falling slowly in large soft masses, clinging to my hair and clothes. The sky was cast in darkness from the thick white blanket that hung in the air. My rental car was covered in several inches of snow already in the short time that I had been there.

"Stay, Kendi." His words cut through the heavy silence. I stilled. I was afraid to turn around, knowing that I would go to him. I wanted to hold him and tell him that everything was going to be okay. I wanted to take the hurt away. But I couldn't tell him the truth, and I knew that he needed that from me. He needed closure, to shut the door on our past so that he could move on. But the truth was the only thing that could set him free. And I wasn't ready to deal with that yet.

His voice stabbed at my heart as he continued. "I need you, just for tonight. Don't go."

I stood, frozen, my back to him. Every fiber of my being wanted to go to him. I longed to feel his arms around me, to breathe in his scent, to…remember. I couldn't fight this pull any longer. I turned and ran to him, tears streaming down my face. He wrapped me into his warm arms, holding me against him tightly. He rested his chin on the top of my head as I buried my face in his chest and sobbed. No longer able to fight against it any longer, I sobbed loud, uncontrollable sobs as he held me against him. We stood like that for what seemed like hours until there were no more tears to cry.

I was cold, numb and wet from the falling snow. Adam leaned down and pulled my feet off the ground, cradling me in his arms. He carried me inside the house and sat me on the couch, tossing my coat aside and removing my wet boots. He kneeled at my feet, placing his hands on my thighs and looked at me in silence.

His eyes penetrated the thick wall that I had built around myself all those years ago, the wall that was supposed to protect me from what I felt in that moment. He still had the ability to see right through me, right into my soul. Waves of emotions lapped at my heart. Love, guilt, regret, heartache, complete agony—I was overwhelmed, ready to burst under his gaze. He gripped my thighs tightly, and a chill swept through my body.

"Let me get you some dry clothes," he whispered. He left the room, and I sat there watching the flames dance in the fireplace, thankful for the moment of solitude. Adam's dog collapsed at my feet, nuzzling my leg with his nose. I absentmindedly ran my hand down his back, petting him into a slumber. Adam returned with clothes in hand. "Here, you can change into these. The bathroom is at the end of the hall."

"Thank you, I'll just be a minute," I said, taking the clothes and heading toward the bathroom. I closed the door, sinking to the floor with my back pressed against it. Burying my face in my hands, I let myself cry for a few more minutes, mourning what I had lost. I pulled myself together, taking a deep breath and peeling myself from the bathroom floor. I cringed when I saw my reflection in the mirror. I looked awful. Black mascara was smudged under my red-rimmed eyes; my nose was red from the cold winter air—my dry lips pale in comparison.

Still, my looks were no match for the despair that I felt on the inside. I splashed warm water on my face, trying to remove the traces of the blubbering mess I had been just a few minutes before. I pulled my damp hair into a ponytail, securing it with the band that I always wore around my wrist. I removed my damp cold jeans and sweater, replacing them with the large worn T-shirt and plaid flannel boxer shorts that Adam had given me. The shirt was big, drowning me, but it was dry so I couldn't complain. I lifted it up to my face, inhaling Adam's scent. I would recognize that scent anywhere, even after all this time. I hung up my clothes on the towel bar to dry and made my way back to the living room, feeling a little self-conscious wearing his clothes. Adam was in the kitchen when I returned to the couch hugging my knees to my chest.

"Hey, I set a blanket out for you in case you're still cold," he called out from the kitchen behind me. I pulled the blanket over my knees, tucking it under my thawing feet.

"I thought that you might like some wine. Is red okay?" he asked, walking toward me with two glasses in his hands.

"Sure, that sounds great actually." I reached out to take a glass from him, his hand brushing mine and lingering for a moment. He sat down beside me on the couch. I took a sip while I watched him do the same. And it occurred to me that I had never seen him drink before. I smiled at the thought.

"What?" he drawled curiously.

"It just seems weird to have a glass of wine with you. You never drank before."

"Well, I'm an adult now. I'm sure there are a lot of things that you've never seen me do." He smiled, his familiar dimples setting my heart on fire.

I took another sip of wine. "This is good, by the way." I was not an expert on wine, but I did drink it quite often and had been wine tasting a few times with Derek. The thought of Derek instantly made me feel guilty. I took in the warm dim lighting, the fire, the wine, Adam sitting next to me and realized that this scenario alone would break Derek's heart, let alone the feelings that were stirring inside of me. I decided that I had to be completely present in this moment, to let this night be the closure that Adam and I needed. I wanted to have this intimate time with him so that we could get everything out in the open finally, but that was all that this night was about. I owed this to Adam and to myself. I could deal with the rest later.

"Thanks, Rick and I made this. We started brewing our own beer and making our own wine a few years ago, just for fun. But now some of the local bars and restaurants actually serve it."

His voice snapped me back to our conversation. "Wow, I can't believe you made this. So, wait, Rick's here in town?"

"Yeah, he moved back after graduating from Arizona. He's been running his parents' farm. He married his college girlfriend, Sara, and they had a baby boy a few months ago."

"Huh, I didn't know that."

"Well, you haven't actually come home in, like, how

many years?" he teased.

"Not true. I was here last year when my grandma passed away."

"Yeah, but one night doesn't count."

I looked at him, shocked. "How did you know that?"

"It's a small town. Nothing is sacred here. And besides, the longer you stay away, the more 'celebritylike' status you have. Which makes you *really* famous. I promise I wasn't stalking you. I wasn't even in town that week." He was smiling, almost giggling to himself.

I frowned at him. "Well, I have a crazy schedule. I can't help it."

"So tell me, Dr. Brooks, what is your crazy schedule like?"

"Crazy, and are you making fun of me?" I eyed him suspiciously, my mouth turned up in a smile that I couldn't hide.

"Hold that thought," he said laughing at my expression as he made his way back into the kitchen only to return with the bottle of wine, refilling both of our glasses. He placed another log on the fire; it crackled and sparked as he sat once more on the couch. He leaned back, propping up his feet on the rustic wood coffee table and reaching his arm across the back of the couch, nearly touching me, because he was so close. "Now where were we?"

"You were making fun of me," I said, taking another sip of my wine.

"Oh, right. Actually, Kendi, I'm really quite impressed with what you're doing. You knew what you wanted all along, and you're actually doing it. You always were stubborn and determined." His face grew more serious, and his fingers grazed my shoulder. "I only know what I hear, so tell me about it."

"Well, not much to tell. I'm in my third year of residency at UCLA in Radiology. I think that I picked the perfect specialty for me. It's hard to believe that I have come this far. It's been a long road."

"Do you like living in Los Angeles?"

"I love it. You can't beat the weather, warm nearly all the time, but never too hot—at least not at the beach where I live. I rent a small apartment above someone's garage. It doesn't sound very glamorous, but it's literally steps from the ocean with a stunning view. I can hear the surf at night from my bed. The traffic is horrendous though, and there are a throng of people everywhere you go, so that can be annoying."

"Still it sounds great. Do you think that you'll stay there?"

"I don't know. It depends on where I can get a job when I finish my residency. I'd love to stay on at UCLA as an attending, or even at USC, but it's pretty competitive."

"I'm sure that you'll be an asset, wherever you end up."

"Thank you." I didn't offer any information about my personal life, especially about Derek, and Adam didn't ask. It really wasn't any of his business anyway; at least that was what I told myself. Instead, I turned the conversation to him. "So tell me about everything that you've been up to since Africa."

"What do you want to know, specifically?"

"I don't know. My mom told me that you resigned from your ministry. What happened, if you don't mind me asking?"

"Honestly I had a change of heart. Some things were happening in my life, and it came to the point where I had to make a choice. Suddenly being a minister felt like too much of a sacrifice. It didn't feel right anymore. It was one of the hardest decisions I've ever made, but I feel that it was the right one."

He wasn't going to elaborate, and it didn't feel right

to ask, but I knew that there was more to that story. For whatever reason he didn't feel comfortable telling me, and I needed to respect his privacy. "So farming?"

"Yeah, I've nearly taken over my parents' business. I think that my dad is ready to retire completely. And I've also started my own business in addition to that. I still love it. It keeps me busier than I would like, but I can always hire more help if I need to."

There was a knock at the door. Adam stood to answer it. "I ordered a pizza earlier. You know, in case you were hungry," he called out over his shoulder. He paid the delivery boy and took the pizza to the kitchen.

I followed him, bringing the wine bottle and our glasses with me.

"I ordered pepperoni and mushroom. I hope you still like that." He handed me a plate. It all felt so surreal. If someone would have told me two days before that I would be sharing a pizza with Adam, chatting it up like old friends, despite the lengthy, life-altering history between us, I would never have believed them.

"Yep, still my favorite. I can't believe that you remembered that," I said as I took a bite, realizing how hungry I was. He reached over and wiped pizza sauce from the corner of my mouth with his thumb.

"I remember a lot of things, Kendi." His tone was more serious. We both paused at his intimate gesture, his blue gaze locked on mine.

I looked away suddenly. Taking my plate and nearly empty wine glass, I sat at the table behind me. Adam followed me. We chatted lightly about nothing important while we ate our pizza and finished off the bottle of wine. I helped him clean up the kitchen, and we retreated back to our places on the couch by the fire.

I propped my feet on the table next to his, and he covered my legs with the blanket, settling back just inches from me, his extended leg brushing against mine under the blanket.

"So are you seeing anybody?" he asked.

And there it was, the question that I thought we were avoiding. "Actually, I am seeing someone."

"Is it serious?"

"I guess so. We've been together for two years. He wants more, but I'm consumed with my residency. It's as serious as it can get for now."

"Do you love him?"

I paused briefly, searching my heart for what I honestly felt for Derek before answering. "Yeah, I do." We both stared at the fire in an uncomfortable silence, until I asked him the same question. "So, what about you?"

"I'm not seeing anyone right now. I was seeing someone. It was pretty serious, but it ended a while ago."

"Is she the reason that you resigned?"

"Part of it, but it wasn't what you're thinking."

"What am I thinking?" I asked, feeling myself getting caught up in him as I stared into his eyes. He looked away, returning his gaze to the fire.

"It wasn't about sex. I loved her, but not the same way that she loved me. I ended it, knowing that I couldn't marry her and give her what she wanted. I resigned because I started to resent my decision. I felt like the choices that I had made for the church were the reasons why I suddenly wasn't happy. I felt like…I don't know. The things that are supposed to fulfill you as a minister weren't enough anymore. It's a long story, but I completely changed my life, and I have no regrets. At least not about that."

"Why didn't you want to marry her? I mean, you loved her, right?"

He was quiet for a long time, and then he turned toward me, his eyes intently fixed on mine. "Honestly?" he asked, and I nodded. "As much as I tried to love her wholeheartedly, I couldn't. You still own my heart, Kendi. Even after all this time."

Hearing his words, I remembered what he had said to me on the porch. That he still loved me. Part of me still loved him too, and I wondered if I always would. He leaned in slowly and gently brushed his lips across mine, holding my chin delicately in his hand. And once again I couldn't breathe, but I didn't run away this time. I kissed him back. Our lips were slow and unsure at first but soon moved with familiarity. I held my hands against his chest, feeling his firm body beneath my fingers. My hands eventually found their way to his hair, my fingertips combing through his silky curls. He moaned at my touch. I wanted to completely lose myself in his arms, but I couldn't quiet the voice inside me reminding me why I had come here in the first place.

"Adam, I need to tell you something," I tried to say against his lips.

"It can wait," he managed to breathe out with my mouth locked on his.

"No, it can't." I pressed my hands against his chest, pushing him back.

He rested his forehead on mine, caressing the back of my neck with his hand, his thumb grazing my collarbone. "Please, Kendi, can we just forget everything tonight? Just for one night?" He kissed me again, and I was lost.

Truth or Dare

I woke early in thè morning. It was still dark outside. I
looked over at Adam, sleeping peacefully beside me. His hair
completely disheveled, his lips slightly parted; it was hard to
take my eyes off him. The sheet was pulled up to his waist,
leaving the smooth cut planes of his chest for me to admire.
God, this man was beautiful. My heart was heavy. I knew
that I had to break his heart today along with mine.

I couldn't keep this to myself another day; as much as
it hurt to open myself up to the pain again, I owed him the
truth. I brushed my hand over my swollen lips and smiled,
thinking about last night. Him kissing me on the couch,
picking me up and carrying me to his bedroom, touching
every inch of my body, slowly undressing each other,
whispering how beautiful I was and how much he still loved
me. It took every ounce of restraint I could muster to tell him
to stop. I knew that everything leading up to that point was
wrong, but it felt so right in the moment. In the end though, I

couldn't actually have sex with him while I was with Derek, the final act feeling like the worst betrayal.

Adam, surprisingly, understood, even though he needed a few minutes to pull himself together. He settled for holding me in his arms the entire night. I almost changed my mind, several times, but eventually we both fell asleep. Derek is the least of my worries this morning though.

I pulled Adam's T-shirt over my head, located my bra and panties and tiptoed into the bathroom. I freshened up, brushed my teeth with Adam's toothbrush, and slipped into my dry jeans and sweater. I didn't want to wake Adam, so I snooped around his kitchen until I was able to brew a pot of coffee. I realized that my purse and cell phone were still in the car, but, looking out at the foot of snow covering the ground, I decided that I didn't need either at the moment.

Marie knew where I was, and I hoped that she knew better than to worry about me. I had lived alone for so long, it hadn't occurred to me to let anyone know of my whereabouts. I sat on the couch and sipped my coffee, anxiously waiting for Adam to wake up as the sun began to cast orange streaks across the horizon. Cooper was sleeping soundly in front of the smoldering fire. My nerves were getting the best of me as I sat and pondered how I was going to start the conversation that I had come here to have. It was not going to be easy, for either of us.

While I finished my second cup of coffee, Adam emerged from the hallway. Barefoot again, wearing only his jeans from last night. My gaze swept across his chiseled torso and toned chest; he was still ridiculously perfect in every way. I brought my coffee cup to my lips, trying to hide the blush that had set in across my cheeks.

"Good morning." He yawned, mindlessly running a hand through his hair. "You made coffee? I could get used to this." I let his words linger in the air, both of us knowing that the night was over and so was our cozy reunion. He poured himself a cup of coffee before approaching me with a kiss on the cheek as he sat down beside me.

"Adam, we need to talk," I blurted out before I lost my nerve, trying to hide the anxiety in my voice.

"I know what you're going to say, Kendi. Save yourself the trouble. I get it."

"No, it's not what you think.... Could you put a shirt on? It's a little distracting seeing you like this." I motioned toward his bare chest with my hand. I couldn't think straight; the urge to reach out and touch his smooth hard chest was clouding my better judgment.

"Seriously?"

"Yes."

"Fine." He shrugged as he disappeared down the hall only to return minutes later sporting a black T-shirt. "Better?" he asked, holding his arms out as he waited for my approval.

"Much. Thank you."

He sat back down next to me on the couch.

My hand was shaking as I placed my coffee cup on the table in front of me and turned toward him, resting my back against the arm of the couch with one leg drawn up underneath me. "Adam, there is something that you need to know...." My voice cracked and tears were already making their way down my cheeks. So much for keeping it together. Adam looked at me with concern in his eyes as he placed his hands on either side of my face and wiped away my tears with his thumbs. "What is it? You can tell me."

I cleared my throat and pulled his hands from my face, interlacing our fingers in my lap. "Do you remember that week, before you left for Africa? When I thought that I was pregnant?"

"Yeah..." His eyes were guarded, already disliking where I was going with this.

The tears were constant now, and I released one of his hands to wipe them away. "Well, I lied to you that day. I *was*…pregnant." I saw the confusion flash in his eyes. I had to remind myself to breathe as I took a deep breath and blew it out forcefully through my lips.

"What do you mean, you were pregnant, Kendi?" he asked cautiously, freeing his other hand from my grip.

I braced myself for the anger that I knew was brewing inside Adam as he considered the options of what I might say next, the hatred that he would feel toward me as my words shattered the undeserving pedestal that he had kept me on all these years. The questions that he had held in his heart all this time as to why I would cut him out of my life so abruptly, finally answered, only to be replaced by new, more painful ones. He stood and stepped away from me.

"Are you saying that you lied to me about not being pregnant and then you had an abortion behind my back? How could you do that?" His hands were now running frantically through his hair, his trademark indication that he was starting to lose the hold he had on his temper. "You know how strongly I feel about that. Is that why you felt the need to lie to me?"

The disdainful look that he directed at me was nearly crushing me, and all I could do was shake my head through my sobs at his accusations. "No, Adam, it wasn't like that," I managed to choke out. "I didn't have an abortion."
He stopped pacing in front of the fireplace and looked at me, confused once again. He sat back down beside me. "Okay, I'm listening. Please explain this to me, because I don't understand what the hell you're trying to tell me."

"I was pregnant, and I had the baby." I couldn't breathe. The weight of the guilt and regret was as if a two-ton brick were sitting on my chest, squeezing the life right out of me. I held my face in my hands, unable to tell him the rest. The pain that I had buried long ago, nearly suffocating me now.

I felt Adam's hands on mine, peeling them gently

from my face. He lifted my chin in his hand until my bleary eyes met his. "Tell me what happened."

His unexpected gentle tone calmed the storm that was raging inside me, and I found the strength I needed to tell him what I came here to say. "I had the baby and…I gave her up…. A nice young couple adopted her." I searched his eyes, waiting for his reaction. He sat frozen, almost breathless. I knew that it would take a minute for my words to sink in. I could see the moisture building as tears made their way down his cheeks.

"Her?" he asked, his eyes softening as he released my chin and in the same moment his eyes grew hard, cold. "You had a baby girl, my baby, and gave her away without even telling me?" His anger was resurfacing as he processed the extent of my deceitfulness. He was on his feet again, pacing with his fingers squeezing the bridge of his nose, as if he was suffering from a headache. "The worst part is there is nothing I can do or say to change anything. You never gave me a choice in the matter. I have a daughter somewhere out there that I never even knew existed. How could you? How the fuck could you do that? I loved you, Kendi, I would've done anything for you. I was ready to give everything up to support you."

"I know. That's just it. I didn't want you to have to give anything up. I thought that once you left, I would have time to think about what I wanted. I needed time to process it, to know what was best, before I turned your life upside down. Two days wasn't enough time, so I lied. I tried to write you so many times during those nine months, to tell you, but in the end I could never go through with it. That's why I came here yesterday, to tell you."

"You should've tried harder to tell me all these years. You should've told me sooner. I can't believe that we spent the entire night together, and you were keeping this from me the whole time."

He was yelling, and I drew my knees into my chest in an effort to protect myself from his words. He was right, and I deserved this reaction from him. I sat quietly, letting him absorb the truth while he lashed out at me.

"I'm so sorry, Adam. I never meant to hurt you. It was the hardest thing that I have ever done, and I have tried so hard to forget and move on with my life. But it's always with me.… She's always with me." I sobbed loudly.

He looked at me, his face livid, angry—his eyes void of any compassion. "No, Kendi, it was the most *selfish* thing that you have ever done." His words cut deep as he jabbed a finger toward me, marking me with blame. "Get. Out. I can barely look at you right now," he seethed.

He left me sitting alone, drowning in the shame from what I had done—from the lies that I had told—as he stormed out of the room, slamming his bedroom door a moment later.

I did what I do best; I ran. I ran out the door slipping on my coat along the way. Shivers raked through my body as I attempted to brush aside the snow from my windshield with my coat sleeve. The sun's reflection off the crystallike snow was blinding, but at least it had nearly melted what had accumulated on the ground, making my departure much easier. I focused on the inhale and exhale of my breath as I drove to my mother's house, trying desperately to keep myself from falling apart. I fought the sobs that shook my body, knowing that—if I let myself fall victim to the pain, to feel it all again—I would shatter into a million pieces.

I snuck in through the front door quietly, hoping that everyone was either still asleep or busy showering but no such luck. My mom, Marie and Scott were sitting at the table talking, coffee cups in hand. At the sight of me, my mother looked almost furious.

"Kendall, where have you been? I was worried about you."

"Sorry. I went to see Adam." My words were barely recognizable as my body shook violently, fighting the breakdown that it so desperately needed.

"Well." She paused, not sure what to think as I stood there in yesterday's clothes with tear-stained cheeks. "You could have called to let us know that you wouldn't be home."

Marie came to me with open arms, knowing all too well that my strength was faltering. "Are you okay?" she asked, wrapping her warm arms around me. I shook my head slowly and started to cry once again, her compassion weakening me. The one person close to me that knew my secret and, yet, she had respected and loved me enough to never discuss it or pass judgment. She had been my rock all these years, and I knew that it hadn't come without the heavy burden of carrying around a secret of this magnitude. She had suffered as well, keeping this from those that we love.

"What is this all about, girls?" my mother demanded. Marie looked at me, and I knew that it was time to tell my story. She held my hand as we walked to the table, silently telling me that she was there to support me. I removed my coat and sat down next to my mother, feeling the weight of what I was about to tell her weighing down my shoulders. I took a deep breath and started from the beginning.

Denial

It didn't take the entire three minutes for the double pink line to appear. I watched in disbelief as the red dye slowly made its way across the tiny square of the cheap plastic contraption that I held in my trembling hand. Under any other circumstances I would probably dispute the reliability of this test, but there was no denying the tenderness I felt in my breasts or the lack of my period, which should have come and gone by now. I couldn't believe that this was happening to me. While sitting in the bathroom alone, waiting for the results of this life-altering test, a vivid vision of my life from that moment on flashed before me.

I could see myself living in this same small town, pregnant, holding a tiny child in my arms while Adam was in the fields farming for long hours every day, trying to make ends meet. I could already feel the resentment building inside, knowing that my dreams were no longer in my reach, and I could envision the insecurity of wondering what Adam felt in his heart. Would he be a faithful husband? Would he be resentful too, toward me, toward our…baby? Of course the "barefoot and pregnant" image was a bit extreme, but, the reality was, we were young, with no college degrees, no jobs. We lived with our parents. It wasn't hard to foresee that the probability of either of us attending college, any college for that matter, or moving away from this town and our parents' support, was slim to none.

It wasn't only my dreams being ripped from my grasp, it was his as well. It suddenly didn't matter what this cheap plastic stick revealed; I could not have a baby, and I could not ask Adam to stay. I could not be responsible for the fallout that he would undoubtedly face with his family, knowing how their disappointment would ruin him. He had to go on his mission. I wasn't sure what I was going to do, but I needed time to figure that out. Adam didn't have the luxury of time; he was leaving in two days. I gathered the evidence along with my despair and buried them deep in the trash can under the bathroom sink, so that he could not see the truth. I walked out and knowingly betrayed him in the worst way possible.

The relief in Adam's eyes told me that I had done the right thing, but I could not have felt worse. I had never felt so alone as I did in that moment, but what choice did I have? I knew that Adam had to get on that plane.

I felt the cold splash of guilt and fear wash over me from the lie that I had cast into our lives in that moment, separating us, unaware of the wave of consequences that would inevitably carry me away from him—leaving, in its wake, a ripple.

~

I glanced around my dorm room, my home for the next ten months. It was small but comfortable, and my roommate,

Tabatha, and I were lucky to get a room with a large bay window that let in an abundance of natural light, which I was told was a necessity in Seattle. Tabatha was from Austin, Texas. She was short and cute, with long curly dark hair, huge brown eyes and full lips. A handful of freckles danced across her nose and cheeks. She had just a hint of a southern drawl, which she contributed to the fact that she had only lived in Texas since the seventh grade when her family had moved there from Columbus, Ohio. She seemed sweet and bubbly, and I instantly felt as if I had known her longer than the two hours it had been since we had met.

I was guessing that she had a sense for fashion, as she tried desperately to stuff three large suitcases full of clothes into her tiny closet, not to mention the shoes, mostly heels, that she was arranging underneath the small twin-size bed. My closet seemed bare in comparison, having brought only the necessities of jeans, T-shirts, warm sweaters and sneakers.

I had Adam's Gonzaga sweatshirt tucked away underneath my pillow, in anticipation for a long, sleepless night. I had spent every night since he had left with it clutched to my chest, my face buried in the worn cotton, trying to hold on to the faint scent that still remained of him. I had not heard from him yet, but he had my new address at school, so it was only a matter of days before I started obsessing over the contents of my mailbox.

Saying good-bye to my family that morning—after they had helped me with the few small boxes and one large suitcase that held all my personal belongings—had paled in comparison to saying good-bye to Adam the week before. Although it was hard not to feel completely alone starting a new life in an unfamiliar place among complete strangers. It was comforting to know that Marie lived nearby, but she had her own life with her demanding job—which she loved—and the potentially serious relationship that she had with Reid, an aspiring architect that she had met through a close friend. We had promised to meet for brunch on Sundays as often as possible.

After Adam left, I couldn't think about anything but the fact that I was pregnant and the desperation of not knowing what to do or who I could trust to talk to about it. It occurred to me now that an entire day had gone by, and I had not thought about it once. The lack of symptoms, as if nothing out of the ordinary was happening with my body, and the nervous excitement of moving into my dorm and meeting my new roommate had proven to be quite the welcoming distraction.

I continued to be distracted as I began my classes and eased into my role of a college student. It was refreshing, meeting new people, almost like I could be whatever I wanted to be, because no one knew the truth about me. Not that I was deceiving in any way—other than the fact that I was hiding my pregnancy, which no one really needed to know. I carried on as if I was not actually pregnant; well, other than abstaining from alcohol, which was not that easy on a college campus. I simply told my roommate and anyone else who asked that I didn't drink, and once I had held my stance through their endless doses of peer pressure, they usually left me alone.

Tabatha kept my social calendar full by dragging me to all the big fraternity parties. I would probably have enjoyed these parties, even sober, but the constant attention from the drunk, horny college guys was exhausting after a while. And dating or hooking up with some guy was not in the cards for me. I lived vicariously through Tabatha and her flirtatious behavior that seemed to attract every frat boy within a ten-mile radius. Apparently she had dated the same guy all through high school only to have her heart broken after graduation. She was making up for lost time, although I could tell that she still loved him from the pain that I saw in her eyes when she spoke of him.

I had become the sober escort for Tabatha and any other drunken female that lived in our building. I didn't mind, although I couldn't help but think of how happy this would make Adam, knowing that I was attending college parties and not drinking.

I received my first letter from Adam during my initial week of school. He described his long and laborious trip to Ghana, the insufferable humidity and the skimpy living conditions. He told me about the wonderful people and his first assignment in the fields, how he felt like he was already making a difference. He shared how much he missed holding me and how much he loved me. He sounded happy, and I couldn't help but feel excited for him, even through my tears. I wrote back to him and told him about Tabatha, my dorm room and classes. The day-to-day campus life. Everything except what I should have told him. I still hadn't decided what I was going to do, so I just kept living one day at a time.

I ran almost every day along the wooded paths that weaved through campus. I even found myself running in the rain. I wasn't really sure why they considered this rain; it was more like a constant drizzle, leaving everything green and wet, the sky a dark layer of clouds. It was the only time that I allowed myself to think about the consequences of my decisions. The decision to have sex with Adam without using protection, the decision to lie to Adam about what that test really concluded and the decision yet to be made but impossible to face. I knew that the clock was ticking; that sooner or later I had to make a decision, but still I kept pretending that it wasn't really happening, ignoring the inevitable.

Luckily my body had not changed at all. I wasn't sure when people started to actually look or feel pregnant, but, besides losing the definition of my stomach muscles and the slight increase in my bra size, I had yet to notice anything else. I had thought about having an abortion several times, but the idea alone scared the hell out of me, and then I usually felt sick just for considering it.

I didn't want to have a baby at such a pivotal time in my life, but, without having an abortion, what choice did I have? I had written a thousand letters to Adam, telling him the truth, asking him what I should do. All of them ended up crumpled in the trash can in my room, unsent. The lie I had told seemed unforgivable, and I wasn't sure how he would react. I feared that, once I told him the truth, he would be so angry that he would turn his back on me, unable to love someone so deceiving. I wouldn't have blamed him. This lie was so much bigger than the lies he had told me, and I had immediately pushed him away after discovering the truth. Only allowing him back into my life when I knew that he was leaving. So I just kept running, waiting for answers that never come.

~

Thanksgiving break was upon us, and I had decided to spend it in Seattle with Marie and Tabatha. Tabatha was staying in Seattle, waiting the few short weeks until Christmas break to fly home to Austin. The dorms were closed for the week, and Marie had to work through the holidays—some big marketing deadline that she had before Christmas. So the three of us spent the week in Marie's small apartment. My mother was not happy about it, but she was hosting our usual family Thanksgiving, cooking for twenty-five to thirty people, so she didn't have much time to argue. I was happy to not be at home surrounded by reminders of Adam. I missed him so much that it hurt sometimes.

Tabatha and I lounged around in our pajamas all day watching Marie's assortment of movies. We took advantage of having a comfortable couch to sit on, a large television to watch and long, hot private showers. We had just finished watching *Pulp Fiction*, our second movie of the day, when Marie emerged through the door, her arms full of groceries.

"Hey, get your lazy asses up and help me with these bags," she huffed. We scrambled to the door and grabbed a few bags from her.

"What's all this?" I asked, peering into the grocery bags in my arms.

"Thanksgiving dinner. I thought that we could cook one ourselves." She smiled. "I invited Reid to join us. He's bringing dessert."

We put on some music, and began slicing and dicing. Slowly the dinner was coming together. Marie and I had helped my mother make this meal a thousand times, but we were not usually the ones to handle the turkey. I let Marie figure out that one; luckily she had a helpful cookbook. I cut up everything for the stuffing, peeled potatoes and put together the green bean casserole, my usual duties. Marie had opened a bottle of white wine and filled three glasses. I picked mine up when she toasted to our own Thanksgiving but then pushed it away. Marie gave me an awkward look, knowing that I liked white wine. Tabatha announced that she would drink mine since I didn't drink.

"Since when?" Marie asked, eyeing me suspiciously. I shrugged and let her question hang in the air. "I hope this isn't because of Adam, Kendi," she added with obvious disapproval in her voice.

"I just decided to focus on school, and I've been running almost every day. I don't want to get out of control and feel hungover all the time." I hoped that she was satisfied with that answer. I had never lied to my sister before, and I felt completely transparent in that moment, like she could see right through me.

"Whatever." She shrugged. "If that's the real reason, then I'm glad. Now I don't have to worry about you waking up in some frat house with no memory of the night before."

I let out a sigh of relief, feeling like I had just dodged a bullet. Tabatha nearly spewed wine from her mouth, and I laughed, knowing my sister had just described a situation that Tab had already found herself in more than once—well, except for the lack-of-memory part.

The rest of the day flowed smoothly. Our dinner looked perfect and tasted delicious. Reid was funny and sweet, and I could see why my sister loved him. I could tell by her body language that they were completely comfortable with one another, and watching them together made me miss Adam even more. When dinner was over and the dishes were done, we sat at the table eating the store-bought pumpkin pie that Reid had brought while Tabatha taught us how to play poker, Texas hold 'em style. We played cards for hours, laughing so hard that tears were streaming down our faces, and I knew that I would remember that as one of my favorite Thanksgivings.

~

I finished my finals feeling confident that I had nailed every one of them. I had done little besides running and studying since Thanksgiving, so I didn't expect anything less. Marie and I dropped Tabatha at Sea-Tac airport and then endured the treacherous drive home for Christmas. The mountain pass was foggy and drenched in snow, resulting in a long drive that took us twice as long as it should have. I cringed as we passed that familiar intersection, the scene of the fatal accident that had changed my life. So much had happened since that tragic day, and I longed to go back in time, to change so many outcomes. The most obvious being in *that* intersection with Mo on *that* day at *that* moment, the moment when I had lost my best friend.

"You okay?" Marie asked. I let out the breath that I

had been holding and relaxed my hands that were fisted around the shoulder strap of my seat belt that rested across my chest, noticing the sting where my nails had broken the skin of my palms.

"Yeah," I answered and closed my eyes feigning sleep, hoping to avoid conversation that might give away what I had been holding on to deep inside.

Marie had the week off from work, so we were driving home together. I hadn't yet decided if I was driving back to Seattle with her before the New Year or if I was going to endure the entire break at home. I was going to play it by ear. I was nervous about going home for the first time in months. Knowing that I would be surrounded by memories of Adam and the idea of someone discovering the huge secret that I was trying to conceal left me feeling anxious. Luckily I had yet to produce a bulging belly like the ones that I saw on television.

Sometimes I worried that something had happened and maybe I was not really pregnant anymore. I felt tired all the time though, sometimes barely able to keep my eyes open during class. And I had easily gained ten pounds; my face felt puffy, and my joints hurt when I ran. I had been living in sweatpants, leggings and baggy shirts, unable to button my jeans anymore. I tried not to dress in front of Tabatha, afraid that she might notice the small changes in my body. Although she had gained a few pounds herself, she could contribute it to her binge drinking and love for junk food. I ate rather healthily, didn't drink and ran nearly every day. I wasn't sure what excuse I could use.

When I walked into the only real home that I had ever known, I was immediately engulfed by the familiar smell of cinnamon, coffee and my mother's perfume. The warmth radiating from the house almost dissolved the cold that had taken residence in my heart, a result from the distance that I had placed between myself and everyone that I loved—a

171

necessity when hiding a painful truth. My mother embraced me before I had a chance to put down my bag. Feeling her arms around me brought tears to my eyes as I realized how much I had missed her. She was teary eyed as well.

"How are my girls?" she asked as she hugged Marie. Scott bounded down the stairs at the sound of our voices. He looked so grown-up, and it seemed longer than the nearly three months that it had been since I had seen him last. He pulled Marie and me in for a group hug, and we both commented on how tall he was. It was hard not to notice that his voice was deeper than before as well.

"Wow, Kendi, putting on the freshman fifteen, huh?" he said, laughing.

"Scott!" my mother objected. "Kendall, you look good with a few extra pounds on you. You're always so skinny. You're almost glowing," she said, gently rubbing my cheek with her hand. I felt my face flush, immediately worried about their observations.

We spent the next hour catching up, each of us taking our turn sharing the new happenings in our life. Marie told us about work and the big promotion that she had just been offered. She blushed as she told us about how serious things were between her and Reid. He was spending Christmas in New York with his family, but they were meeting up for New Year's Eve in Seattle.

Scott told us about the end of the football season. He had been a starting running back, and they had nearly won the state title. He was taking the season off from basketball—it really wasn't his thing—and was getting ready for track season in the spring. After a little prodding from Mom, he told us about his new girlfriend, Lexi.

Mom told us about work and all the latest gossip that was floating around town. She was not really one to gossip, but she knew that Marie and I loved to hear all the ridiculous rumors.

I talked about how well I did on my finals and the new classes that I had registered for. Scott asked how Adam was doing, and so I shared the contents of his last letter. The truth was that his letters were coming less often as time went on. His last letter had contained a thin colorful tribal necklace, a Christmas gift, that I was wearing under my shirt. He had written about the latest crop that he was able to implement and how he was learning the language. He had shared how strongly he felt the Holy Spirit as he continued to teach the people about his church. He had told me how much he missed me and that he still loved me, but those words were mentioned less and less, the majority of his letters focusing on his faith.

I could feel every mile, every ounce of ocean that separated us in his last letter. I had sent him a care package of Christmas cookies and hard candy, a leather-bound journal, and a picture of Tabatha and me that had been taken in front of the campus rose garden in September, while it was still warm and sunny. I had told him as much truth as I could. The depth at which I missed him, the detailed memories of our relationship that I thought about nearly every day, the vivid dreams that I had about him and the disappointment that I felt when I awoke only to discover that I wasn't really in his arms just moments before. I focused on my emotions rather than the physical part of my days, hoping to somehow close the distance that I felt from him. Deep down I knew that it wasn't just the miles or his growing faith that separated us now; it was the weight of what I wasn't saying in my letters.

Christmas was busy and fun, as always. We spent Christmas Eve at my grandparents' house as we had every year that I could remember. On Christmas Day, we opened presents in front of the fire, and my mother's family came for dinner. The phone rang constantly, always my high school friends wanting to get together. I told everyone that I was sick and needed to stay home, and then we would end up chatting about the last few months over the phone. It was hard not seeing Liz and Tracy—even Chase had called—but I just couldn't face anyone. I told my mom that I felt like I was coming down with something and spent most of my time in my room, staring at the wall of pictures that I had missed.

I ran my hand over the pictures of Mo and me, wishing that she were here to talk to. I knew that I could trust her with the mess I had made of my life, and she would know exactly what to do. She had always known what to do in a crisis; she had prided herself on that. I looked at the pictures of Adam as well, cataloging every detail in my mind. His dimples framing his smile of perfect white teeth, his deep blue eyes—so intense—his crazy dark curls that I longed to run my fingers through... He was perfect, and I missed him so much.

I missed the way that he made me laugh without saying anything at all and the way he made me feel so small engulfed in his long arms, yet so safe at the same time. I missed feeling his lips against mine, the warmth from his skin, the way he played with my hair—twirling it around his fingers and then smoothing it out with his hand. I decided in that moment that I was going to tell him in my next letter and let him decide for himself what he wanted to do. I couldn't keep it from him any longer.

I decided to spend the rest of my break at home, relishing in the comfort of its familiar walls and my mother's cooking. I spent my days playing video games with Scott on the new system that he had got for Christmas, reading my new book and sleeping. I spent an afternoon with Morgan's family, sharing all the details of college life, trying to ignore their pained expressions as their thoughts drifted, no doubt, to the fact that Morgan should have been there sharing the same stories.

The weekend before classes were scheduled to start, my mother drove me back to Seattle with Scott in tow. We all spent the night crammed into Marie's small apartment, Mom and Scott returning over the mountains the following morning.

Marie dropped me off at the dorm, but, before I could get out of the car, she asked, "Is everything okay with you, Kendi?"

"Yeah, I'm fine," I responded a little too quickly.

"Because you know if you aren't fine, you can talk to me. I'm always here for you."

"I know, and I love you for that." I tried to smile but I was reeling inside with the idea of telling her everything in that moment. Instead, I gave her a brief hug and stepped out into the freezing rain. I needed to tell Adam first, and, as I made my way up the stairs to my dorm room, I decided to write him a letter that instant and actually send it.

I sat down and wrote the most difficult letter that I had ever written, knowing that he would actually read this one, my resolve to finally come clean unwavering. I told him what I should have told him that day I took the test and every day since then. I begged him not to hate me, hoping against all odds that he could forgive me. I sealed the envelope, which was the closest that I had ever come to actually mailing him a letter containing the truth and left it on my desk, as I started to unpack my bag full of clean clothes.

Tabatha came barging into the room, breathing heavily from the two flights of stairs she had just walked up, dragging her huge suitcase behind her.

"Hey, Kendi, you're back," she said, running over to give me a hug.

"How was home, Tab?" I asked as I hugged her too.

"Great. You'll never guess what happened."

It was amazing how her tiny body could fill the entire space of a room, her strong presence exuding confidence and enthusiasm.

"What?" I asked, a million ideas running through my

mind.

"I hooked up with my ex. I ran into him at a party, and he told me that he can't stop thinking about me and that he still loves me, and then I went home with him."

"Wow, so are you guys back together?" I asked.

"I don't know. I told him that I needed time to think about whether or not I wanted to have a long-distance relationship. I told him that I would write to him. Watching you write love letters to Adam and seeing how excited you are when you read his letters is inspiring. It seems so romantic," she said, raising her shoulders and opening her eyes wide and dreamily.

I wanted to tell her how depressing it could be and how *not* romantic it was, but I didn't want to burst her bubble, so I just smiled.

"Speaking of letters…I stopped at the mailbox, and someone had a love letter waiting for them already." She waved an envelope in front of me, and I recognized my name written in Adam's handwriting.

I snatched it out of her hands before she could tease me with it any longer and sat down on my bed to open it.

Tabatha started to unpack her suitcase, hanging her clothes up piece by piece in her overflowing closet.

I lay back against my pillow and started to read Adam's letter.

> *Kendi,*
> *I hope that you had a wonderful Christmas. We tried to show the people here a traditional Christmas, but it wasn't quite the same. I miss the snow and the smell of the Douglas firs, but mostly I miss you. I miss you so much. I hope that you got everything that you wanted, and I hope that you had a good time with your family and friends from home.*

I need to tell you something, and I hope that you can be understanding and open-minded, because I am not sure that I could survive without your support.

I have been called to serve as a minister of faith here in Ghana. This is a huge honor. I will be studying to become a minister while I am here, and I will be serving as one when I return. I am not sure where I will end up yet, but I have plenty of time to figure that out. I hope that this doesn't change the way you feel about me. I still love you so much, and I want nothing more than to share my life with you, but this is the path that I have chosen, and I hope that you can live with that.

There is more.... Because of the schooling that I will be going through as well as fulfilling my mission duties in the fields, I will be here an extra twelve months. I know that this is a lot to digest, Kendi. I can just imagine your shock as you are reading this. Please don't give up on me. I am really excited about this new calling, and, even though I miss you like crazy, I am so happy right now.

I hope that you can find it in your heart to be happy for me too!

I love you, and I will be waiting to hear from you.

> *Always,*
> *Adam*

I was in shock as I stared at his letter. I wasn't expecting that at all. I read it again and again, trying to comprehend what his words really meant. The letter changed everything between us. I wanted to feel angry that he was making this choice, but it wasn't fair, knowing that I was struggling with my own choices and keeping secrets that could destroy him, destroy us. But I couldn't deny how much it hurt that I was not his first choice, that he was not desperate to come home to me. That he was happy with his decision, the decision to become a minister without anyone forcing his hand.

"Are you okay, Kendi?" Tabatha asked as she sat beside me on my bed.

"Not really. Adam just told me that he's staying another year, so he'll be gone a total of three years," I said, without looking up from his letter.

"Oh, my God. That's like an eternity. What are y'all going to do?"

"I don't know." I shrugged. "I think I'll go for a run." I folded Adam's letter, reinforcing the folds over and over again, still stunned from his news.

"I'm sorry, Kendi. Do you wanna come with me to the café for dinner later?"

Tabatha was not fazed by my sudden need to run. She knew that running was my outlet; just like I knew that chocolate was hers. She usually kept a few Hershey bars under her mattress for emergencies.

"Sure, I won't be long." I was already in my running clothes, planning to go for a run at some point that day. I had missed running during the two weeks spent at home in the freezing, snowy weather. I laced up my running shoes, grabbed Adam's letter and the one that I had just written to him and headed down the stairs.

It had stopped raining temporarily, but I zipped up my windbreaker just in case. I tossed the sealed envelope addressed to Adam in the large trash can outside my building and stuffed his letter in my jacket pocket. I started to run, heading for the nearest path. Tears were already clouding my vision before I reached it. My life had just become so much more complicated. I could not send that letter to Adam. He

178

was happy, and this would crush him. It would completely change his life and the path that he had just chosen for himself. I couldn't tell him.... I just couldn't.

I was starting to feel winded and my side was cramping up, a result of taking two weeks off. I stopped to catch my breath and decided to sit on a bench for a few minutes. I felt an indescribable movement from inside, a subtle flutter at first, followed by something pushing against my belly from the inside. I instinctively reached under my shirt and jacket and held my hands against the skin of my abdomen, just in time to feel it again. This was unmistakably the baby moving inside me. I gently pressed my hand against the tiny movement, and it pushed back again a moment later.

The reality of this pregnancy finally hit me, coupled with the fact that I was alone, and I suddenly felt scared, more scared than I have ever been in my life. I started walking, lost in my despair. At some point it started to rain again, and I pulled my hood over my head, still walking without any real destination in mind. I eventually found myself outside Marie's building and realized that I had been walking for over two hours. I was drenched and cold as I pushed the button for her apartment.

She buzzed me in, and I rode in the elevator to the fourth floor, knocking on her door a few minutes later.

"Oh, my God, Kendi. You're soaking wet and shivering. Did you walk here? What's wrong?"

Her questions came at me rapidly, as she took in the sight of me. I couldn't speak. The thoughts were there to answer her questions, but my brain wasn't connected to my mouth at the moment. She brought me inside and pulled my wet jacket off me, wrapping me in a warm blanket. She removed my shoes and socks and set them aside.

"Kendi, talk to me. You're scaring me. What happened?"

She sat next to me on the couch, holding me like a

small child as my body shook uncontrollably. Slowly my body temperature returned to normal, and I tried to speak, but the words were barely a whisper. "Adam's...not...coming home...for three years."

"What? Is that what this is about?" She seemed confused by the state that I was in.

"I'm...preg...pregnant." Just saying it aloud for the first time left me in uncontrollable sobs.

Marie didn't say anything; she held me tight against her and let me cry for what felt like hours.

When the tears finally stopped coming and I was able to catch my breath, she walked me to the bathroom and started the shower for me. "Take a hot shower. You're still shivering. And then we'll talk. I'll make some hot tea. Everything's going to be okay, Kendi."

I just nodded and started to undress as Marie left the room. The steaming-hot water felt good on my cold skin. I stood under it until I felt it turn cold. Marie had set a towel and some pajamas on the counter for me. I slowly got dressed and brushed my hair, pulling it up into a bun. I felt so tired. I just wanted to sleep, but I knew that Marie was probably ready to explode with questions. I sat back down on the couch, covering myself with a blanket and waited for the inquisition to begin. Marie handed me a steaming cup of peach tea, my favorite. I wrapped both of my hands around the cup, trying to draw as much warmth from it as I could.

Marie was so motherly. She always had been. She was nearly five years older than me and looked more like my father, while I had more of my mom's features. Marie had thick strawberry-blond hair, always cut at chin level, with light blue eyes. Her skin was pale but smooth, like porcelain, and she stood an inch taller than me. She was always a little more curvy than me but in all the right places.

"I called Tabatha to let her know that you were here. I didn't want her to worry," she said as she sipped her tea.

"Kendi, tell me what happened."

I told her about that night in August in Adam's bedroom, the pregnancy test, the lie I told Adam, the letter I got from him today and feeling the baby move for the first time.

When I was done, she was speechless. She sipped her tea in silence.

"Say something," I pleaded, afraid of what she thought of me.

"What should I say, Kendi? Why didn't you come to me sooner?"

"I don't know. I was scared."

"Well, you need to tell Adam. You can't keep this from him. He will find out eventually, and, the longer you wait, the worse it will be."

"No, I can't tell him. Please don't ask me to do that."

"How are you going to keep a baby from him, Kendi? Like he won't figure it out."

"I can't have a baby, Marie. I'm eighteen and just starting college."

"Well, I hate to state the obvious, but you *are* having a baby. It's too late to have an abortion." We both cringed at the word. "Have you thought about adoption?"

"I haven't thought about anything, obviously," I said, feeling frustrated and confused.

"We need to tell Mom," Marie said.

"No, please. It will kill her. And how's she going to keep this to herself? No one can know, Marie. Swear to me that you won't tell anyone about this, or I will never forgive you," I said, holding my finger up in warning.

"Kendi…" she started to protest.

"Swear to me," I demanded, cutting her off.

"Fine, I swear. I won't tell a soul. But you need to see a doctor, and we can look into your options. We can't use your insurance or Mom will find out." She was holding her fingers to her lips, thinking intently. "We can go to the clinic at Harborview, the county hospital, and pay cash. We're going tomorrow though. I'll call in sick."

I agreed—Marie didn't give me much choice—and that was the end of our conversation. I didn't feel alone anymore, knowing that I had Marie by my side, but I was so terrified of what the future held. I was still plagued by the uncertainty of what I was going to do.

Exposed

The next morning Marie woke me from a dreamless sleep before the sun was even up.

I groaned, covering my head with the pillow. It felt like I had just fallen asleep, and already it was time to get up. I was dreading the day. I knew I needed to face this head-on, but I wanted to crawl under a rock and continue to hide.

"Come on, Kendi, the clinic's going to be busy. The earlier we get there, the less we'll have to wait." Marie was already dressed, her hair styled perfectly as always.

I shuffled slowly into the bathroom to brush my teeth and hair. I pulled my hair into a ponytail and applied a touch of mascara and lip gloss. Marie had set out a pair of black leggings, a long sweater and a fresh pair of socks. After I was dressed and ready to go, I met her in the kitchen, where she forced me to eat a bowl of oatmeal with blueberries and a glass of orange juice. I usually didn't eat this early in the morning, but Marie insisted that it was going to be a long day. We left her apartment with to-go mugs full of steaming-hot coffee and drove to Harborview Medical Center.

Sitting in the county clinic, it was hard to feel inconspicuous. The room was packed with men and women who appeared in desperate need of a shower and young girls that looked barely old enough to drive. The smell was hardly tolerable, antiseptics mixed with foul body odors and stale cigarettes. We were catching plenty of stares while we waited to be seen, reading magazines that Marie had brought from home. Marie's fancy designer coat and Coach handbag were not helping us blend in.

When I finally heard my name called, I felt like I was going to be sick. My stomach was in knots, and the oatmeal that Marie had forced down my throat was threatening to make a reappearance. She pulled me from my seat and led me to the doorway with her arm around my shoulder, whispering that everything was going to be okay.

We were pointed to a cold, sterile room with an exam table and a single chair that looked like it had seen better days. The medical assistant asked why I was there, and I was unable to speak. Marie explained to her that I was pregnant and had not seen a doctor yet. When she asked when the date of my last menstrual period was, Marie looked at me for an answer.

"I don't remember, but I know when it happened. August 12th." I remember the exact date because it was the first anniversary of the accident, the same day that Adam and I had made love in his room, the one and only day that I had had sex in the past year. It was a day that I would never forget.

The assistant made some notes in a chart and then checked my blood pressure and heart rate. She left a gown for me to wear and then slipped out of the room. I changed into the thin cotton gown that was completely open in the back, and Marie and I went back to our magazines while we waited for the doctor; the only sound in the room was the tapping of my foot on the step of the exam table. After what felt like hours, the doctor finally entered the room.

"Hi. Miss Brooks? I'm Dr. Hoffman."

She held out her hand, and I shook it gently, telling her to call me Kendi. Dr. Hoffman looked to be my mother's age with short dark hair. She wore small black rectangular glasses and a warm smile.

"Well, Kendi, let's do an ultrasound so that we can confirm the pregnancy and make sure that everything looks okay all at the same time. Okay?"

"Okay," I responded.

She wheeled a large machine from the corner of the room, setting it up next to me, and asked me to lie on the table. I felt the rigid steel table against the skin of my bare back as she draped a sheet over my legs and pulled my gown up to my chest. Marie came to stand next to me, and I felt her take my hand in hers.

"This is going to be cold," Dr. Hoffman warned as she squeezed a clear jelly on my exposed abdomen. She pushed down hard against my skin with the transducer and started tapping keys on the machine. "Well, it looks like there's a baby in there. And I would say that you're about twenty-two or twenty-three weeks along by the measurements. The baby looks healthy. Let's check the heartbeat." She tapped a few more keys and a loud shock-wave sound emerged from the machine, followed by a fast, steady beat. "Heart rate sounds strong and healthy. Would you like to know the sex of the baby?"

"Um." I looked at Marie, not sure what I wanted.

She just shrugged her shoulders at me, silently telling me that it's my decision.

"No, I don't want to know," I finally said, shaking my head.

"Okay," Dr. Hoffman said, her voice void of any

judgment or concern. She wiped the gel from my belly and pushed the machine back to the corner of the room. "So, Kendi. I was concerned because you're nearly twenty-three-weeks pregnant and haven't had proper prenatal care, but, now that I've seen the ultrasound, it seems that you have been taking good care of yourself. The baby is thriving and appears to be healthy, but I'm going to prescribe you prenatal vitamins to take daily.

"And you need to come in for a checkup once a month for now and more often as your due date approaches. We also have a few blood tests that you'll need to get at the lab, just normal precautionary tests."

I sat up, pulling the thin gown down over my legs. She held up a chart full of dates and continued. "It looks like your due date is May 5th. Do you have any questions?"

I couldn't speak. I had so many questions but I didn't know where to begin.

I heard Marie ask, "Do you have any information that you could give us in case she decides not to keep it…the baby?"

Dr. Hoffman looked at me then and asked if that was what I wanted. I nodded.

"Well, I have some brochures about adoption. We have several resources available for adoption agencies, lawyers and social workers. I can get those for you on the way out. It can be a very difficult process for a birth mother, but if that's what you truly want, there are many good couples out there waiting for a healthy baby to adopt." She handed me a prescription with her business card and said, "It was nice to meet you, Kendi, and please call me if you have any questions. We'll see you again next month. I'll leave information at the front desk for you about the adoption process, along with a list of resources, lab orders and some information for you regarding your pregnancy, the dos and don'ts, and what to watch for. Good luck." And she left the room.

I started to cry. I was not really sure why I was crying, but I couldn't seem to stop.

"Oh, Kendi. It'll be okay," Marie assured me, while wrapping her arm around my shoulders. "Why don't you get dressed? I'll check us out, and then we'll go have a nice lunch while we look over the information that Dr. Hoffman left for us. Okay?"

"Okay," I managed to choke out through my tears.

"I won't lie, Kendi. This is going to be hard no matter what you decide to do, and I will be here for you the entire time in whatever way you need me, but I also need you to be strong." She kissed me on the cheek and left me alone in the room to get dressed.

I had always thought of myself as a strong person, blocking every punch that life had swung at me, and, when I got knocked down, I always landed on my feet eventually. This didn't feel like the usual punch; this felt like a bulldozer, and I wasn't sure how I was going to recover this time.

After careful review of all the information from the clinic, Marie made a few calls and scheduled an appointment for the next day with an agency that seemed like a good fit. We decided that we could collect all the information, asking all the questions that we had, and then I could decide what I wanted to do. Marie was taking another day off from work to go to the appointment with me, and I felt that I was intruding on her life, but I couldn't do this alone.

As tired as I felt, I couldn't sleep. Every time that I closed my eyes, I saw myself standing in an open field at a crossroads, lost and unsure of which path to take. I immediately forced my eyes open. I placed my hands on my belly and tried to picture myself with a baby, but the image was blank. I just couldn't see myself as a mother. I tried to imagine giving this baby away, to someone who *could* picture themselves as a mother, and it seemed to make more sense. The only thing that I was sure of at that point was that I was having a baby, and, no matter what I chose to do about it in the end, I knew that I had to let Adam go. I had known this since the day I walked out of that bathroom. I had just wanted to hold on to him as long as I could. Ironically reading his last letter, it had felt like he was the one letting go.

The adoption agency was located in a brick building on a quiet tree-lined street in the lower Queen Anne neighborhood. It was nice. I wasn't sure what to expect, but, after our experience at the clinic yesterday, my expectations were low. I was pleasantly surprised.

As we waited on the tan leather seats in the reception area, I concentrated on each breath I took, unable to focus on anything else. *Just breathe*, I told myself. I heard my name called, a repeat of the day before. Marie and I followed a short, heavyset woman into a large office. The office was bright, full of light pouring in from the large windows that looked out onto the street; the color from the tall trees gave the room a natural feel. The woman motioned us toward a large table with several comfortable-looking chairs that sat in the center of the room. Marie and I settled into the two closest to where we stood.

"Hi, Miss Brooks. I'm Susanne Waters. Welcome to Northwest Open Adoption Agency. I am a counselor here, and my sole purpose is to help guide you to make the best choice for you and your baby, whatever that might be. We offer support for pregnant mothers who decide to keep their baby as well as facilitating an open adoption plan with a family of your choice, if you should choose adoption."

"Open adoption? What does that mean?" I asked quietly.

"Well, that is the type of adoption that we offer here. An open adoption allows you to choose the parents who will raise your child and provides you with access to their files containing their personal information, medical files, etc., to help you make that choice. And they would have access to your files as well. You would be able to meet them, and you can decide how involved you would like them to be during your pregnancy. Doctor visits, ultrasounds, things like that.

"Together you can decide what type of contact you would like to have with your child after the birth, or you may choose not to have any contact at all. Although we recommend some sort of contact or update at least three times a year. We find that open adoption gives birth mothers a piece of mind knowing that their child is safe and happy, and it gives the children a sense of security and confidence knowing who their birth parents are and where they came from. These are all things that we can cover later. I have some forms for you to fill out, and then we can talk more about your options and how you're feeling about your pregnancy."

She handed us a thick file folder and a pen, and left us alone to fill out the numerous forms in the folder. Most needed just my basic personal information: name, birthdate, address, phone number. Others were medical forms asking me questions about my health and my family's medical history. Marie and I filled this out to the best of our knowledge. There was a form strictly about the pregnancy: date of conception, due date, father's name, father's date of birth and father's contact information. I looked at Marie, unsure of how to fill in the blanks under Birth Father.

She suggested that I skip over it for now.

When Susanne returned to her office, she silently reviewed the forms before speaking to us. "Everything looks good, Kendi. What can you tell me about the birth father?"

I looked at Marie and then back to Susanne. "I'm not really sure who the father is," I said, feeling ashamed for what she must have thought of me rather than the fact that I had just lied to her.

"Okay," she said, void of any judgment.

She must have heard that often. She made a few notes in the area that I left unanswered. We talked for over an hour about everything from what my living situation was to what my dreams and goals were in life. We talked about my family and the fact that I didn't want anyone to know that I was pregnant. We talked in detail about the adoption process and what kind of support the agency offered birth mothers at no expense. I left feeling hopeful.

The whole package that had just been presented to me sounded easy and uncomplicated and free. I would know who was raising the baby, and I could walk away with the peace of mind knowing that it was safe and loved. The solution sounded too perfect for this predicament that I was in. I knew exactly what I wanted to do, and I told Marie as much in the car on the way home. Susanne had told me to spend a few days thinking about what I wanted. She had also given me a small book to read with testimonials written by other birth mothers and adoptive parents, so that I had a deep understanding of what would take place and what I could expect emotionally. I didn't need a few days. I couldn't keep this baby.

The Plan

That night, while sitting at Marie's kitchen table eating Thai food out of little paper boxes with chopsticks, we talked about what I was going to do about school. I wouldn't be able to hide this pregnancy for much longer.

"I have to finish this quarter. I'm already registered and my room is paid for."

"What are you going to tell Mom?" Marie asked as she tilted her head to the side and stuffed a huge bite of pad Thai noodles in her mouth.

"I don't know. I could tell her that I'm overwhelmed and taking on too much. Maybe she'll understand if I take spring quarter off to catch my breath."

"What about your scholarship?"

"It only covers one more quarter. I guess I'll lose it. I could get a job after…afterward and take summer courses. That would make up for the scholarship, and I could catch up from missing spring quarter."

"Well, it sounds like you have it all figured out. Excuse me." Marie tossed her chopsticks into one of the empty boxes as she stood up and walked into her room, closing the door behind her.

I sat there staring into a box of cashew chicken, wondering what had just happened. She was fine a minute before, and now I felt like she was mad at me.

I knocked softly on her door and opened it slowly when she didn't respond. She was sitting on the edge of her bed with her face in her hands, crying.

"Marie, what's wrong?" I asked as I sat beside her.

"Everything," she mumbled into her hands. "I am just so sad that this is happening to you, Kendi. You've already been through so much." She looked at me, her blue eyes full of compassion. "I don't think that you realize how hard this decision is going to be, this choice that you're making. I know I said that I was going to be here for you no matter what, and I will. But I'm in over my head. You should do this the right way. You should tell Mom, and you should definitely tell Adam and let him make this decision for himself. This isn't right, Kendi."

I let out a long sigh. "I can't do that. It has to be this way, Marie. If you're not okay with this, tell me now, and I'll do this without you."

She was quiet for a moment, and I was scared of what she might say next.

"I don't understand it, Kendi. But you can't do this alone. Please, just promise me you'll think this through carefully before you make any decisions."

I felt relieved to still have her support. "I promise. And thank you for being here for me. Do you think that I could stay with you at the end of this quarter, until I go back to school in the fall? I know that it's a lot to ask, but I don't have anywhere else to go. I can't go home."

"Of course, Kendi. I kind of planned on it already."

"Thank you. For everything, Marie." I put my arm around her shoulders and pulled her toward me. She rested her head against my shoulder, and I became overwhelmed with the love and gratitude that I felt for my sister. I knew that what I was asking of her was beyond her realm of comfort. She was sacrificing a lot to respect my wishes, knowing that keeping this secret meant that my lies became her lies, my shame became her shame, and the guilt that I was already drowning in would inevitably pull her under with me.

~

Winter trudged on bringing more freezing rain and even a dusting of snow now and then. I longed to see the sun, just to feel its warmth on my face for a few minutes. I continued to run as much as I could, but sometimes it was just too cold. At night, while Tabatha was out at a party or watching the Huskies battle it out on the basketball court, I took advantage of the privacy and laid in my bed reviewing the countless applications that Susanne had given me for prospective parents. It wasn't an easy task finding a couple that would raise my baby.

I searched each application, not sure exactly what I was looking for, but sure that each one wasn't the right couple for my baby. I guess that I was looking for a piece of Adam and me in every picture, every description. I was getting frustrated and starting to feel that maybe this wasn't a good idea, when I glanced down at the next application. Charles and Heather Petersen. It was their picture that caught my eye first. She was pretty but in a very natural way. Long blond hair and hazel eyes that radiated kindness. He was broad shouldered with short dark hair, warm brown eyes.

I read through their application and felt a connection that I hadn't with the others. They both were born and raised in Lynden, a small town just south of the Canadian border. They were high school sweethearts, had attended college at Western and had been married for nine years. They lived in Bellingham. He was owner and founder of a successful export business, and she was a pediatric nurse.

They had been trying to conceive for seven years in every natural and scientific way possible, always unsuccessful. Their story broke my heart and gave me a sense of hope at the same time. I can't place the exact reason that they stood out to me more than the others, but I felt like I had found the right couple. I immediately called Susanne at the number she had given me and told her that I wanted to meet the Petersens. She assured me that she would set up a meeting with them as soon as possible.

The following week, Marie and I went to the agency to meet Charles and Heather Petersen. I was nervous, suddenly feeling insecure. What if they didn't like me? What would they think of me, that I was willing to just give away my baby? When Susanne introduced us, I could see that they were just as nervous as I was. I could sense hope in Heather's eyes but also fear, and I wondered how someone survived the heartache that they had suffered time and time again.

They had brought pictures of their home, pictures of their parents and siblings, nieces and nephews. I pictured the baby surrounded by a big family. They asked questions about me and my life. I hadn't included any information about where I was from in my file, and I wasn't about to tell them now. I mentioned that I was local and that I was a student at Udub, and that was it. They asked about the birth father. I wondered how many times I would have to lie about Adam. They asked about the pregnancy, how I was feeling and if I knew the sex of the baby.

I liked them instantly; they seemed to be good, honest people. At the end of the meeting, I told Susanne in private that I wanted to proceed with the adoption process with the

Petersens. Susanne was thrilled, and we scheduled another meeting with the couple and their lawyer, so that we could discuss the terms of the adoption. Susanne asked me to think about how involved I wanted to be in the baby's life once it was born, so that we could discuss it at the next meeting. I wasn't sure if I wanted to be involved at all.

~

"Hey, Tab, you should know that I'm going to take spring quarter off from school. I'm moving in with Marie until fall. I just turned in my paperwork today," I casually informed her while we were pulling our clothes out of the dryer in the laundry room of our building. I had been avoiding the conversation for days, but, now that it was official, I had to break the news to her.

"What?" she asked, completely shocked at my news. "Why would you do that?"

"I'm just feeling overwhelmed and need a break. I'll catch up over the summer."

"Maybe you should've stuck to three classes rather than the crazy five you've been juggling these past two quarters," she said, shoving her designer jeans in her laundry basket.

"I know. I'll slow down next fall when I come back. So you're going to have the room to yourself next quarter. What do you think about that?"

"I think that I'm going to miss you like crazy!" she said sincerely and then her face grew serious. "Can I ask you something, Kendi, without you getting upset with me?"

"Of course." I braced myself for her question, knowing that I had to be honest with her.

"I don't know how to word this any differently so I'm just going to ask. Are you pregnant?"

I had known that it was coming, but the words still

took my breath away. My belly was growing more with each passing day, and it was only a matter of time before she acknowledged the obvious. I blew out a long breath through my lips and answered, "Yes."

Her brown eyes grew wide as she processed my response. "Wow. When did this happen? I mean you haven't even looked at a guy since I met you." Before I could even respond, she had connected the dots. "Oh, my God, it's Adam's, isn't it?"

I could only nod.

"Does he know? What are y'all going to do?"

I took a deep breath. "Tab, you can't ever tell anyone about this. My sister is the only one who knows. Adam doesn't know, and I'm not keeping this baby. Can I trust you to keep this to yourself?"

"Of course, Kendi. So this is why you're 'taking a break'?" she asked, making quotations with her fingers.

"Yeah, pretty much," I admitted. "The baby is due May 5th."

"I wish that you would've told me sooner. I feel like such a bitch for always pushing the parties, the drinking and the guys on you when you had all this going on." She motioned toward my growing belly.

"It's okay, Tab. You're not a bitch, at least not all the time." I smiled at her, trying to lighten the mood. She threw a T-shirt at my face, and we both laughed. And that was the last time that she brought it up. I was so grateful that she didn't treat me any differently. She still teased me to no end about being a prude and a bore, the usual. And there was this unspoken truth between us that, although she was going to pretend as if this wasn't happening—as I had done for the past six months—she did know, and she supported me.

~

Heather and Charles were so kind to me, easing me into the legal proceedings gently and making sure that my young mind understood everything that was discussed. I could tell that this process was not new to them, and I wondered why they were still childless if they had gone through the adoption process before.

We had decided that they would accompany me whenever possible to doctor appointments with the new obstetrician that they had referred me to. I declined politely when they asked me to move into their home when I finished school this quarter. I couldn't imagine how awkward it would be to live with them for the remainder of my pregnancy, but apparently it was common with young, single birth mothers. I was thankful that I had Marie.

When the subject of the nature of my relationship with the baby after the birth was brought into question, I wasn't sure how to respond. I didn't want to be involved; I wanted to move on and never look back. Marie did not agree with this decision. She begged me to take as much contact as they were offering, knowing that I could decide differently later on. She had a good point; I had no idea how I would feel once the baby was born.

So I agreed to the terms that they were generously offering. Heather encouraged me to have some kind of relationship with the baby. She said that she wanted to be open with her child from the start about the adoption and who I was. I wasn't sure that I understood her logic, but she seemed to feel strongly about it. The lawyer suggested contact between me and the Petersens, a minimum of three times a year, but no more than once a month. This could be in the form of a letter with pictures, phone calls or a face-to-face visit.

They decided that they did not want to know the sex of the baby; they wanted to be surprised. I was thankful for this. I didn't want to picture a little boy or a little girl growing inside of me. I couldn't help but notice how reserved Charles was in comparison to the first time that I had met him, most noticeably when we discussed the birth procedures. I agreed to having them at the hospital when I went into labor, but I did not want them in the delivery room. That was beyond my comfort level. I was worried that this wasn't really what he wanted. I decided to ask Susanne about this in private. I had grown to depend on her to answer every question that I had, no matter how ridiculous it seemed.

With the legal matters squared away for the adoption, I focused all my energy on my finals. The quarter was coming to an end, and I had five huge exams to get through. I studied every spare minute I had. Taking a quarter off from school wasn't going to look good; the least I could do was finish this quarter strong. I was definitely looking pregnant, and I tried to ignore the stares and whispers from those around me. Tabatha was great at taking that attention from me. She tried to embarrass herself on purpose to distract the rumor mill long enough to get me to and from class. I was used to the way rumors spread, having grown up in a small town. I just wasn't used to being the subject of the gossip.

I finished finals uneventfully and began to pack my belongings before the dorms closed for spring break. I had to turn in my ID badge by the end of the day.

"I can't believe that this is your last day as my roommate," Tabatha whined. "Who am I going to make my evening coffee runs with, and who is going to make sure that I get home safely from campus parties?"

"You'll be fine. Besides I haven't been to a party with you in months."

"True. You just had to go and get yourself knocked-up and ditch me on the party circuit." She smiled as I cast her an incredulous look for her crass comment.

"Kidding," she moaned. "On a serious note, Kendi. I'm worried about you. Can I come hang out with you at

Marie's? Someone's got to keep you from wallowing in self-pity while you sit around and get fat." She laughed but I could sense the sincerity of her concern.

I walked over and threw my arms around her. "I would love for you to come see me. I haven't decided what I'm going to do to keep myself busy for the next six weeks, and I'm going to miss you."

She helped me carry my stuff down to Marie's car, and then the three of us walked to administration to turn in my badge. We stopped at our favorite coffeehouse on the way back to the dorm for one last cup of joe. As I looked around at the mix of college students sipping their coffees, discussing their spring break plans or the latest party that they had attended, I couldn't help but feel envious of the simplicity of their lives. I missed waking up each day knowing that the most difficult decision that had to be made was what I was going to wear. Everything had gotten so complicated. This wasn't how my first year of college was supposed to be.

Choices

It was hard not to feel depressed as I watched my body become unrecognizable. My belly was huge, my feet were swollen, my cheeks were chubby, and my breasts were starting to look like the world's worst implants. I tried to spend as much time outdoors as possible. The days were getting warmer, and I spent hours walking around Marie's neighborhood, looking in shop windows and people watching.

With so much free time, I found myself thinking of Adam. I missed him terribly. The day that I signed over the baby to the Petersens—the preadoption papers, nothing was final until the baby was born—I knew that I had to let Adam go, and I did. I never replied to his letter that explained his plans to become a minister and stay in Africa an additional year. He had written a handful of letters since then, which I tucked away in a shoebox unopened.

I didn't have the heart to read his thoughts when I did

not intend to write him back. I couldn't stomach the hurt he must feel knowing that I hadn't written him a single letter since Christmas. I didn't know what to say to him, how to tell him good-bye without an explanation or, worse, give him one full of more lies. So I just didn't tell him anything. This only added to the overwhelming guilt that I was feeling already.

I dreamed of him nearly every night. My dreams were so vivid. When I woke up, it was hard to decipher what was in my mind and what was real. I had very physical dreams, where his touch felt so authentic. Adam kissing my lips, my neck, whispering in my ear, as my body shivered from his breath on my cheek. Adam taking my body for his own, in the way only he knew how. I would wake up breathless, the longing nearly choking me.

And then there were the dreams where I walked out of the bathroom and told him that I was pregnant, and he was ecstatic. The dreams where he was here with me, watching my belly grow, placing his hands against my skin as he marveled at the feel of the baby's movements from inside. Awakening from these dreams resulted in severe rounds of hysteria that were nearly impossible to recover from. Marie would come home from work to find me still in bed with the curtains drawn. I just wanted this to be over so that I could move on with my life. So that I could be young and free again.

My mother called nearly every day. She had been extremely upset when I had told her of my plans to take a break from school. I played up the idea of how overwhelmed I was and how stressed I was feeling. She insisted that I come home, but I told her that I wanted to get a job to save money for school. She couldn't deny that I would make more money in Seattle than I could ever make taking a job back home. She called for constant updates about my job hunt. I just kept telling her that nothing had come up yet. I tried to avoid lying to her as much as possible, but it was inevitable. I wondered if this was just the beginning. If my life would always be one big fat lie.

My favorite days were when Tabatha skipped classes to hang out with me. She would paint my toenails while she told me everything that was happening at school, and then we would watch old movies until Marie came home from work. Tab usually had a letter or two from Adam in hand when she arrived. I had forwarded my mail but they still seemed to end up in my old mailbox on campus. I put them in the box unopened with all the others, while trying to ignore the hopeful look that Tabatha gave me each time.

"Come on, Kendi. Aren't you even a little curious about what he has to say?" she asked.

"Curious or not, it's too hard. I don't deserve to have him in my life. It's better this way."

"The poor guy. Can't you at least write him and tell him good-bye or tell him that you are moving on?"

"Whatever I tell him will be void of the truth, and he will still be left wondering why. Can we not talk about this, Tab?"

"Fine. But I'm just sayin'," she said as she plopped down on the couch next to me.

"I know." I breathed out in frustration. The truth was I had considered reading his letters a thousand times, but something always stopped me, although I didn't have the strength to throw them away. At first I didn't know what to say to him, and now it had been so long that it seemed like whatever I did say to him wouldn't be enough.

I rode the bus to Capitol Hill where my new doctor's office was located. Heather had referred me to Dr. Pierce, a highly recommended obstetrician who practiced at Swedish Medical Center. Initially I wasn't thrilled about having a male doctor, but I didn't have much of a choice since the Petersens were footing the bill. Dr. Pierce had experience with newborn adoptions, and was extremely comfortable with Heather and Charles's role in the situation.

Heather was meeting me at Dr. Pierce's office that day. She tried to drive down from Bellingham for most of my checkups. It seemed silly for her to come all that way for a twenty-minute doctor visit, but she insisted, and who was I to deny her. It was nice to have someone with me. I had insisted on going to my appointments alone so that Marie didn't miss any more work than absolutely necessary.

After my appointment Heather invited me out to lunch. She drove us down to the waterfront where we enjoyed lunch at a small restaurant, watching the ferries come and go through the bay windows while we ate. We chatted about how I was feeling and what I had been doing with all my spare time. She told me about her latest patients at the hospital and her father's birthday party that they had attended over the weekend. She was sweet and easy to talk to.

I asked her if they had gone through the adoption process before, remembering how knowledgeable she seemed. She admitted to me that they had been through this a year before with another young girl. She had moved in with them, they had painted the nursery, and, the day the baby was born, the mother couldn't go through with it. She had kept the baby and moved back home with her parents.

Heather had tears in her eyes as she told me the story. I was shocked. The lawyer had repeatedly told me that nothing was legal or permanent until after the baby was born, that I could change my mind when the time came. I couldn't imagine doing that to Heather and Charles. I knew how much they wanted this baby, how much they deserved to have this baby. As if reading my thoughts, she reached across the table and placed her hand on mine.

"You know, Kendi. I would understand if you couldn't go through with it too," she said softly. "This is your life, your choice, and we are so grateful to you for even considering us to be your baby's parents."

I looked into her hazel eyes, filled with sadness. "Heather, I don't know what to say. I want you to raise this baby. I know that you and Charles will be great parents. I need to finish college, and I want to try to get into medical school."

She smiled at me, but her features were still laced with uncertainty. "You're extremely smart and driven. I'm sure that you'll have no problem getting into medical school. And you're always welcome in our home, if you want to see the baby."

"Does Charles want that too? He doesn't seem happy about our arrangement."

"Oh, Kendi, he is happy. He's just very guarded this time. We've been through a lot, and he doesn't want to get too attached, in case…you know…"

"In case I change my mind?" I finished her sentence for her, and she nodded. "I guess that makes sense."

Her face suddenly lit up with an idea. "Hey, why don't you let me take you shopping for some maternity clothes to get you by for the next month or so? What do you think?"

I had been practically living in the same pants for weeks; new clothes did sound nice. "Okay, if you don't mind," I said.

"I would love to." She seemed excited at the idea of shopping. "Let's go up to Fifth Avenue, and then I'll drive you home when we're done."

We spent the rest of the afternoon at a maternity boutique where Heather bought me a pair of jeans with an elastic band around the waist and several cute tops that hugged my belly just right. She also took me to Nordstrom where she insisted on buying me several new outfits in my normal size for after the baby was born. This included a pair of designer jeans that cost more than my whole wardrobe put together. And then shoe shopping.

I wasn't comfortable with Heather buying me things at first, but, once I realized how much she was enjoying it, I relaxed and decided to just go with it. I had a really great time. By the time she dropped me off at Marie's apartment with several shopping bags in hand, it was dark, and I was exhausted.

~

Two weeks later as I was vacuuming the apartment, trying to earn my keep, I felt a dull ache in my belly. I didn't think too much of it at first, but it continued to get worse.

An hour later, the dull ache was replaced by cramping, and I decided to call the doctor's office. They instructed me to come in right away to make sure that everything was okay. I called Marie, and she agreed to meet me there. I took the bus as I had done several times before. As I stepped off the bus, I felt a slow wet stream make its way down my leg. I wasn't sure what was happening, but I was scared.

By the time I reached the office at the end of the block, the pain in my abdomen had intensified. The assistant took one look at me and ushered me into an exam room. They helped me change into a gown, and, in minutes, Dr. Pierce was at my side telling me that it looked like my water broke and that I was in labor. They hooked me up to a machine to monitor the baby's heartbeat and checked my blood pressure. Dr. Pierce checked my cervix and confirmed that I was dilated four centimeters. Everything was happening so quickly.

"Kendi, we're going to take you across the street to the hospital in a wheelchair. Do you want to call anyone?"

"The baby isn't due for another two weeks. Is

everything okay?" I asked in a panic.

"Everything's fine. Due dates are not exact, and the baby is full term and healthy."

"Okay. My sister is on her way here, and I should probably call Susanne at the agency."

"We'll send your sister over to the hospital when she arrives, and I'll have the front desk contact the agency. We have their information on file. Don't worry. Everything is going to be fine. Let's get you over there and settled in. I think that this baby is coming real soon."

I tried so hard not to cry. I needed Marie to be there. I couldn't do this alone.

The nurse sat me in a wheelchair and pushed me out of the building and across the street to the hospital. She checked me into the maternity ward. I was sweating and gasping for breath as the contractions swept me into endless segments of agony. They were coming faster and stronger while the nurses hooked me up to machines and started an IV in my arm. Marie finally appeared in the doorway, and I lost the hold I had on my tears at the sight of her.

"I'm here, Kendi. It's okay, I'm here," she said reassuringly as she made her way to my side. At that moment another contraction seized my abdomen as I cried out in pain, sweat dripping from my brow. Marie squeezed my hand tightly and whispered comforting words through my cries. When it was over, she retrieved a cool cloth and mopped the sweat from my forehead.

A nurse approached to check on me, and Marie asked if I could get something for the pain, an epidural. The nurse needed to check my cervix first. She told us that I was dilated nine centimeters already and that we didn't have time for an epidural. She left to page Dr. Pierce.

I survived several more contractions before Dr. Pierce arrived. Bile was rising in my throat from the pain, and I wasn't sure how much more I could take.

Susanne poked her head in while the nurses were getting the room ready for the delivery.

She informed us that she would be right outside if I needed anything, and that Heather and Charles would be arriving any minute. What I needed was to get this thing out of me so that I could breathe again. Dr. Pierce put on a gown and a pair of gloves while the nurses held up my legs. He asked me to push slowly but hard the next time I felt a contraction.

I can't say what happened after that except that I nearly passed out from the pain of it. I had never felt such excruciating pain in my life. I could hear a baby crying from somewhere in the room, and Dr. Pierce was still giving me instructions to push. The pain in my abdomen was fading, although my vagina felt like it was on fire. When Dr. Pierce was done he covered me up with a blanket and came to sit beside me. I could still hear the baby crying from nearby.

"Kendi, everything went beautifully. You did great."

"Is the baby okay?" I asked, worried from its violent cries.

"Yes, the baby is perfect. Just not liking the sponge bath at the moment." He smiled at me and then switched to a more serious tone. "Would you like to hold your baby or would you like to wait for the Petersens? This is your decision."

I looked up at Marie; she had tears in her eyes and was still holding my hand. "I don't know. I don't know what I want to do," I answered honestly.

"You should, Kendi. You will never get this moment back," Marie encouraged me.

"Okay," I said, unsure if it was the right thing to do or not.

Dr. Pierce nodded at the nurse across the room, and, before I knew it, she was placing a tiny bundle in my arms. "It's a girl," the nurse practically gushed. Dr. Pierce and the nurse both stepped out of the room at the same time, leaving me alone with the baby and Marie.

I pulled away the thin blanket from her chin so that I could take in every inch of her sweet face. I gently peeled the blue-and-pink-striped beanie from her head and gasped at the amount of hair that stuck to the tiny crown of her head. I could see Adam in her big dark eyes and the unmistakable curls of her dark hair. I took in her familiar full lips and the shape of her face, and there was no denying that this was my daughter.

This tiny bundle pulled on the strings of my heart with a familiar melody. I leaned down and kissed her forehead whispering, "Hey, sweet baby girl," as warm tears made their way down my cheeks. I was caught off guard by the boundless love that filled my heart for this tiny person that I had just met moments ago. I heard a knock on the door pulling me back to the heartbreaking reality of the situation. The door opened slowly, and I could see Heather and Charles poke their heads in.

"May we come in?" Heather asked quietly in her sweet voice.

I swallowed the lump in my throat and told them to come in. Heather rushed to my side and glanced at the baby with her hands clasped in front of her chest.

"Oh, my goodness. She is beautiful, Kendi." Charles walked up behind her hesitantly and asked how I was feeling.

"I'm okay. Just tired I guess. Would you like to hold her?" I asked, not sure what to do or say in that moment.

"Yes, we would love to," Heather whispered, looking back at Charles. She gently took the baby from my arms and cradled her against her chest, kissing her head and then her cheeks. Heather had tears in her eyes. I had no doubt that she would be a wonderful mother, but my heart was breaking. A piece of my soul had just been ripped from my arms leaving me hollow, empty. I wiped away the tears on my cheeks with the back of my hand as they continued to fall, and I felt Marie's arm around my shoulders.

The nurse returned to the room to let us know that the baby would be going to the nursery, and the Petersens were welcome to accompany her. I watched, unable to turn away from my daughter, as she was transferred from Heather's arms to the young nurse's, placed in a small cradle with clear plastic sides and carefully wheeled from the room. Heather asked me if I needed anything. I shook my head, unable to speak.

"Kendi, we're here for you if you need anything," Heather said. "You and the baby will be here for a few days. We want you to spend as much time with her as you need to while you're here. Nothing will be finalized until you're both discharged. Please. I want you to be sure of this choice that you're making, because once I take her home, I'm not sure if I could survive it if…if you change your mind."

I nodded in understanding.

"She's beautiful, just like you." She squeezed my hand and left the room with Charles. I knew that she was trying to protect herself and Charles from what had happened last time. I knew that she wanted me to be sure of my choice, to feel confident that I was doing the right thing. I honestly had so many mixed emotions right then that I didn't know what the right thing was anymore. I completely lost all sense of control; sobs took over my body as Marie held me in silence. Moments later the nurse was back to clean me up and check my vitals. I was starting to feel the pain and aches from the quick and brutal labor that I had just experienced, so she gave me some medication for the pain. I eventually drifted off into a dreamless, drug-induced sleep.

~

In the quiet early morning hours, I held her tiny body in my

210

arms. She seemed to fit so perfectly, snug against my chest. Her tiny pink lips parted as her breath peacefully passed between them while she slept soundlessly. I hadn't expected my heart to feel so connected to this tiny person that had been kicking me for months. I shouldn't have held her again, but Susanne had insisted. She said that it was the only way to be sure that I was doing the right thing.

It was too late though; I had promised the Petersens this gift. How could I take away that promise and knowingly break their hearts? I knew that they would love her, that they could give her everything that she needed. I knew this with every ounce of my being, and yet part of me wanted to hold her forever so that my own heart didn't shatter into a million tiny pieces. I couldn't help but think of how differently this moment could've been, if I had made different choices from the beginning.

Suddenly college didn't seem so important or Adam's mission in Africa. The tiny baby girl in my arms seemed to fill the space of the entire universe, and her importance could not be measured. How could I have not seen this sooner? I would like to think that I did this for her, that I was trying to make the best choice possible for her, so that she could have a life full of things that I could not offer.

But the truth was that I had made this choice for me and for Adam, so that we could continue down the road that led to our intended lives and purpose, to our dreams. It was a choice made in utter selfishness. And that realization was drowning me in guilt and regret, but I deserved these feelings. I had brought them into my heart all on my own, and now I had to live with my choices.

Forty-eight hours. That is the length of time that I spent with my daughter. Marie never left my side. The baby had spent some of that time in the nursery, where I was told that Heather and Charles fed and rocked her. The hours that she spent in my room, I held her and told her in hushed whispers how my heart swelled at the sight of her and how sorry I was for this choice that I had made.

I told her how loved she would be by everyone in her life, that a day would not go by that I wouldn't think of her. And that I would never stop loving her, and maybe I could be strong enough to be part of her life in some small way. The ache in my heart was too strong to be a part of her life in the way that our contract stated. I knew that I needed time and distance, and I hoped that someday I would be able to be there for her.

Charles and Heather did not return to my room, until I asked for them. The nurse was getting my discharge papers ready. Susanne and the Petersens' lawyer were in my room with the adoption paperwork. The lawyer reviewed the contract, and Susanne asked me once again if I was sure that this was what I wanted. I was unable to hide the tears that seemed to bleed from my heart as I nodded. I asked to see Charles and Heather and the baby one more time before I signed the papers. Susanne brought the three of them into the room a few minutes later.

"Hi," Heather whispered. The fear in her eyes was unmistakable, and the silence hung heavy in the air.

"Hi, Heather," I said with more confidence than I'd had since I met them. I placed my hand on her arm that was cradling my daughter. "I haven't changed my mind," I said quietly. I could see the relief flash in her eyes. She appeared so fragile in this moment, like at any second she might crumple to the ground. And I realized that, while she held my whole heart in her arms, I held her heart in my hands. The two of us so vulnerable, each in our own way. I knew that I would be forever bonded to this woman, the woman who my daughter would call mother.

"Have you given her a name yet?" I asked, my voice barely a whisper even through my best attempt to appear strong.

Heather turned her head and looked at Charles, as if to ask his permission to answer my question. The look he gave her was guarded but she turned back to me, "We would like to name her Brooklyn Grace. We want her to have a piece of you in her name, and Grace is my mother's name."

My eyes filled with tears once again. "It's beautiful. Thank you." I turned to Susanne. "I'm ready to sign the papers."

I felt Marie's hand on my shoulder. "Are you sure, Kendi?"

"Yes, I'm sure." The bedside table was wheeled toward me, a pen placed in my hand. I signed my name several times, a yellow tab showing me each place that required my signature. When I was done, I glanced up at Heather and Charles through bleary eyes. Tears streaked down Heather's face, and Charles's eyes were filled with moisture as he held his wife at his side. "May I have a few minutes alone with her?"

Heather wiped the tears from her face with one hand. "Yes, of course." She handed me the tiny bundle. "We'll be right outside."

Susanne and the Petersens' lawyer followed them out the door. Marie leaned over and kissed the baby's forehead. She pulled a small camera from her purse. "Do you mind if I take a picture?"

"Of course not." I looked down at my daughter, sleeping soundly in my arms. I removed her hat, releasing her tiny dark curls. I could hear the quiet *click* from the camera as Marie took just one picture. She squeezed my shoulder and left the room.

"Brooklyn Grace." I sighed. "What a beautiful name for a beautiful girl." I couldn't say good-bye, couldn't seem to form the words on my tongue. Although my mind was screaming it into the empty depths of my soul, I just sat in silence and cradled her, memorizing her delicate features, her scent, the feel of her soft skin against my own, the way she firmly gripped my finger in her tiny pink hand. It felt as if hours had passed while I held her, but, when I heard the door open and the sound of Marie's voice as she called my name, it seemed not nearly long enough.

"Are you ready?" Marie asked softly.

"Yeah, I guess so," I answered, knowing that I would never be ready for this moment.

Susanne, Heather and Charles returned to the room. I had wanted to write Brooklyn a letter, a keepsake that she would have when she was older, but I hadn't been able to find the right words. I knew that I would have many chances to write to her, our contract giving me that right. I kissed my sweet baby girl's cheek and handed her back to Heather.

I pulled the blankets from my legs and slipped out of the bed to stand on my feet. I removed the sapphire ring from my finger—the one Adam had given me—and held it out to Heather. "Please, give this to her one day. It's the only thing I have that means anything to me." Like the blood that ran through her veins, Brooklyn, Adam and I were bound together now by this one small token. *Always*.

"Of course," Heather said, opening her palm so that I could place it in her hand.

I heard Charles's deep voice, cracking as he tried to speak. "Kendi, words cannot express our gratitude. Susanne has our contact information, please keep in touch. We hope that you will always be part of our lives."

I could see his struggle, trying to keep his composure as the realization was settling in that they were going to walk from the room with this baby girl in their arms. My baby girl.

"Good-bye, Kendi," Heather said as she reached out with one arm to embrace me. As she pulled away, I once more stroked Brooklyn's cheek. Charles pulled me into a firm hug as well, and then they walked out. As I heard the door shut, I dropped to my knees, the overwhelming grief

stripping me of my strength to stand.
I was broken.

Questions

I pulled my seat belt tighter around my hips, feeling the airplane's speed pick up as we raced down the runway. I leaned my forehead against the icy window and watched the endless snow-covered fields disappear as we made our ascent into the clouds. The plane jerked and swayed until it found a comfortable cruising altitude, and I let out a deep sigh, thankful to be going back to California. I was exhausted from the emotional events of the past two days. I had peeled back the bandages and aired my open wounds for people to see. Although no one could possibly comprehend the depth of the emotional scars that were still present ten years later.

The disappointment that my mother felt toward me for the choices I had made was hard to stomach. She was hurt. Hurt that I felt that I could not confide in her, hurt by my deceit, hurt to see her daughter live with such pain, hurt for the granddaughter that she would never know. The shame I felt in revealing this part of my life to my mother—that I had buried for ten long years—had nearly killed me, and yet I felt free finally. The heavy burden that I had been carrying around with me had been lifted; I could breathe again.

Allowing myself to remember Brooklyn's face and the unbearable pain that I felt when she was gone was like rebreaking a bone—already fractured, beginning to heal—but it felt good to allow myself to think of her. My mother was understandably upset, but she still had hugged me tightly when I had left, assuring me that there wasn't anything that I could do to make her love me any less. Her unconditional love only made me feel worse for keeping this from her for so long.

She was openly appalled that I had kept this from Adam. She made me promise to make this right with him, reminding me that he deserved better than that. She was right of course, as mothers inevitably are. He did deserve better. I wasn't sure if he would find it in his heart to ever forgive me.

Now that Adam knew the truth, there was one more person that I needed to share this part of me with. I owed Derek the truth as well. I knew that our relationship could never move to the next step without showing him every piece of me, and, as much as I had tried to deny it all these years, this was a huge part of who I was and who I am now. I feared that Derek would never see me the same once he knew the truth, but that was a chance that I had to take.

My mind drifted to Derek's face and all the moments that we had shared these past two years. He was the first person that I had allowed myself to have a meaningful relationship with after Adam. I had dated plenty in college and medical school, but those relationships were purely physical, and I had walked away the moment I felt that they were getting too predictable. The hurt that I had suffered by simply loving freely and deeply had burned me too many times. I had not allowed myself to love again.

I am not sure why Derek was different. I was so far

away from home, yet the memories still burned in my mind, and I wanted a new start. Derek was that for me, and I was starved of something beyond a physical connection. Although in the beginning, our physical chemistry was what kept me coming back for more, but slowly a much deeper connection had developed.

Derek was very successful and could be serious at times, but he was also a big kid at heart and so much fun. He had introduced me to a life that I had never known. He had taught me how to surf, snow ski and kayak. He had introduced me to five-star hotels and expensive, celebrity-filled restaurants. Of course material things did not weigh on me like other girls, but it was nice to be pampered, and we always had a lot of fun. Derek had worked hard for the life that he had. He had been raised in a middle-class home much like my own. So he was appreciative of everything he had and did not live extravagantly. He was a simple guy who enjoyed the simple pleasures in life, and he was kind and loving.

I loved him, but, after seeing Adam, I feared that I would never love Derek the way he deserved to be loved. The passion that stirred inside me in Adam's presence I had never felt with someone else. Maybe it was always that way with our first love. Maybe our adult relationships are supposed to be more about friendship and commitment, and our maturity keeps us from the irrational love and passion that we feel in our youth.

I heard the pilot announce our approach in Los Angeles, pulling me from my wandering thoughts. I glanced at my watch, noting that it was almost seven in the evening. I was working the night shift the rest of the week and into the weekend, my penance for taking off a few days while my colleagues covered my shifts at the hospital. I was already looking forward to my own bed and a hot shower.

As I walked toward baggage claim, following the

signs leading to a taxi that would take me to my beachfront apartment, I couldn't help but smile when I saw Derek waiting for me. He was leaning against a pillar in a navy polo shirt that was casually untucked, low-rise jeans and leather flip-flops, his legs crossed at the ankles. His dreamy tan face was pulled into a warm smile that reached his nearly gray eyes. His light-brown hair was styled perfectly, sexy gelled peaks framing his face. He held a small sign in one hand, propped against his midsection, that read in bold letters Got Brooks? I slowly strolled toward him, pulling my carry-on behind me.

"Hey, what are you doing here?" I asked as he pulled me into his arms, my feet leaving the ground as he spun me around. When my feet touched the ground again, he leaned down and kissed me.

"I missed you and thought you could use a ride home. The taxi line is a bitch this time of night."

"I missed you too."

He took my suitcase and walked me to his car, his arm around my lower back.

This felt safe and familiar, and I felt the tension of the past two days melt away as I leaned against him, my hand resting in the back pocket of his jeans.

On the drive to my place, he asked me about the funeral. It seemed like weeks ago. I described the service and the speech that I gave, purposefully leaving out the part about Adam; I wasn't ready to dive into everything yet. Derek told me about his trip to New York and the company that his team had just brought public after months of hard work and due diligence. It sounded like a very successful launch, and I was happy for him.

Derek pulled his car into my designated guest parking space next to the garage and killed the engine. "Mind if I come up for a little awhile?" he asked, knowing me well enough not to assume that he was invited to stay.

"Not at all," I replied, giving him a quick kiss on the mouth.

The warm salty air was welcoming after the arctic chill that I had just come from. I said as much to Derek. He laughed, reminding me that he had been in New York, where the northeast had its own version of cold. Once inside my dark apartment, Derek suggested that I should take a nice hot shower while he made me something to eat. With the steaming-hot water spraying over my head, I tried to wash away the last few days. I debated about what to say to Derek and when. I would just have to find the right time, whenever it presented itself. I quickly dried my hair and pulled on a pair of jeans and a T-shirt.

When I emerged from the bathroom, I was shocked at the scene in front of me. The room was dark, candles of all different shapes and sizes were lit around the room and I could smell something yummy coming from the kitchen. "Derek?" I called out hesitantly, not sure what to think.

Derek casually strolled into the room and reached for my hands. He led me to the couch and sat down beside me.

"What's all this?" I asked, my eyes scanning the room.

He took a deep breath and released it slowly. "Kendi, I know that we've talked about this, and you keep saying that you're not ready…but I'm ready enough for the both of us. I just reached the top of the world in my career this past week, the place that guys in my field only dream about. And I realized that it means nothing to me if I don't have you to share it with. My existence means nothing without you." He dropped down to one knee, holding a tiny box in his hand.

My heart completely stopped beating in my chest.

"Kendi, will you marry me?"

I clasped my hand over my mouth to hold in the gasp that my body desperately needed to expel. "Derek." I dropped down to my knees on the floor in front of him.

"There's something that I need to tell you before I give you my answer." I took the box from his hand and placed it on the end table next to me. He looked confused and defeated as he lowered himself all the way to the floor, stretching his legs out on either side of me. I clasped his hands in mine and placed them in my lap.

"Okay, I'm listening," he said, clearly nervous about what it was that I had to say.

"There's something about me that I never told you. I never told anyone until today."

~

I told him the complete story about my past, about Adam, the pregnancy and adoption. It was much easier to talk about everything now. I felt emotionally disconnected from the story as if I were telling someone else's secrets. The look on Derek's face was hard to read and my fear of what he saw now when he looked at me was the one thing that brought me to tears. He started to speak, but I interrupted him, letting him know that there was more I had to say.

As if I hadn't dropped enough in his lap already, I confessed that I spent the night with Adam and explained Adam's reaction that morning when I finally revealed the truth to him. The hurt in Derek's eyes was undeniable now. I knew that I had pushed him away at this point, so I waited patiently for him to respond.

He stood up and moved to sit on the couch, leaning back into the cushions. "Kendi, I don't know what to say."

I pulled myself up from the floor and sat next to him. "I know that it's a lot to process. I'm so sorry about keeping this from you. I haven't talked about it in ten years. And I'm sorry about last night. I don't know what happened. I just got caught up in the past."

"Do you still love him?" he asked, his eyes burning

into me.

It was a valid question, but still… "I don't know," I answered honestly. I wasn't sure about anything right now.

"Well, that's not very convincing." He scrubbed his face with his hands, his fingers rubbing across his eyes.

As I watched his every move, I silently wished that he would wipe away the look of disappointment that he held in his eyes, taking with it the shame that was consuming me. He clasped his hands in his lap and looked right at me. "You're right. This is a lot to take in. Oddly I'm putting myself in Adam's shoes, and I can't imagine what he must be feeling right now. I can't grasp the idea that the warm, compassionate and loving person that I fell in love with and want to spend the rest of my life with could do something like this, something so dishonest and wrong. I feel like I don't even know who you are."

"Derek, I'm still me. I was eighteen and scared. It was complicated. Don't think that I haven't regretted my decision every day for the past ten years. Please try to understand."

"That's just it, I don't understand. And to think that you spent the night with him last night… I don't know what to think about that."

"I didn't have sex with him. I couldn't do that to you, Derek."

"That doesn't make me feel any better. You obviously feel something for him."

I didn't say anything. We both sat in silence for several minutes as I wiped away the tears that spilled down my cheeks. I finally couldn't take it anymore. "Say something," I pleaded.

"What do you want me to say, Kendi?" he asked.

He was so calm, always in control. Part of me wanted him to yell, to rip into me for what I had done, for the hurt that he must feel. But that was not him, and somehow it made me feel worse. "Say that you still love me and that we can get through this."

"Of course I still love you. I love you so damn much." He held my hand in his and brought it to his lips. "I think that I need some time. I need to figure out what this all means for us. And I think that I deserve this time."

I sucked in a breath at his conclusion. "I understand," was all I could say.

He kissed me softly on the lips, his hand brushing my cheek. "I'll talk to you soon."

"I love you, Derek," I whispered against his lips, reassuring him as I kissed him one more time. He stood, retrieving the small box from the table and making his way to the door.

I sat there, watching him go.

He stopped in the doorway and turned back to look at me. "What would your answer have been?"

Silence hung heavy in the space between us as I contemplated my answer. "I can't answer that right now." I shrugged.

He gave me the saddest smile, as if he already knew what my answer would be and closed the door behind him.

I pulled my knees into my chest and sobbed. I had hurt so many people in the past twenty-four hours. I was caught in the swirling vortex of my lies, sucking in everyone that I loved with me. How did my life get so messed up?

I eventually made my way into the kitchen to find warm pasta in the oven and a green salad set aside for me. Derek was too good to me. I didn't deserve him. I tried to eat a few bites, but I wasn't in the mood to eat. I cleaned up the kitchen, happy to have something distracting to do. When I was done in the kitchen, I unpacked my suitcase and put away my clothes. I slipped into a pair of cotton shorts and a worn UW T-shirt and crawled into bed.

I reached over into my nightstand and felt around

until I found what I was searching for: a book, its pages faded and frayed at the edges. Opening the book to a marked page somewhere near the middle, I found the worn photograph. I brushed my finger over the picture of a young college girl holding a beautiful baby with a handful of dark wavy hair. I flipped off the bedside lamp and held the photograph against my chest as I drifted off to sleep, dreaming of her face.

Rally

I woke early, thankful for a day off from the hospital. I had been working impossible hours, offering to cover fellow residents' shifts for months in an attempt to keep my mind busy so that maybe I wouldn't notice the constant ache in my chest. Three months had slipped by in the blink of an eye, and I was left wondering how I got here, to this place where everything was such a mess? My residency was the only thing that I had in my life that made any sense, so I clung to it.

I sat on the small deck that attached the stairs to my apartment and sipped my coffee, listening to the waves crash against the sand not far from where I was. I never tired of this view, the one place where I found peace in the constant crazy of my life. My mind started to drift to the places that I had been trying to avoid for months, but I couldn't help but think about Adam and whether or not he would ever forgive me. I hadn't heard from him since that day, not that I was surprised.

I hadn't seen Derek since he had proposed. I was giving him the time that he needed. I occasionally received a text from him with a simple message like *Thinking of you… Miss you. I hope that you are doing well.* And I would respond desperately with *I miss you like crazy. Please call me. Hope you are doing well too.* It was probably for the best.

I needed this time to figure out what I wanted. I missed Derek terribly, but I still didn't have an answer to his question. And I didn't want to hurt him any more than I already had. I was still trying to sort through the emotions that Adam had stirred, the love that I continued to feel for him. His touch had ignited a part of me that had been asleep since that last summer that we had spent together. I guess that it didn't really matter. He probably never wanted to speak to me again. I didn't blame him.

My thoughts carried to Brooklyn. I gasped at the instantaneous stab of pain that I felt just from the image of her perfect face that I brought to the forefront of my mind. When I felt my heart overflowing with a sea of emotions, I decided to take a walk and try to make sense of what I was feeling. It had been so long since I had allowed myself to have these thoughts; I decided to give myself today to live in them. I knew that opening myself up to the past would leave a gaping wound in my soul, but I needed to feel something, anything, just for today.

Wearing only a pair of short cutoff jeans and a tank top, I pulled a thin white sweater over my head and slipped my bare feet into a pair of flip-flops. I quickly weaved my long hair into a loose braid that hung over my shoulder, to keep the strands from blowing into my face from the sea breeze, and made my way across the warm sand to the ocean's edge. I strolled along the shore, my flip-flops now dangling from my hand, feeling the cold waves lap against my feet. I walked lost in my thoughts, picturing every detail of the day that she was born and every day that I had lived without her, this missing piece of my heart.

Vacant

I had been reluctant to leave the hospital, afraid that, once I left, it would feel as if the past two days had never happened. As much as I wanted to forget, to dull the unbearable pain in my heart, I also didn't want to let *her* go.

Susanne had given me a file folder containing the Petersens' home address and phone number, so that I could contact them if I wanted to. As much as I wanted to hold *her* in my arms that instant, I knew that each time I had to say good-bye would crush me all over again. And the thought of hearing Heather's voice over the phone, sharing moments of my baby's life that I wasn't there to witness firsthand, created an ache beyond measure.

Marie took me to her apartment. I could see that she was hurting by the way that she looked at me, her eyes full of empathy. I spent two weeks in bed, letting my body recover and hoping beyond all else that my heart would recover just as quickly. Marie finally pulled me out of bed, her firm voice threatening to drag my mind from the coma that possessed me.

"All right, Kendi, enough is enough. You need to get a job and start helping out around here, and you need to register for your summer courses. Take a shower and eat something for God's sake. You've already lost every pound you gained and then some."

I took her advice, one step at a time. I took a shower, spending time washing my hair and shaving my legs, something I hadn't done since, well, since that day. I couldn't even think it—let alone say it—the pain threatening to swallow me up whole, leaving behind no trace of the girl that I once was.

I found a job as a barista at a quaint little coffee shop down the street. It was warm and comforting, and I hoped that somehow it would ebb the numbness that was slowly taking up residence in my heart. It was busy, and I welcomed the distraction. In the evenings, singer-songwriter types played their acoustical guitars and sang their ballads of love into a microphone, while I served espresso and lattes to loyal fans. The pay was surprisingly good, and the people that I worked with were young college students, like me, just trying to get by.

Marie strategically invited Tabatha over in an attempt to cheer me up while Marie was out. If anyone could bring a smile to my face, it was Tabatha. Marie was spending her weekends trying to make up for lost time with Reid. She had admitted to me that they "took a break"—her way of keeping my pregnancy from him—and now she was trying to patch things up. I felt guilty for causing so much stress in her life. She had been such a huge support for me. I owed her so much. I hadn't realized how much she had sacrificed for me, supporting me in my decision. My love for her was unending, and I hoped that one day I could give back everything that she had given me.

Tabatha filled me in on all her latest conquests. She was not giving her ex-boyfriend a second chance. She was leaving soon, heading back to Austin for the summer break. We had decided to room together again in the fall, requesting this in our fall registration forms. It was comforting to know that I would have a good friend by my side next year. Although I couldn't help but feel so different from the girl that I once was in Tab's presence.

She, however, was ecstatic to have a drinking partner, a partner in crime as she had put it. She said this as we drank the margaritas that she had mixed for my benefit, and I commented on how much I had missed drinking and its numb, fuzzy affect that blurred the jagged edge of life. Tabatha didn't ever bring up what had happened, and I loved her for that, but sometimes I saw her concern in the way that she looked at me. I knew that she wanted to ask me about it, but she was waiting for me to bring it up. She could keep waiting, because I didn't think that I would ever be ready to talk about it.

I went to my follow-up appointment with Dr. Pierce a month after…after it had happened, as scheduled. He cleared me for physical activity and sexual intercourse. He gave me a prescription for birth control and encouraged me to take it, even if I felt like I didn't need it right then. He also encouraged me to take advantage of the free counseling that the agency offered. Apparently it was normal for any woman to feel depressed after giving birth because of our hormones. I didn't need a medical degree to know that what I felt was not from my hormones.

He said that he would like to continue to be my doctor for my annual checkups, and I agreed. The office switched the medical insurance on file to my own insurance that my mother paid for. I was comfortable with this decision, only for the sheer fact I didn't want to have to explain what I had been through with a new doctor. Dr. Pierce knew my medical history, and hopefully we would never have to discuss it.

I started to run again. I found the reprieve that I needed from the crushing pain in my heart when I ran. I ran fast and hard, lengthening my distance each day. There were days when I wanted desperately to keep running, to leave it all behind. But even I wasn't naive enough to believe that I wouldn't still see *her* face in my dreams or search for her each time I heard a baby cry.

The return of my busy schedule once summer quarter started felt familiar, and I was able to throw myself back into my studies, taking advantage of the distraction as I pushed my memories and emotions from that day deeper and deeper into the dark abyss of my soul.

By fall I had caught up on my course work, as if I had never missed a beat. And I had registered for five classes again, even though I knew how much work was required to pass all five courses. I was standing in the admissions office, checkbook in hand, ready to pay for my room and board and expensive tuition. An older woman with short auburn-colored hair and heavy makeup punched the keys rapidly on her computer as I waited.

"It looks like your tuition and housing have already been paid for this quarter, Miss Brooks," she said, glancing up at me from her computer screen.

"There must be some kind of mistake. I haven't paid it yet." I handed her my student ID card so that she could check the spelling of my name and my student ID number.

"Let me see," she mumbled as she continued to type on her keyboard. "No mistake. It has been paid in full, and it looks like it was paid anonymously through a Seattle law firm. I don't know what else to tell you, but you don't owe anything at this time."

"Huh, that's strange," I said completely puzzled. "And my meal plan?" I asked.

"Yep, paid. The same amount that you bought last year. Lucky girl. Is there anything else that I can help you with?" She waited for my response, obviously anxious to help the next person in line.

"No. Thank you for your time." I stuffed my wallet back into my handbag and slowly made my way to the bus stop. Maybe Marie had paid for my tuition. She was doing really well at her company, but why would she use a law firm? I knew that my mother couldn't afford the tuition herself, but I couldn't think of anyone else that would do this.

While we ate dinner that night, I brought it up to Marie. "You didn't happen to pay my tuition this quarter did you?" I asked, searching her eyes for an honest response.

"No, why would you ask? Do you need help paying for school? You said that you had enough money saved for this quarter."

"I do, but, when I went to pay, they told me that everything had already been covered. Tuition, housing and my meal plan. Everything. I just assumed that it was you."

She shot me a dubious look. "That's crazy. Who would've done that? You know that it can't be Mom."

"I know. It was paid anonymously through a Seattle law firm."

"Kendi." Marie set down her fork and reached out to touch my hands that were resting on the table. Her eyes filled with empathy as she looked at me intently. "It could be the Petersens."

Her hesitation as she said their name stopped my heart in my chest. My breath seized and I couldn't respond to her revelation.

"Think about it. Their lawyer was from that fancy firm downtown."

"But…but why would they do that?" I stammered. "I don't want their money," I followed up with more resolve in my voice.

"I'm sure that it's only a nice gesture on their part, Kendi. You gave them the greatest gift of their life. They feel indebted to you."

She tried to calm the storm that was brewing in my heart. I couldn't stop the pain from cutting through my numb existence as the memories of the Petersens and the role that they had played in my life blew into my mind like dark, ominous clouds. I didn't want them to feel like they owed me anything for *her*. No amount of money could ever fill the void that I felt inside, the hole inside me, empty because I had given them the most significant piece of me. I didn't want this. I wasn't sure what I felt, but grateful was not on the top of the list.

I tried to return the gift and pay for things my own way, but apparently that was not an option, and very strict instructions were noted with the anonymous payment. I thought about contacting them to say, "Thank you, but it was not necessary," but I couldn't bring myself to do it. I wasn't ready to reach out to them. I had received a few letters from them; they were thick with the feel of pictures inside. I couldn't bring myself to open them.

I placed each one in a wooden box that my grandfather had made for me—a treasure box from the days when I was a child and obsessed with pirates and Tinker Bell. Maybe someday I would be able to read them, and I would be able to respond. I was sure that eventually *she* would want to know who her birth mother was. Hopefully by then I would be stronger, and I could embrace my limited role in her life. For now I placed these letters in my treasure box, my box full of hopes.

College was passing by quickly. Tabatha and I were inseparable. She kept me in check, setting me up on dates, dragging me to parties, trying to breathe life back into my young soul. I usually drank way too much, in an attempt to dull the continuous ache, and I dated way too many boys, trying to fill the empty void inside with another's touch. In the end I would still wake up in the morning the same incomplete mess that I was the night before. It was fun though, and that is what I had wanted all along. To have a fun college experience. To live in a big city and meet new people. To work my way into med school. So that is what I did, one day at a time. I stuck to the plan with my chin up and eyes focused on the road ahead of me.

Regrets

It was fall. My first year of med school. I had finished my undergraduate degree in three years, the sweat and blood of an enormous course load had paid off. I had studied for months for my MCATS and walked away with an honorable score, not bad for a less-than-brilliant college coed. The University of Washington had offered me a spot in their prestigious medical program, bringing me so close to my dream. My tuition had been magically and anonymously paid for each quarter.

I had never contacted the Petersens until after graduation. I had sent them a simple card with a picture of me in my graduation cap and gown. I had written a simple "Thank you" and signed my name. I couldn't find any other words to express the new feelings of gratitude that I felt toward them. They had changed my life. I was starting med school without the heavy debt of student loans.

The small wages that I had earned and managed to save over the past few years, coupled with the money that my grandfather had given me, was enough to pay for the first few years of med school. I pushed myself hard to succeed but I knew that my true motivation came from somewhere else. A place inside me that desperately wanted to forget, a place inside me that longed to feel whole again, a place that fought like hell to make it all worth it.

Tabatha and I had decided to rent a two-bedroom apartment in the U District that year. We could still walk to class and crawl home from most of the bars. It was small and old, but it was clean and had a limited view of Lake Union. My mother had given us a comfortable couch and table with four chairs. We had a small television that rested on an old end table, and, after an expensive shopping trip to Target, we now had dishes and other kitchen necessities. I was unpacking the remainder of my boxes, hanging up clothes in my new and improved closet, when the phone rang. It took me a minute to locate the cordless handset that Tab and I had just purchased.

"Hello."

"Is this Kendall?" a familiar female voice asked.

"Yes, it is," I answered trying hard to place the caller's voice.

"This is Lynn McCoy, Adam's mom."

My heart sunk in my chest at the sound of his name. My mind started to race with the reasons behind her call. Did something happen to him? Does she know about the baby?

"Hi, Lynn," I managed to say through the chaos playing out in my thoughts.

"Hi. I hope that you don't mind my calling you. Your mother was kind enough to give me your phone number. I have a favor to ask you."

"Oh, what kind of favor?" I asked, curiosity replacing my dark thoughts.

"Adam is flying home this Friday. He's arriving at Sea-Tac airport at eleven o'clock in the morning. I was hoping that you could join us in welcoming him home."

Of course he was coming home. Three years. It had been three years. I felt tears sting my eyes as I tried to compose myself to respond to her request. "I don't know, Lynn. We haven't exactly kept in touch."

"I know, but it would really mean a lot to him to have you there. Just think about it, Kendall. South African Airlines flight number 7410 arriving at 11:03 from Dulles airport."

I quickly grabbed a pen and wrote his flight information on a cardboard box that sat half empty beside me. "Okay, I'll think about it. Thank you, Lynn."

"I hope that we see you there. Take care."

"You too." I hit the End button on the phone and let out a sigh. Adam. He was coming home. His face filled my mind. I missed him, but what would I say? What could I say? I had never responded to his letters. They had started to arrive in rapid succession to Marie's address that summer, and, when I moved back to the dorms that fall, I had asked Marie to start marking them Return to Sender. I couldn't bear to look at them anymore.

The letters had continued to come for months, and then they just stopped. I still had seven months of unopened letters packed away somewhere. Although I had never read them, I still could not bring myself to throw them out. I frantically started to rip open random boxes, searching for those letters. I felt a sudden need to read his words, to know what he was thinking and feeling, to have some small piece of him. I found the old worn shoebox that held a thick stack of letters bound together by a large rubber band.

The first one was a letter that I had already read, the letter telling me that he was going to study to be a minister and was staying an extra year. The ink was smeared in places—either from the rain or my tears, I wasn't sure. I read his words, reliving the hurt from that day, the day that had set things in motion. The next several letters were full of questions, the desperation building in each letter: Did I get his letter? What was I feeling? Why hadn't I written? Was I okay?

His letters eventually became declarations of his love and what he felt for me. He wanted to know if I had moved on. Letting me know that, if I still wanted him, he would come home; he needed me, and he didn't want to lose me. This shocked me, his willingness to give it all up in an attempt to keep me in his life. Would things have turned out differently if I had received this letter that winter? If I had known that he was willing to come home on his own accord, that he would own the regrets that resulted from that decision rather than direct them at me or the baby.

The dates on his letters began to reflect his attempt to write to me daily. These letters contained highlights of his everyday life, and each one ended with a poem—poems from the collection that I had gifted to him when he had left for college. He was reciting the poems that I had written for him. I was tortured by his love for me and his pain that I felt in his words. I had hurt him by letting him go, trying to save him from the pain of what I had done. My overwhelming guilt reared its ugly head once again.

He could never know what had happened, what I had kept from him for the past few years; it would kill him. As much as I longed to see him, I knew that I couldn't face him. I couldn't answer his questions without hurting him more than I already had.

I finished unpacking and broke down all the boxes, setting them in a stack in the corner of the living room. Tabatha would be home any minute. We were having dinner at Marie's tonight.

This morning had been my last day of work at the coffeehouse. I couldn't keep up my hours there during med school. Tabatha had spent the summer in Seattle fulfilling her internship that she had landed as an event planner for some upscale company on the east side. Today was her last day of work too, and we were celebrating.

I was anxious to discuss the phone call I had received today and the contents of Adam's letters. Tabatha and Marie were the only two people in the world that I could talk to about this, and I needed to tell somebody.

Dinner was fun as it usually was when the three of us got together. When the wine was poured, Marie made a toast. "To the end of summer and to the year to come and…" She dangled her left hand in front of us. "And to me becoming Mrs. Reid Bennet."

Tab and I both gasped at her news. "Oh, my God, Marie. Congratulations." I beamed at her. "Let me see that thing." I took her hand in mine and examined the beautiful sparkle of the large carat attached to her finger. "Nice work, Reid. How did he ask you?"

"Last night he took me up to the top of the new building that he's working on downtown. It's still under construction, so we were wearing hard hats and everything. Anyway he said that he had something to show me and took me to the roof. The sun was setting, and the view was amazing. He got down on his knee and asked me to marry him. Of course I said yes."

"Marie, I am so happy for you," I said, rising from my seat to give her a hug. Tab threw her arms around us both, pulling us into a group hug. And I was happy for Marie. She deserved someone like Reid. In light of Marie's exciting news and the glow that radiated from her happiness, I kept my news to myself. Tonight was about Marie.

~

Tabatha and I had finally finished organizing the apartment; everything was in its place. The aroma of coffee radiated from the kitchen from our new coffeemaker, and we were enjoying the luxury of a lazy morning before our new crazy schedule began the following week.

"We have to go out tonight, Kendi. It's our last Friday night before you become a lowly med student slave. Come on," Tabatha begged me for the hundredth time, trying to convince me to take the town by storm. "We can go to that new club in Belltown. It'll be fun." She flashed me her sadistic smile, the one that she used when she needed to remind me that she wasn't giving up and that she would eventually get her way.

"Fine," I conceded. "But you have to help me get rid of all these boxes today, and we have to call the cable company. I'll die if we don't get the cable hooked up soon. I'm missing all my shows."

"I'll take the boxes down to the recycle bin while you call the cable company, and then we're going to get a pedicure for tonight, my treat."

"Okay. Deal," I agreed.

Tabatha slipped on her sandals and began bundling up the dozens of cardboard boxes that were lying flat in the corner, while I picked up the phone and dialed the cable company.

"Be right back. I'll have to make two trips," she called out to me from the doorway.

I waved her off as I listened carefully to the automated message listing the menu options for my call.

Ten minutes later, I was lying on the couch still clutching the phone to my ear, waiting out the eternal hold that I was placed on, when Tab appeared back in the doorway, breathing heavily from the trek up the stairs. "I think that you got the better end of this deal," she said, huffing, wiping the sweat from her brow.

"I don't know. You should hear the awful music that's blaring in my ear."

She picked up the remainder of the boxes and disappeared once again. I heard a voice on the other end of the phone. Finally. As soon as I ended the call, Tabatha strolled back into the apartment, slamming the door behind her. She was carrying one of the cardboard boxes in her hand. "Forget one?" I asked, gulping down the lukewarm coffee left in my cup.

"What is this, Kendi?" she asked holding out the box to me.

I saw my handwriting on one of the flat panels of the box, and I immediately knew what had her so worked up. I just stared at her, not sure what to say.

"South African Airlines?" she said in a questioning tone. "Tell me this is not flight information for Adam."

"The one and only," I deadpanned, trying to hide the pain in my voice. I had thought about him all week. I had woken up that morning, sick with the idea of him being so close to me. The truth was, I wanted to see him more than anything, but I had made my choice the day that I had told that first lie, and now I had to live with it.

"Why didn't you tell me that he was coming home?" The hurt in her voice was evident.

"I was going to tell you the other night at Marie's, but I didn't want to burst her bubble. His mom called me the other day and asked me to come to the airport to welcome him home."

"I take it that you're not going, since his plane lands in about"—she glanced at her watch—"sixty-five minutes."

"I wasn't planning on it," I admitted.

"Why not, Kendi? I've been listening to you cry over this boy for three years, and now he's going to be less than twenty miles from you. You should go."

"I can't, Tab. You know it's more complicated than that. I can't tell him. I just can't."

She looked at me with deep understanding in her eyes

and reached for my hands. "Kendi, you don't have to tell him today. You don't have to say anything, but don't you think that you should at least see him? Maybe this will be a chance for you to have some closure."

"I don't know, Tab. I don't think that I'm strong enough to face him."

"Oh, please, you're like the strongest person I know. You can do this."

Maybe she was right. Maybe seeing him would help me move on. I let out a loud sigh. "Okay, I'll go. But you're driving me. The thought of seeing Adam again is making me feel sick to my stomach."

She smiled at me, happy that I was taking her advice. "Fine. I'll drive. Let's get you in the shower. We only have thirty minutes to get you dolled up. You have to make a huge impression. It's been three years since he's seen you."

I rolled my eyes at her and forced a smile, but inside I was falling apart.

Running a few minutes behind schedule, Tabatha raced down I-5 toward the airport. I felt like we were on the autobahn, the world whirling by at record speed. My hands were trembling, my heart racing at the idea of seeing Adam after all this time. I took slow deep breaths, trying to calm the nerves coursing through my blood.

Tab pulled the car up to the terminal and turned toward me. "Kendi, you'll be fine. I'll park the car and meet you at the gate, okay?"

"Okay." My voice was barely audible as I opened the door and slowly climbed out of the car. The door had not even closed yet as Tabatha hit the gas and sped toward the parking garage.

I glanced at the monitor and noted the gate number, my knees shaking so hard it felt like they would give out on me any minute. *I can do this*, I told myself as I inhaled deeply through my nose, trying to calm myself. I walked quickly through the terminal, knowing that his plane was landing that very minute, and I wanted to be there when he stepped off the Jetway. Of course his gate would be at the very end of the terminal. I walked as fast as my trembling legs would carry me, but it took forever.

I rounded the last corner and spotted his gate number up ahead. I was just a short distance away when I saw him. He was standing in the center of a small crowd, hugging several people around him. I knew it was him, from his crazy dark curls that fell over his forehead, much longer than he usually wore it. I slowed my pace and took in the sight of him from afar, my heart pounding in my chest. I felt my face flush with heat, tears of joy wetting my cheeks.

Feeling that familiar pull, I continued to walk toward him. I hadn't realized just how much I still loved him until that moment. I was closing in on him, passing the last gate before I reached him. I could make out the faces of those gathered around him now. His mom, his dad, Josh, his two older brothers, a woman that I didn't recognize, holding a toddler in her arms. The crowd parted, and I could see Rick and a girl that Adam had just pulled into a firm hug, his lips brushing her cheek.

As she stepped back, wiping tears from her eyes, I saw that it was Katie. I stopped dead in my tracks. What was she doing here? I stepped behind a pillar, its massive size obscuring me from sight but allowing me to peer around its edge to see Adam. The pained expression on Josh's face told me everything that I needed to know, as I turned away from them and slid my back down the pillar until I was sitting on the floor, knees drawn up to my chest. There was no way that Adam would want us both here. He wouldn't do that to me. And his mother would not have invited Katie, knowing her role in Adam's past. Which led me to the only logical explanation.

Adam had asked Katie to be here, and his mother had

asked me. Adam didn't know that she had called me, that I might be here, but he had wanted Katie here. I should never have come. The hurt that I felt knowing that he was just steps away, but that I could not face him, especially with Katie here, was unendurable. The idea that she had once meant nothing to him seemed like such a loaded lie after watching their exchange. Her presence here alone screamed significance.

I had no right to feel betrayed. The depth of my betrayal was far greater. I had let him go. Another decision that I could add to my list of regrets. I knew all this, and yet I still felt so wounded. It took every ounce of will I possessed to stand and walk away from the only man that I had ever really loved.

And still loved.

Letters

I shuddered from the memory of that day. There were so many painful moments in my past that I had tried to forget, knowing that they were the result of the choices that I had made. I found myself at the pier several miles from my apartment. I hadn't realized that I had wandered that far, so I turned around and slowly made my way back home. The sun was directly overhead, revealing how long I had been walking, and I could feel my skin absorbing every degree of heat that it radiated. I reached my apartment and took the stairs two at a time, watching each step that my sandy bare feet landed on, careful not to fall.

When I reached my deck, slightly out of breath, I looked up to find Adam sitting in one of the chairs, staring out at the ocean. My breath escaped me, and I heard my flip-flops crash against the wood of the deck as they fell from my grip, the sound bringing Adam's face toward mine. I stood there, in complete shock by his presence, unable to move or speak. He turned away from me, his eyes once again taking in the view. I couldn't read his expression, but I could sense an overwhelming sadness in his tone as he spoke.

"I can see why you like it here so much. This view is breathtaking."

I moved slowly, lowering my body into the chair beside him, keeping my eyes on the beach. "What are you doing here, Adam?" I asked, curiosity swelling inside of me. I was afraid of what he had come here to say. It wasn't his anger I feared or the amount of resentment that would be in his eyes when he looked at me—it was the questions that he had come here to ask. The questions that I was afraid to answer, afraid of where they might lead.

When he didn't answer me, I kept talking, filling the silence that not even the crashing waves below could drown out. "I tried to call you so many times, but you never answered or returned any of my calls. I can't tell you enough how sorry I am."

He still refused to look at me, his eyes staring out into the distance. "I was going to call, but I don't even know what to say to you. I called your mom and asked for your address, and here I am. I guess I just needed to see you." He finally turned and looked at me, his gaze burning into mine as I watched the moisture build and spill down his cheeks.

"Kendi, I need to know everything. I need to know everything about her. I've been trying to wrap my head around the fact that I have a daughter somewhere out there. Now that the anger is gone, I just feel sad and useless. There's nothing that I can do at this point. I need to know what you know, so that I can try to make sense of these feelings that I have."

I saw something in his eyes. That shattered look, revealing the fissures that spread throughout his insides, breaking apart his heart and soul, stripping him of his completeness. I knew that look. I saw it every time that I

250

looked in the mirror. We were both missing a piece of our soul, and I wondered if we would ever feel whole again.

"I know, Adam," I admitted with a sigh. He did need to know everything and there was so much that I needed to tell him.

He leaned back in his chair, his gaze fixed on the beach. He was lost in thought, as if he didn't see the view in front him but something else entirely. He reached up and pulled at a dark curl on his forehead with his fingertips, twirling it absentmindedly.

I took a moment to look at him. And I didn't mean his deep blue eyes or his dark wavy hair that I longed to run my fingers through or the way the ridge of his muscles showed through his dark T-shirt or the tightness of the skin on his legs that his khaki shorts left visible. I meant I *really* saw him. I took note of the pull I felt in his presence. That undeniable feeling of wanting him and not just in a physical sense. Years had separated us, and yet I felt like I knew him better than I had known any other man.

The tenor of his broken voice interrupted my thoughts. "You know I wrote you every day for a year, even after the letters were sent back to me. You can't imagine how much I wanted to get on a plane and come home to you, to beg for you to take me back. I knew that I had lost you, but I didn't know why. I had no idea the decisions that you were making without me."

"I had finally worked up the nerve to tell you everything when I was home that Christmas. I wrote it all down, and I was just about to send you my letter…then I got your letter about your extension and the ministry. I told myself that I could never tell you. I let you go that day. You had made decisions without me too, Adam. I take full responsibility for what I did and for not telling you. But you broke my heart that day."

He looked at me as if he was seeing me for the first

time. "I'm so sorry, Kendi."

"I'm sorry too, Adam. I'm sorry about everything, and I'll understand if you never forgive me. I haven't been able to forgive myself." I could feel my emotions bubbling to the surface, tears wetting my cheeks. I turned away from him and we both sat in silence, fighting against the pain of our regrets that our past had handed us on a silver platter, forcing us to taste its bitter bite on our tongues.

We sat like this for a while listening to the sounds of the ocean, the voices of people passing by on the strand. I knew that it was time to share what I knew of our daughter, to delve into a part of me that I kept closed off from the world in order to hide the shame and guilt that ate away at me one tiny fragment at a time. I reached for Adam's hand, and I felt him tense at my touch.

"Come inside. I have something to show you." I stood and led him through the door into my small apartment. I offered him something to drink as his eyes scanned the room, taking in all the details of my home.

"I'll have some water," he replied, clearing his throat. I made my way into the kitchen, watching him as he ambled around my living room picking up framed photographs that were displayed throughout the room: my favorite picture of Mo and me sitting in the grass in front of the high school; a photograph of Derek and me on the slopes in Aspen bundled in our ski gear; a family photo from Marie's wedding. I returned to the living room carrying two cold water bottles and set them down on the table next to the couch. Adam held up a photograph of Derek and me, taken at a fund-raiser we had attended the year before.

"Is this him?" he asked.

"Yes, that's Derek," I replied sadly, realizing how much I missed him.

"You look beautiful, Kendi." He motioned toward the photo of me in a red silk gown, my hair swept in a fancy up-do.

"Thank you." I felt myself blush.

"Still can't take a compliment, huh?" he teased me, his mouth pulled up on one side giving me a clear view of his dimple.

He pulled so many different emotions out of me that I felt crazy. "Make yourself comfortable, I'll be right back."

I went to my bedroom and retrieved an old wooden box from the back of my closet and the picture from my nightstand. When I returned, Adam was sitting on my couch, sipping his water from the bottle. It felt a bit surreal to have him in my apartment, like two worlds were colliding, my past and my present.

I sat next to him and set the box between us.

"What is this?" he asked, curiosity filling his eyes.

I held out the picture in my hand. "This is Brooklyn Grace, your daughter."

He looked at me, stunned, as he took the worn photograph from my hand. I watched him brush his finger across her face, his eyes taking in every detail.

My tears fell effortlessly as I swiped them away with my fingers, waiting for his response.

"My God, Kendi, she is so beautiful," he whispered through tears of his own. "And you...you're so young. I can't imagine what you're feeling in this picture."

I stared at the picture in his hands, remembering every emotion as if it was yesterday. "She was born on April 21 at 4:35 in the afternoon. She weighed six pounds, two ounces, and measured nineteen inches in length. She was perfect and so tiny. She has your eyes and obviously your hair too. The two days that I spent with her were the most precious and most agonizing of my life, and I have never been the same since."

"Were you alone?"

His question warmed me, knowing that he was

thinking of me in some small way. "Marie was there. She's the only one who knew. I don't know what I would've done without her."

"No one else knew?"

"No, I told my Mom and Scott—and Derek—the same day I told you."

"You're so brave, Kendi. But then again, you always were." His eyes had not left the photograph. "Where is she, Kendi?" he asked as he looked up at me, his eyes so intense it took my breath away.

This was what I had feared. I knew that he would want to know where she was; I knew that just telling him about her would not be enough. I opened the box and began to pull out stacks of envelopes, all unopened. Envelopes addressed to me from The Petersen Family with a Bellingham address.

"What are these, Kendi?"

"These are letters about your daughter. I could never bring myself to open them. You can have them." I handed the letters to him.

He was still stunned. "You know where she is?"

"Yes, it was an open adoption. I chose them to raise her, and I signed papers that would allow me to have contact with her. I couldn't…I couldn't open myself up to that pain again. I haven't seen her since the day I placed her in their arms. She's ten years old now." I felt so ashamed admitting this to him.

"What did you tell them about me?"

I looked at him, pausing, as he searched my eyes for answers. "I told them that I didn't know who the father was," I choked out. I was drowning in the depths of self-reproach. It had rolled off my tongue so easily back then; now, sitting here, staring into Adam's eyes filled with hurt that I had put there, it was hard to accept that I could have lied so easily. I had been raised to always be honest, and I had told lies that had torn lives apart. Adam must have hated me.

He was quiet for a moment, absorbing the sharp edge of my words. "I want to see her," he said quietly, almost a whisper.

"Adam," I started to protest but he interrupted me, his voice firm.

"You can't keep her from me, Kendi. You owe me this much. Please, do whatever it is that you have to do to make this happen."

"Are you sure that's what you want, Adam? Because I can tell you exactly how it feels to hold your child in your arms, to know that she is a part of you, and then the unbearable pain that follows when you have to say good-bye. You don't want to know what I know, to feel what I feel, trust me." I sobbed uncontrollably.

His words cut me to the core, harsh and angry. "You never gave me that chance, Kendi. I will never know what you feel, because you took that from me. Don't pretend that you're trying to protect me. You're only trying to protect yourself." He rested his elbows on his knees and buried his face in his hands. A moment later, he lifted his face, his hands pressed together against his lips as he whispered, "I have to know that she is okay."

"She is, Adam. Heather and Charles are amazing. I would not have trusted just anyone to raise her."

"You don't know that, Kendi. You have no idea. You haven't read these letters, and you haven't seen her. I need to see for myself that she is happy and healthy, that you made the right choice."

"If that's what you really want, I'll call the agency," I said, unable to fight him any longer. I had carried her in my womb for nine months, had given birth to her; and I had not checked on her once. I had not even glanced at these letters to read about her life, scanned the photos for her smile. I had known of her existence for ten years; I had dreamed of her face nearly every night, wondered about her incessantly, but I had never checked on her.

Adam had known of her for a few short months, and he instantly felt this need to protect her, this innate fatherly instinct consuming him. He didn't trust my judgment, and I could not blame him. I found solace in the connection that I felt with Heather and Charles, the comfort of knowing that they were good people and would be great parents. I understood now that Adam needed to know this for himself.

"Yes, this is what I want," he said confidently, as he collected the letters from the couch and stood. "I'm staying at the Ocean Inn down the street for a few days. Let me give you my cell phone number."

I scrambled to my small desk in the corner of the room and produced a pen and piece of paper, writing down his phone number as he recited it to me in an even tone.

"Please call me when you have information about the possibility of me meeting my daughter." He turned toward the door, and I called out his name, not sure of what I wanted to say, but I wasn't ready for him to leave yet. He turned back to look at me, waiting for me to speak. The seconds ticked by, silence hanging in the air. At my lack of response and the desperation in my eyes, he walked out the door.

I called the agency, and surprisingly Susanne was still employed there. I told her of the new circumstances—that I knew who was the birth father—and he was asking to meet Brooklyn. I wasn't sure what the protocol was for this sort of thing or how bad this looked from a legal standpoint, given the fact that I had lied. Susanne said that she would contact the Petersens and their lawyer, and get back to me.

Her call came within an hour. I was shocked, not expecting to hear from her for a few days. The Petersens were actually thrilled to have their daughter meet her birth father, and they wanted to know if I would be there as well. They wanted Adam to sign a waiver, relinquishing his parental rights though, just as I had, before he would be allowed to meet her. The question of whether or not I would be there weighed heavy on my mind as I tried to focus on the rest of our conversation.

I had not even considered accompanying Adam on this journey that he so desperately wanted to pursue. I wasn't sure that I had the strength to see Brooklyn again. I was afraid of her resentment toward me for giving her up; I was afraid of the disappointment that Heather and Charles might feel because of my lack of involvement all these years; and I was afraid for myself. I was afraid of the depth of my love for Brooklyn and how that love would inevitably swell at the sight of her and how that love would break me into pieces again. I didn't think that I could survive it this time. Adam was right; every one of my reservations was in an attempt to protect myself, exposing just how selfish I really was.

I called Adam at the number that he had given me. He answered on the first ring. He was walking along the beach and promised to be at my place in a few minutes.

He appeared at my door, hair in disarray from the wind, the letters still in his hand. "Hi," he said quietly.

"Hey."

"What did you find out?" he asked immediately, not wasting anytime, as he stepped into my living room, setting the letters on the table.

"Well, they actually want you to meet her, but you will have to sign paperwork, waiving your parental rights beforehand."

"I'm not sure that I can do that."

"Adam, you don't have a choice. If you want to meet her, this is the only way."

"I have to see that she's okay first, before I sign anything."

"Adam, these are her parents. It's been ten years. You can't change that now, no matter what. It wouldn't be fair to anyone." I instantly regretted my choice of words, knowing that none of this was fair to Adam.

He ran his hands through his hair as he considered this. The turmoil that he was facing inside was evident in his body language. "Fine, I'll sign. But I want to see her as soon as possible. When can we go?" He looked at me waiting for my answer, his hands resting on his hips.

"I wasn't planning on going with you," I whispered into the space between us.

"Oh, you're going with me, Kendi," he said with conviction.

"I can't…" I started to say, shaking my head.

"Think of our daughter for once, Kendi. Think of me. She deserves to know who we are."

I turned my back to him so that he could not see the shame in my eyes as I shed tears for my baby that I had failed time and time again. He was right. I had to do this for her.

I noticed the letters that Adam had set down. Several envelopes had been ripped open, their contents spilled out on the table. I could see a picture of her, her unmistakable deep blue eyes calling to me from a few feet away. I picked it up and looked into the eyes of a toddler; she couldn't have been more than two. Her smile matched my own, full pink lips parted to display only a few front teeth. Her cheeks chubby, her dark hair long and beautiful, falling around her face in thick curls. She looked so much like Adam it took my breath away. My heart filled and burst all in the same moment. I felt Adam's hands on my shoulders as he stood behind me, looking at the picture that I held in my hand.

"Incredible, right?" he said with pride in his voice.

I nodded, unable to speak through my emotions.

"I love her so much, and I've never even met her. How is that possible?"

My heart broke at his words. It broke for him, knowing the joy that he would feel when he did meet her and the pain that would follow when he said good-bye. My body trembled from the silent sobs that escaped me. Adam wrapped his arms around me and pulled my back against him.

I felt his breath on my ear as he quietly spoke to me. "You're not alone this time. We can do this together, Kendi." The comfort of his arms around me and the compassion in his voice undid me. I collapsed against him, his strength supporting me, holding me. And I knew that I could do this with Adam by my side.

All This Time

I was nervous as we boarded the plane at LAX together. Adam had been staying at the hotel near my apartment for the past few days. I had been working long hours at the hospital during the day, scrambling to cover my shifts that I would miss while I flew back to Washington to deal with yet another "family emergency." We had spent the evenings together at my apartment, reading the letters about our daughter, admiring the pictures that Heather had sent. Watching Brooklyn grow up from the tiny baby that I remembered to this amazing and beautiful ten-year-old was extraordinary. Although I couldn't help but regret all the years that I had wasted in fear, when I could have known her in some small way.

Adam read the letters aloud to me. We laughed at all the cute moments that Heather described, like the way that she pronounced certain words when she was learning to speak or the way she performed ballet to anyone who would watch in the supermarket. We also cried at the tenderness of Heather's words as she described how Brooklyn began asking questions about us, specifically me, when she was old enough to understand what being adopted meant.

Heather and Charles had adopted a baby boy when Brooklyn was two, and they had been open with both children from the very beginning about being adopted. Brooklyn's brother, Kyle, had monthly visits with his birth mother and grandmother, which left Brooklyn with many questions about her own birth family. This broke my heart. The idea that all these years I had been hurting her by staying away.

Heather begged me several times to consider writing Brooklyn a letter, so she had something from me, but she would always end with the assurance that she completely understood why I stayed away. That she could not begin to imagine what I felt. Her understanding could hardly assuage the guilt that I felt.

The most recent letters included small notes from Brooklyn herself, her penmanship improving with each letter. She played soccer, took ballet lessons and piano. Adam couldn't help but comment that she must get her musical talent from him. I felt so free in these moments, sharing these letters with Adam——the only person who could ever understand what I felt reading intimate details about the life of a child that I had birthed but had not known.

I was slowly opening my heart again, allowing myself to bask in the love that I felt for Brooklyn. Its warmth thawed the numbness inside me. I could feel everything. Even the cuts that still bled from the past, but somehow it didn't hurt as much with Adam here beside me. He was still guarded. We spoke openly about our daughter, but not of us. With every small brush of a leg or hand, I felt his body tense. I knew that I had hurt him beyond repair; my betrayal cut so deep that he would never be able to forgive me, to love me again. Our current bond and renewed friendship was only for the sake of knowing our daughter.

Adam and I sat in silence while we ascended into the air, the vast blue of the Pacific Ocean stretching on for miles beneath us. Once the jets quieted and the plane leveled, Adam's voice interrupted the comfortable silence that had settled over us. "I remember the long flight home from Africa. I hadn't heard from you in over two years but I thought of you that entire trip home. I was secretly hoping that you would be there in Seattle when I landed, even though I knew it was a long shot."

"Adam." I turned from the window to look at him. It was the first time that he had said anything about us in days.

"It's okay, Kendi. I totally understand why you weren't there. It doesn't matter now. I was just thinking of that day."

"I was there," I whispered, staring straight ahead, remembering that day.

"What? What do you mean you were there?" I could feel his eyes on me from where he sat.

"I went to the airport to see you that day."

"What happened?" he asked.

I turned toward him and took in his confused expression as he tried to put together the pieces from that day so long ago. "I saw you with your family, and then I saw you with Katie. And I left."

His eyes moved away from mine as he ran a hand through his hair, processing what I had just told him. "I can't believe that you were so close to me that day. You have no idea how badly I wanted to see you." He let out a loud sigh before he continued. "Seeing you would've changed so many things. Why did you leave?"

"It would've changed nothing, Adam. It doesn't change the past."

"It changes my past, Kendi. And you didn't answer

my question. Why did you leave?" He looked at me, searching my eyes for answers.

"I saw what was going on between you and Katie, Adam. How could I face you after everything that had happened, when you had obviously moved on and with her of all people?" I tried to hide the hurt that I felt from this; I didn't deserve to feel hurt by Adam's choices.

"I'm so sorry. She insisted on being there. Nothing was going on between Katie and me. We had been writing back and forth for over a year. That's it."

"What did you mean by my presence changing your past? Adam, what did you mean?" I asked again when he was silent.

"Katie and I had a very close friendship when I got back from Africa. It eventually turned into something more."

"So you guys dated?"

"Yeah, you could say that."

"What aren't you telling me, Adam?"

His evasiveness filled in the blanks for me.

"She's the one? The one that wanted to get married? The serious relationship that you had?"

He nodded and waited for my reaction.

I looked back out the window but could not focus on the mountainous terrain that passed by below us; I couldn't focus on anything but the image that I had in my head. The image of Katie and Adam sharing their lives, making plans for their future. He had shared with her what I had only dreamed of during that time. Wanting Adam in a way that I knew would never be possible after betraying him the way I did. I don't know why the hurt cut so deep.

I had known that he had almost married someone, but knowing that it was Katie triggered something inside me. The physical relationship that they'd had in high school had changed everything between Adam and me. It had taken Adam from me in the end, forcing him to leave on his mission. And the fact that he'd had a relationship with her, a very serious relationship after everything that we had gone through, left me questioning every single thing that I thought I knew of him. I fought the tears that threatened to spill from my eyes and turned to look at him. "You still haven't answered my question."

"If I had known that there was any chance for us, I would have never dated her in the first place. I was so lonely when I got home, and she was more than happy to be there for me as a friend, and then she started to push for more. Before I knew it, she was ready to become a pastor's wife and live the life that it entailed. I told you though, in the end, I couldn't see past you. I only ever wanted you, nothing else could compare to the way you made me feel. It ended badly, as you can imagine."

I couldn't help but flinch every time he used the past tense in reference to me. I knew that he didn't feel that way for me now. I knew that something resembling hate filled the space where his love for me had once resided. "Adam, there was never a chance for us, not after what I had done. If I had told you about the pregnancy and the adoption back then, would it really have changed anything?"

"I don't know. But I can't help but think that we wasted all these years apart. We could have known our daughter on some level, and we could have tried to right the wrong between us."

"And now?" I asked.

"Now? Well, it just seems too late for all that."

The sadness I saw in his eyes chipped away another fragment of my heart. "Why did you really resign, Adam?"

"Do you really want to hear this?"

"Yeah, I think I do."

"After I ended things with Katie, I went a little crazy. I felt this deep-seated resentment toward the church and God, for taking me from you. It was like all this time I had thought that I was doing the right thing and fulfilling a calling that only my faith led me to understand. But I couldn't shake the feelings that I still had for you. I knew that, if I truly believed in my work, then it would have been enough for me. My faith, and certainly not Katie, hadn't been able to dull this ache I had inside from losing you.

"I tried so hard to forget you. I slept with a lot of other women, hoping that I could feel something, anything, for someone that wasn't you. At that point, I couldn't live with being a hypocrite, standing in front of my congregation preaching about things that I wasn't sure that I believed in anymore. The shame I felt from my sins became too much."

"You told me that it wasn't about sex."

"It wasn't. It was about so much more than that."

I sat back in my seat, trying to digest what Adam had just told me. Trying not to picture him with other women. I'd had my fair share of lovers over the years, in an attempt to fill a void of my own. Adam and I were not that different.

Something was weighing heavily on me though. It wasn't the other women or even the relationship with Katie, which was much harder to accept than the meaningless encounters; it was something else entirely. He had given it all up: his dream, the path that was so important to him that I hadn't wanted to interrupt it or burden him with a pregnant girlfriend or a baby. He had just walked away. It was hard not to feel that all our sacrifices were for nothing.

I was still working toward my dream but at what cost? I wasn't sure how I felt about the past. I had so many regrets, and yet I was doing what I had set out to do from the beginning. I was so close to finishing my residency—my goal that I had been working toward for as long as I could remember. I was happy and in love; at least I'd thought I was, until I ran into Adam at my gramps's funeral.

My typical response in that moment would be to walk —run—away from Adam, his presence too much while I was sifting through our past, trying to make sense of all the wrong turns that we had taken. But I was trapped on the damn plane, trapped between his body and the window. I could smell his cologne and feel each place that his body met mine from the cramped seating arrangements. Our legs, just above the knee. His elbow against my arm on the armrest.

I wanted to reach over and hold his hand, lean my body into his, to feel him. And yet at the same time, I wanted to shake him and beg him to forgive me, to tell me how we got here. How we were so far apart, bitter and angry with our decisions, and yet our love still lived inside us. It didn't seem fair that, after all the hurt and pain we had put each other through, we couldn't seem to let go. I buried my face in the window as if I was interested in watching the endless mass of vapor that we were passing through, anything to avoid conversation with Adam. I didn't think that I could bear to hear any more about the past.

~

We managed to endure the remainder of the flight in silence. Before I knew it, we were landing in Bellingham. I was nervous. I had both looked forward to and dreaded this day for years. I was finally going to see my daughter. I wanted her to like me, to accept me. I wasn't sure what to expect, and that scared the hell out of me.

Arms Wide Open

Adam drove the rental car through the streets of Fairhaven, an old neighborhood in Bellingham. We were meeting Charles, Heather and their lawyer at a café. They wanted to meet Adam, and we both had paperwork to sign before we met with Brooklyn. I stood on the sidewalk, straightening my short gray cotton dress that I had paired with my favorite black riding boots. Deciding what to wear when meeting my ten-year-old daughter for the first time since her birth was not easy. I settled for nice. Not too casual and not too dressy.

Adam came around to my side of the car, wearing dark charcoal dress slacks and a bright blue button-down shirt. His hair was damp and styled, his best attempt to tame his curls. He looked handsome and eerily calm. He led me into the café with his hand resting on my lower back. Once again I felt comforted by his presence.

I immediately spotted Charles and Heather at a corner table near the back of the café. Heather gave me a subtle wave as we made our way in their direction. They stood when we reached them. Their lawyer, Tom Stephens, extended his hand as he introduced himself to Adam and me. I introduced Adam to the Petersens, and, while Charles politely shook Adam's hand, Heather wrapped him up in an unexpected hug and then embraced me as well.

"Oh, my God, the resemblance is remarkable," I heard Heather say aloud to no one in particular.

I felt tears well up in my eyes as I remembered her from all those years ago. At the time, I had pitied her, wanting to give her what she couldn't have but desperately wanted, and now I found myself envying her, wanting what she had. Such a stark contrast to what I had felt when I was young and naive, unaware of the effect of my decision.

"Kendi, you look beautiful. It is so good to see you," she whispered in my ear.

I wasn't sure what to say so I replied, "It's good to see you too." My heart was hammering in my chest as we all sat down to discuss the business portion of our reunion.

Their lawyer cleared his throat. "I have new documents for you both to sign. I'll give you time to read over them. Let me know if you have any questions."

Once the paperwork was out of the way, I heard Heather ask Adam questions about himself. Where are you from? What do you do? He answered each one, adding in his usual wit and charm, and, before I knew it, the awkward tension lifted, leaving everyone at ease. Adam was amazing with people, just another of his many talents. Before long, Mr. Stephens announced that his work was done, and he had a long drive back to Seattle. We said our cordial good-byes to him, leaving the four of us in another awkward moment, not sure how to proceed.

Heather's voice broke through the uncomfortable silence. "Well, why don't you two follow us to the house? It's not far from here. The kids are expecting us, and they are so excited to meet you!"

~

Moments later Adam and I were back in our rental car, following the Petersens' Land Rover through a beautiful and upscale neighborhood bordering the water. I had forgotten how lush and green the Northwest was. My nerves were getting the best of me, and I let out a loud sigh. Adam placed his hand on my wildly bouncing knee and asked if I was okay.

"Yeah, I'm just a little nervous and scared." I was touched by his concern for me. I didn't deserve it. "How about you?" I asked in return.

"I'm really nervous too, but mostly I'm excited. The Petersens seem really nice, and I can tell that they're good people."

"They are, Adam." We turned onto a long paved drive that led to a large stucco house surrounded by evergreens and a perfectly manicured yard lined with colorful flowers.

"Here we go," I heard Adam say.

We stood in a huge foyer, with ceilings two stories tall. A beautiful staircase led upstairs and straight ahead, through a short hallway, the room opened up to a kitchen, living room and dining room framed by a wall of windows that overlooked Bellingham Bay. The sweeping view was breathtaking, and I felt a sense of pride knowing that Brooklyn was living here in this gorgeous house, surrounded by such beauty. It was a far cry from the modest home that I had grown up in, surrounded by fields of wheat and sagebrush. This house was enormous and beautiful, but it was also warm and homey.

I could feel the sense of family in the colorful construction paper drawings that hung on the bare walls of the kitchen and the Legos that littered the coffee table in the living room. Off to the side of the massive space sat a baby grand piano covered in framed photographs. I couldn't help but peek at them, a glimpse into Brooklyn's life. Through the wall of glass near me, I heard children's laughter, followed shortly by two kids bounding through the sliding glass doors. They both stopped and stood before us.

My gaze immediately locked on Brooklyn's. Her huge deep blue eyes and long dark curly hair was a sharp contrast to her brother's pale skin and fine blond hair. She was so petite, reminding me of my young self. I swallowed back the tears and reached my hand out to her. "Hi, Brooklyn. I'm Kendi."

I waited for her to shake my hand as she paused, her eyes full of wonder. I was suddenly scared of what she was feeling. Was she disappointed, angry? I stood waiting for the resentment that I had feared was coming. Without warning, she leaped toward me, wrapping her small arms around my waist, burying the side of her face into my belly, the exact place where I had given her life.

I could barely hear her tiny voice when she muttered against me, "You finally came."

I was in awe, not sure what to make of this moment. My hands were outstretched, not knowing where they should be. I looked up from her mound of dark curls, to see Charles and Heather standing aside with their arms around Kyle, giving us our space, tears glistening in their eyes. Adam had a painful look on his face, struggling with new emotions that he could not place.

My attention returned to my beautiful baby girl as I knelt down and enfolded her in my arms, stroking her thick curls down her back with my hand. Tears of joy and sadness and regret washed over me as I held her small frame against me.

After several minutes had passed, Brooklyn released me, looking into my eyes with the same intensity that I had seen in Adam's eyes countless times. I wiped the wetness from my cheeks with the back of my hand as her face stretched into a smile, showcasing a pair of dimples that were all too familiar. She looked so much like Adam that it was astonishing.

"I can't wait to show you my new Barbie house," she chirped in her cute little voice.

And just like that, the very intense, grown-up moment melted away, reminding me that, no matter the circumstances, she was only ten years old.

I laughed with relief. "I would love to see your Barbie house." I brushed my hand across her cheek, remembering what she looked like the last time I had held her. Seeing how much she had grown and changed reminded me of how much time had passed. All this time I had never stopped loving her.

Adam knelt down beside me and introduced himself. Brooklyn ran her hand over Adam's hair and then combed her fingers through her own curly locks. "We have the same hair," she said matter-of-factly.

"Yes, we do," Adam said in a broken voice. I could tell that he was struggling with his emotions. "And I think we both have these," he said sticking his finger in her left dimple. She laughed.

I could hear laughter coming from everyone in the room and within that laughter was an awareness that we were all a part of something—together—in a strange, unordinary but extraordinary way.

Brooklyn grabbed Adam's hand and reached for mine with her other hand. "Come on. I'll show you my room."

I held her hand in mine and looked at Heather as if I needed her permission or blessing.

She nodded. "You guys go ahead. We'll get some snacks and drinks ready."

The three of us walked hand in hand up the stairs to Brooklyn's bedroom. It was hard not to notice her excitement as she showed us her beautiful room, adorned with pink everything. We sat on her floor admiring her new Barbie house, asking her a million simple questions about her life, when something caught Adam's eye. He reached for it, pulling it away from Brooklyn's neck. A charm that hung from a simple white gold chain. He held the charm in his hand, silent wonderment in his eyes.

I looked more closely to discover that the charm wasn't a charm at all but my sapphire ring. The one that I had given to Heather, for Brooklyn, the day she was born.

Adam looked into my eyes, unspoken questions lingering between us.

I shrugged and flashed him a look of "It's the least I could do." He smiled at me. A variety of emotions fleeted across his face. I felt connected to him and to Brooklyn. The three of us may not be a traditional family, but we were bonded by blood and circumstance, and I knew that this moment would be forever etched in my memory.

An hour later we were sitting outside at a large teak table sipping ice tea and devouring Heather's delicious homemade snacks. It was a perfect warm, sunny day in the Pacific Northwest, a rare occurrence this time of year, making it nearly a crime to spend the day indoors. An expansive green yard stretched out before us, ending at a cliff that lead to the cold blue waters of the bay below. The view was incredible, and I found myself staring out into the infinite expanse of the ocean waters, inspired by its endlessness. The colors were so vivid here—the deep greens of the bountiful trees, the intense blue of the sky that bled into the dark blue of the ocean.

Brooklyn and Kyle challenged Charles and Adam to a game of soccer, and the four of them ran for the lawn, Charles setting up the goals at each end. Heather and I watched in amusement as the two men scrambled to keep up with the kids. I was impressed with Brooklyn's skills. She was built like me, petite in every way, but, watching her run circles around the guys, dribbling the ball back and forth between her quick feet with obvious confidence, reminded me of Adam and the way he had dominated fields and courts of any kind back in the day. She had undoubtedly inherited his innate athletic talent. My eyes drifted between Brooklyn and Adam, my love for each of them overwhelming me.

"What's the story with you two?" Heather asked as we both watched Adam pretend to miss the soccer ball, falling on his rump, pulling Brooklyn and Kyle down with him. Their playful laughter drifted across the lawn as Adam tickled them endlessly.

"It's long and complicated." I sighed.

"Do you love him?" Heather cut to the chase.

I looked at Adam before I answered. I felt my heart fill with warmth, and I knew without a doubt what I felt for him. "Yeah, I do. Which is crazy, because, up until a few months ago, I hadn't seen or heard from him in over ten years. It doesn't matter how I feel though. He doesn't feel the same way. It's too late for us."

"It's never too late to build and nourish relationships, Kendi. Today alone should be a testament to that. Just look at Brooklyn. She's so happy to finally meet you. You should tell him how you feel. I see the way he looks at you. He might surprise you."

"Trust me. It's a miracle that he's even speaking to me right now."

"Kendi, help us!" I heard Brooklyn squeal. I looked at Heather, and she nodded toward the pile of bodies on the grass in front of us.

"Go," she said.

I ran over to help free the kids from Adam's arms, and he somehow managed to pull me down with them. The kids thought that this was hilarious.

"Get her," Adam yelled.

And I instantly felt little hands tickling me under the arms and chin.

"Her secret spot is right here," Adam whispered as he tickled my sides, leaving me breathless as I laughed until I cried. I turned on them, trying to tickle Brooklyn and Kyle, but they squealed and ran away to kick the soccer ball to Charles.

Adam and I both fell on our backs sprawled out on the lawn, trying to catch our breath. We were quietly giggling, looking up into the clear blue sky. Our fingers were touching where they rested in the grass, and I felt Adam take my hand in his and interlace our fingers. I turned my head to the side to find him looking at me, his dimples in full form from the huge grin that spread across his face. He looked happy. I smiled back at him, and he squeezed my hand before releasing it to stand up. I looked up to see him standing over me, offering me a hand. I reached for it as he pulled me to my feet.

"Thanks," I said, as I brushed the grass off my dress and joined Heather back at the table. I wasn't sure what that moment meant for Adam and me. I couldn't wrap my head around the peace and calm that filled me, driving away the storm of emptiness and guilt that I had become familiar with. Today was starting to feel like one of the best days of my life.

Letting Go

We rode back to the hotel in complete and utter silence. I was awestruck by Brooklyn's perfection. I couldn't articulate the feelings that I was experiencing. I was expecting sheer heartbreak from meeting her and leaving her—again. But instead I was enraptured by this beautiful girl who only emanated curiosity and love toward me, nothing close to the disappointment or resentment that I was expecting. Charles and Heather had raised an amazing child, and, for the first time since the day Brooklyn was born, I felt confident that I had made the right choice, the right choice for Brooklyn.

And everything was different now. I wanted to be a part of her life. I was strong enough to embrace my role in her life, to be there for her in whatever way she needed me. The day had flowed so well that Heather had invited us to stay for dinner. The evening had ended with Adam playing the piano for us, teaching Brooklyn a simple duet that they played together until it was perfect. The melody would be echoing in my mind the rest of the night.

The warmth that I had felt cooking and sharing a meal with the Petersens was so inviting, leaving me with a yearning for what they had. Though Adam and I had given Brooklyn life, it had felt like we were her aunt and uncle, linked in some way, a part of the family. I knew this was only the beginning for all of us. We said our good-byes and promised to see each other soon. Brooklyn asked me to come to her ballet recital the following month, and I gave her my cell phone number, inviting her to call me or text me anytime.

Adam was so quiet, and I wasn't sure what he was feeling. He was completely captivated by Brooklyn, and, watching them together, I had no doubt that he would be an amazing father. We parked the car in the hotel parking lot, walking side by side through the lobby doors and rode the elevator to the fourth floor in silence.

Where I felt elated, I was concerned that Adam felt my betrayal on a much deeper level now that he had met Brooklyn, and I worried that he was hurting from leaving her, the way that I had feared. I told him good-night and that I would see him in the morning as I opened the door to my room. Adam said good-night quietly and walked slowly to the other end of the hall toward his own room. He looked sad, his head bent down, his hands in the pockets of his dark charcoal dress slacks. I watched him until he disappeared into his room. I let the door close slowly and walked into the quiet of my hotel room. I pulled back the covers and collapsed onto the king-size bed, pulling off my boots and tossing them aside.

I couldn't help but feel that this was the end of the road for Adam and me. We would both continue our contact with Brooklyn, separately. There was no reason for us to see one another again. I was sure that Adam was still angry with me for the choices that I had made, keeping this secret from him for ten long years.

But I had seen something in his eyes today that I couldn't explain. Contentment maybe. Not a trace of anger or resentment, but I couldn't deny the air of melancholy that had surrounded him on the drive to the hotel. I wanted to wrap my arms around him and kiss away his despair, but I was caught up in my own emotions from the day. I honestly still loved him. The truly, madly, deeply kind of love. How was that possible after all this time?

Spending these past few days with Adam had rekindled a fire inside me. Where I had once only wanted closure, I wanted Adam. I knew that I wanted something that I could never have. I had two choices at this point. I could hide in my room all night, say good-bye in the morning and go on with my life, putting it all behind me by throwing myself back into my work, finishing what I had started.

Or I could take Heather's advice and tell Adam how I felt and hope that someday he would be able to forgive me and, at the very least, we could be friends once again. The thought of going back to my life without Adam or Brooklyn after this day—feeling more complete than I had since giving her up—generated a loneliness that felt far worse than the emptiness that I was used to.

I decided to be honest with myself and Adam, the need to tell him how I felt outweighing my fear of rejection. Still barefoot I grabbed my key card and opened the heavy door to my room, my heart drumming in my chest with anxiety. Deep in thought, swirling words around in my head of what I might possibly say to Adam, I abruptly walked into something or rather someone. Startled, I looked up into a pair of smoldering deep blue eyes. Adam pushed his foot against the door before it closed and slowly backed me into my room, our gazes locked.

Before I could even say his name, I felt strong arms pulling me in closer and soft, warm lips crashed against mine. Instantly intoxicated by his smell, my lips responded desperately against his. I heard the door latch close, and, in the same moment, Adam pushed me back against the wall. His hands were in my hair, his lips forcing mine apart as his tongue expertly found its way into my mouth. I pulled him closer to me, my fingers running frantically through his dark curls.

He brought his hand to my face, fingers wrapped around the back of my head as his thumb grazed my cheek, prompting me to open myself up more to him as he kissed me with a fevered passion. My body ached for him, a powerful need building within me fueled by the heady emotions from the day. I wanted to feel every inch of him against me, without any barriers, physical or mental.

As if reading my mind, his hands found the hem of my dress, pulling it slowly up the curves of my body. I raised my arms straight in the air above me as he continued to peel my dress over my head, pulling his lips from mine only for a brief moment. When I felt the soft cotton fabric graze over my fingers, my eyes found his blazing in return, filled with unmistakable desire.

Standing in front of him in only my bra and panties, feeling vulnerable but desired, I leaned back against the wall. He intertwined our fingers, still above my head as his lips found mine once again; his hands eventually worked their way down my arms to the rest of me. He gently caressed each naked curve of my body, his gaze taking in every inch of me. He leaned in, stroking my neck with his tongue as I tilted my head, giving him better access.

I ran my hands up his back, underneath his already untucked shirt, my fingers feeling every cut of his defined body. I brought my hands between us and unbuttoned his shirt with nimble fingers, pulling it down his arms until it dropped to the floor. My hands molded against the bare skin of his chest, working their way up to his neck as I pulled his lips back to mine.

Feeling his arousal pressing into me, I released his slacks, letting them fall to the floor, and went in search of bare skin inside the cotton of his boxers. Adam moaned against my lips. Releasing my bra, he trailed kisses down my shoulder across my chest, until I felt his wet lips against my breast, taking my nipple into his mouth. My body was consumed with pure longing, the ache between my legs nearly bringing me to my knees.

"Adam," I managed to whisper, a small whimper, pleading with him, for what, I wasn't sure. Just when I thought that my legs would give out on me, not able to tolerate the heated desire coursing through my blood another moment, Adam, in one small swoop, cradled me in his arms and carried me to the bed, his lips never leaving mine.

He settled me on my back, and, once his boxers left his body, he was lying next to me, pulling me against him, hands exploring fervently. Within minutes Adam was on top of me, filling me, moaning my name. I was consumed by our past and all that we had endured together and apart, overwhelmed in this heated moment by my love for Adam.

Hot tears spilled from my eyes, and I felt Adam brush them away gently. I opened my eyes at his endearing gesture to find his own eyes filling with moisture, the intensity of his gaze burning into me. We were so connected in the moment, two bodies melting into one, two souls reunited. On the edge of our desire, we both fell seconds apart, crashing into one another. Adam spilling into me as my body trembled against him. He held me firmly in his arms sending chills down my spine as he gently kissed my neck and shoulders.

I stayed in Adam's arms, feeling every inch of his body against mine as our breath evened out and the thunderous beat of our hearts grew silent. It was hard to ignore the intensity of our connection, reaching a level of transcendence beyond anything that I had ever experienced. I tried to put into words what I was feeling. "Adam."

"Shh." He placed his finger over my lips to stop me from speaking. "Don't say anything, Kendi. Just let me hold you a little bit longer."

I buried my face in his chest and breathed him in as his words ran through my mind. *A little bit longer.* Before what? Before we talk about what just happened? My mind eventually quieted, giving in to the exhaustion of an emotional day as I drifted peacefully to sleep in Adam's arms —the only place I wanted to be.

~

I woke a few hours later, remembering the warmth of Adam's body next to mine. I reached out, but the bed was empty. I slowly sat up, rubbing my eyes as they sought unfamiliar objects in the darkness. I could barely make out his silhouette, sitting quietly in a chair in the corner of the room, a fraction of light filtering in through a break in the heavy drapes behind him. His face was resting in his hand as he leaned against the arm of the chair, his eyes taking me in from across the room. "What are you doing over there?" I asked, confused.

"Watching you sleep," he responded, the melancholy from earlier returning in his voice.

"What is it, Adam?" I pulled up the sheet and held it against my chest, suddenly feeling very exposed and vulnerable. He made his way over to me, sitting on the edge of the bed, fully dressed. He reached over and turned on the bedside lamp, its soft light illuminating the space around us. I could see his thick hair twisted in every direction, his eyes dark in the dim light. I took in the beauty of his face, instinctively wanting to reach out and touch him, but his mournful expression stopped me. Instead, he brought his hand to my face, brushing his thumb across my cheek, and

282

then, as if he had suddenly thought better of it, dropped his hand to his lap. The pained look in his eyes tore me apart inside, and I was afraid of what he might say next.

"I have so many mixed emotions about today, or I guess I should say yesterday," he said glancing at the digital clock next to the bed. It was two o'clock in the morning. His eyes rested on his hands in his lap as he picked at one of his nails absentmindedly. "It's hard not to think about what could have been. If you had made different choices, if that was us with Brooklyn, raising her."

I sucked in a breath and released it, anticipating what he was getting at. He looked up into my eyes once again.

"But the problem with the image that I see is that it's one of who I am now, where I am now. And right now there's definitely a place for her in my life. But I'm trying to put myself back to that year, where I was at the time, who I was then. And I was so selfish and determined. I wanted so much to please my parents, practically begging for their approval. I wanted to somehow assuage the guilt that I felt for betraying you and my brother. I wanted to make things right. I was so wrapped up in myself.

"When I was in Africa, I got caught up in the honor that they were bestowing upon me. I lost myself somewhere along the way, and, because of that, I lost you." He reached out and cupped my cheek in his hand. He took a deep breath and returned his hand to his lap, and I felt a chill run through my body at the loss of heat from his touch.

"I will never feel that your choice to keep your pregnancy from me and to keep Brooklyn from me all these years was the right thing to do, because it was wrong on so many levels. But I also can't help but put myself in your shoes. We were so young, and you must have been so scared, afraid of dragging me away from my dreams. I see now that your choices were not selfish at all but in my best interest, or so you thought at the time. And I want you to know that I forgive you, Kendi."

I gasped at his words, tears streaming down my cheeks. This was the last thing that I had expected to hear from him. Loud sobs escaped me, and I buried my face in my hands. I could almost feel the heavy weight of my guilt lift from my body as his words washed over me. Wiping the tears from my eyes with my fingertips, I looked up at him as he continued. His mouth turned up on one side, a partial smile that touched his eyes as he brushed away a missed tear from my cheek with his thumb.

"It's hard to ignore how happy Brooklyn is and seeing with my own eyes the caring and loving parents that Charles and Heather are, knowing that you found them and that you made all these grown-up decisions on your own.... I know that we could never have given her the life that she has. She would have been loved for sure, but that may not have been enough.

"I can't imagine what it must have been like for you, making that choice all alone. When I think of you as the strong, kindhearted and beautiful girl that I fell in love with —I know that you were trying to make the best decision for both of us, and you did the right thing, Kendi. For all of us. I see that now. I wish that you would have told me, that we could have made this decision together, but we can't go back and change the past."

Taken back by his unexpected compassion, I was at a loss for words. I said the first thing that came to mind. "I'm so sorry, Adam. I truly am sorry. I never meant to hurt you. I wanted to protect you." I choked on my own words, struggling with my emotions.

He reached for me, pulling me against him. "Shh. It's okay. I forgive you," he reassured me in an attempt to comfort me, his arms softly stroking my back.

I threw my arms around his neck and buried my damp face against his shoulder. I had prayed for this moment for so long. He could not possibly understand what his words meant to me. My heart was overflowing with love for him. I pulled my face from his shoulder, running my fingertips through his hair; I slowly leaned in to kiss him.

I felt his hands on my shoulders, holding me back before I heard him sigh and whisper, "God, Kendi."

I rested my forehead against his, giving him a moment to collect himself, for what I wasn't sure.

"I should go back to my room."

"Why? Adam?" I wanted to tell him that I loved him, but the words were caught in my throat, fear gripping my insides.

"I'll see you in the morning." He kissed my forehead and made his way toward the door.

"What happened tonight, what was that, Adam?" I called out to him.

He turned to face me, clearly torn up inside, sadness heavy in his eyes. "That was me letting go." And with that said, he walked out the door.

I didn't know what to feel. Angry, sad, relieved. His forgiveness was more than I deserved, but I wanted so much more than that. Wanting him to open up his heart to me again was obviously too much to ask. I lay back in bed, hugging a pillow close to my chest, wondering what I was supposed to do next. How was I supposed to move on after that? I could still smell him on my skin, feel the ghost of his touch—his warm lips against mine. I eventually drifted back to sleep, replaying Adam's words in my mind.

~

I woke early before the sun, groggy from a nearly sleepless night. I decided to take a cab to the airport, avoiding the uncomfortable and inevitable good-bye with Adam. He was flying to Spokane that morning, around the same time as my flight to Los Angeles. The last thing I needed was a dramatic airport good-bye. I sent him a long text on the drive to the airport.

> *I feel like we have said enough good-byes for one lifetime. I didn't want to leave without saying something. Thank you for this past week and for convincing me to come with you to see Brooklyn. It was the best decision I have made in a long time. And thank you for telling me how you felt last night. You have no idea what your words mean to me, how they have already changed me. I truly am sorry, Adam. For everything.*
> *Until next time…*
> *K*

While sitting on the plane, watching people pass by in the aisle to find their seats, my cell phone buzzed continuously. I checked the screen to find several missed calls from Adam. I powered down my phone and dropped it back in my bag. I wasn't sure what was left to say, what he could possibly need to tell me at this point. I could still feel his hands on my skin, my body still abuzz from his heated touch. The passion that we had shared the night before was mind blowing, and I knew that it was going to be so much harder to move forward with those memories fresh in my mind. But I wouldn't take it back; I wouldn't change what had happened between us.

Upon arrival in L.A., I turned my phone back on and immediately noticed that I had a text waiting. Assuming the text was from Adam, I was shocked to see Derek's name on the screen. *Can we talk? Have dinner with me.* After waiting to hear those words from him for months, this was when he decided to contact me? My head was all over the place because of the past few days, but I responded anyway. I found myself disappointed that the text wasn't from Adam. He hadn't left a voice mail either. I guess that he'd said everything that he needed to say.

Derek wanted me to meet him at our favorite beach restaurant near my place the following night. I let him know that I would be there. I knew what I needed to say to him, but I was unsure of what it was he wanted to say to me; nerves pooled in my gut from the uncertainty of it all.

Still Waters

I rushed through my makeup routine, coating my eyelashes
with mascara and brushing a clear gloss across my lips.
Glancing in the mirror one last time, feeling satisfied with
my dark skinny jeans and sheer black tunic, I walked the two
short blocks to the restaurant. I was excited but feeling
anxious to see Derek. It had been a few months, longer than I
had expected when he had said that he "needed time." Derek
was waiting for me outside when I reached the double glass
doors that led into our favorite seafood bistro.

"Hi, beautiful," he greeted me with an inviting hug.
"Mmm, I missed you," he mumbled as he inhaled the
familiar perfume on my neck and kissed me on the cheek.

"Hi," I said with a grin as I hugged him back, happy
to see him. He looked incredible in his expensive jeans slung
low on his hips and a baby-blue button-down shirt. His hair
was perfectly styled, showcasing his gorgeous eyes. My
feelings for this man came rushing back to me. I couldn't

help but notice that they felt only skin deep in comparison to the intense emotional roller coaster that my heart rode every time that I was near Adam. I couldn't deny the physical chemistry that Derek and I had, but was that enough?

"Shall we?" he asked, releasing me and guiding me through the doors with his hand resting on the small of my back. We were led to our favorite table near the back of the restaurant.

Derek ordered a bottle of wine for us, and we put our menus to the side, already knowing what we were going to order. "So how have you been, Kendi?"

"Good. Busy. So much has happened since I saw you last. How have you been?"

"Crazy busy. We've been hammering out all the fine details with NetTech's IPO. I've been in New York for weeks."

"I'm really happy for you, Derek. I know how hard you've worked on this account."

"Thanks, it's good to be home though."

The waitress arrived with our bottle of wine, uncorked it and poured a small amount in a glass for Derek to taste. He nodded at her, satisfied. She filled both of our glasses, placing the bottle on the table as she left us to our conversation.

"You look beautiful, Kendi. Something's different with you, and I can't put my finger on it. Does this have anything to do with everything that's happened since I saw you last?"

"Maybe," I admitted. "I saw my daughter, Derek." I was nervous to tell him, not sure how he'd feel about my past, but I couldn't hide the smile on my face as I thought of Brooklyn.

"I went to Bellingham and spent an entire day with her. She's ten now and so amazing. And something has changed. I feel…I don't know, lighter somehow. Does that sound crazy?"

He looked genuinely happy for me, but there was a hint of sadness in his eyes. The waitress returned to take our order, and, when we were alone again, Derek responded. "No, it's not crazy. I see it in your eyes. That's great, really, Kendi. I *am* happy for you. What brought all this on? I mean, after all these years, why now?"

I took a deep breath before I told him the hard part. "Adam showed up here last week." He cringed at the sound of Adam's name. "He wanted to know all the details, and he wanted to meet her. He insisted that I go with him, so I did." I looked into Derek's eyes waiting for his response.

"So you two went up there together?" he asked hesitantly.

I nodded.

"And now?"

"And now nothing. We went our separate ways. He told me that he forgives me for everything, telling me that giving up Brooklyn was the right thing to do. Although I don't think that he'll ever really forgive me for lying to him."

"How do you feel about him, Kendi?"

It was hard to look into Derek's eyes and tell him the truth, knowing that it would hurt him. But I didn't have any other choice. "Honestly? I still love him. I know that's not what you want to hear, but I do. I'm sorry, Derek. It doesn't matter how I feel though. Adam and I have too much past between us, so there's no starting over or going back."

"Where does that leave us?"

"I don't know." It was an honest answer. I didn't know. I loved Derek. It was different than what I felt for Adam, but I loved him nonetheless. It wasn't like I had to choose between Adam or Derek; Adam wasn't an option. But was that fair to Derek, knowing that, if given the choice, I would choose someone else?

Our dinner arrived, interrupting the uncomfortable

silence between us. I moved my food around on my plate, having lost my appetite from the turn in conversation. We ate in silence. I finished my wine, and Derek poured me another glass, always the gentleman. I put down my fork finally and looked at Derek, waiting for him to say something, anything. I needed him to make the choice. I needed him to choose to be with me or not, because I couldn't make that decision for us.

"Kendi, I was hoping that this time apart would seal the deal for you. I was hoping that you would be just as miserable without me as I have been without you. But, instead, I feel like it confirmed what you feel for someone else. How do I compete with that?" He tossed his napkin on his plate in frustration.

"You shouldn't have to," I said, wishing that things were different. I didn't deserve Derek. He deserved to be with someone who loved him completely, and maybe I could do that one day, but I knew that I couldn't give him that right now. I had to let him go. I reached my hand across the table and held his hand in mine. "Derek, you deserve so much more than I can give you right now. I love you. I do. But I have a lot to sort out right now, and you shouldn't have to wait for me to do that. Maybe if the timing was different... I don't know what else to say."

Derek pulled away his hand, reaching for his wallet. He threw a stack of bills on the table and stood, reaching for my hand.

"Come on. I'll walk you home."

I took his hand, and we made our way outside. We strolled hand in hand toward my apartment, breathing in the thick salty scent of the ocean. We walked in silence, but my mind was reeling from the anticipation of how this night was going to end.

Derek escorted me up the stairs to my door. I turned toward him. "Do you want to come in?"

"I probably shouldn't." He pulled me into his arms and rested his chin on my head, his hands clasped on my lower back.

I felt my tears building, knowing that a good-bye was looming in the air.

"I love you so much, Kendi. But I can't share your heart with someone else. I need to know without a doubt that you only want me, that I'm enough for you. I know that you can't promise me that, and I understand, I do. I might regret this for the rest of my life, but this has to be good-bye."

I was sobbing into his chest. I knew that he was right. It was over, but it didn't make it any easier. I wrapped my arms around his waist, pulling him tighter against me. We held each other for what had seemed like forever, neither one of us wanting to let go.

He finally pulled away, and I looked up at him through my tears. Gently wiping them from my cheeks, he leaned down to kiss me.

I poured every ounce of love that I felt for him into our kiss. We kissed long and hard, until I could feel everything that we had slipping away.

He must have felt it too, releasing me with the gravest look in his eyes. "Good-bye, Kendi."

"Bye, Derek," I whispered, as he turned toward the stairs. He didn't let go of my hand until I was no longer within reach, and then he was gone.

~

I went straight to bed, exhausted from such an emotional week. I held my worn photograph of Brooklyn and me from long ago close to my heart, drawing comfort from the memory rather than the soul-shattering torment that this same picture had seemed to confront me with in the past. I had finally accepted the idea that I could not change the past, but

I could move forward and embrace the future. A future with Brooklyn in my life. I had called my mother and Marie when I'd returned from Bellingham, sharing all the details of our reunion. It felt liberating to voice the emotions that I had experienced that day, opening up a part of me that I had kept closed off all those years. They were both looking forward to the day that they would meet her.

I closed my eyes and took in a deep breath, still clutching the photograph against my chest. I couldn't ignore the quiet calm that pervaded my mind and my heart. I was completely alone. I had managed to lose both Adam and Derek due to my secrets and lies. The past really does catch up with us, eventually. I couldn't deny the change I felt in my heart though, now that I had been honest with myself and everyone that I loved.

I could breathe again without the weight of the repressed guilt and shame that had threatened to suffocate me for so long. The truth had set me free. It had stilled the ripple cascading through my life, quieting the storm inside my soul. I felt complete, whole. I knew that time would mend what was broken, helping me to let go of the men that I had loved but lost. But for once, *I* was no longer broken, I was healed. And the peace that I found in that made it all worth it.

Epilogue

I rushed from the cab, holding my jacket over my head to block the rain from hitting my face. I was running late. My flight was delayed, and I had come straight from the airport. I had texted Heather to let her know, and she had promised to save me a seat. Quickly leaving my damp coat and suitcase at the coat check, I made my way into the auditorium. I spotted my empty seat in the second row from the front. I quietly made my way down the center aisle of the performing arts center, my eyes scanning the group of dancers on the stage until I found Brooklyn.

She looked beautiful. Her thick curls were pulled tight into a neat bun; her bright pink sequined costume shimmered in the theater lights; her petite form moved with such grace as she twirled and pliéed. Her face lit up when she noticed me walking toward the stage, and I acknowledged her with a small wave as I took my seat next to Heather. Heather patted my leg as I set my handbag at my feet, her eyes not leaving Brooklyn's performance. Charles was beaming behind the small video camera as he proudly watched his daughter. He winked at me and returned his gaze to the dancers. Kyle sat next to him, playing a small handheld video game, clearly bored with the ballet recital. My eyes quickly returned to the performance.

Brooklyn looked so grown-up dancing on the stage, and I was so proud of her. My cheeks were aching from the huge grin stretched across my face. The music ended, and the eight identically dressed girls bowed as we clapped for them. They left the stage, and a new group of ballerinas took their place. The music was live, and, as it moved into the next piece, I noted how beautiful it was. Off to the side of the stage a small orchestra was assembled around a black grand piano. It was hard to see, as it was obviously not intended to be the main attraction but only an accompaniment to the dancers.

Heather leaned over to whisper to me now that Brooklyn was no longer on stage. "How was your flight?"

"Long. I couldn't get here fast enough."

"Brooklyn was so excited that you were going to be here."

"I wouldn't have missed it. I'm honored that she invited me," I whispered with my hand over my heart, emphasizing what her invitation meant to me.

The audience was applauding once again, and we directed our attention again to the front of the auditorium. Brooklyn was back on stage a moment later with a group of girls, dressed in a completely new black ensemble. With her hair pulled back and the small trace of makeup that she was wearing for her performance, her blue eyes stood out, shimmering under the lights. Those eyes. Adam's eyes.

His face instantly filled my mind as I watched Brooklyn dance with perfect poise. I had not heard from him for over a month—since the last time I was here in

Bellingham. I had returned to Los Angeles and poured myself into work, spending endless hours reading X-rays and assisting with special procedures, loving my new rotation. I had tried, unsuccessfully, to push my recent memories of Adam to the back of my mind.

I had spent countless hours talking to Brooklyn on the phone, each of us taking turns asking questions as we got to know each other. Most of her questions had been easy to answer, but occasionally she had asked the hard ones, bringing me back to that year when I was pregnant with her. I had tried to answer her as honestly as I could, keeping in mind that she was only ten. I had enjoyed every minute of our conversations, leaving me a little sad when it was time to hang up. Heather and I had talked quite often as well. I had so much respect for her as a mother and as a friend.

The recital went on for several more group performances, and then a young girl took the stage for a solo performance. Heather leaned in once again and whispered, "Brooklyn has a solo next."

I instantly felt nervous for her, and, by the tapping of Heather's foot, I knew that she felt the same. Applause filled the auditorium as the young girl bowed and left the stage. The lights dimmed, and I watched Brooklyn confidently walk to the center of the stage and lock herself in a pose, waiting for the music to start. I heard Heather suck in a breath next to me as she raised her hands to her mouth in anticipation for Brooklyn's performance.

The piano started playing a familiar melody, and I suddenly recognized it as "Clair de Lune." The piano played alone and intensely as Brooklyn danced elegantly to the music against a backdrop of a calm lake glowing in moonlight. She was stunning in a midnight-blue costume embellished with sparkling glitter as she twirled in a spotlight that mimicked the moon behind her. She took my breath away, and I felt tears sting my eyes.

The piano ended its haunting melody, and Brooklyn held her pose until the lights came back on. The audience stood, giving her a standing ovation. She bowed and then extended her arms toward the piano. The pianist stood and walked up the few stairs to the stage as Brooklyn ran toward him.

I gasped, my hand gripping my chest as I realized that it was Adam. He was wearing a dark suit, looking just as confident as his daughter as he marched toward her. He kneeled down to embrace Brooklyn, pride gleaming from his eyes as he held her. I stood still, overcome with emotion at the sight of the two of them on stage sharing such an intimate moment, as if the auditorium wasn't filled to the brim with spectators. I was moved beyond words, tears spilling down my cheeks.

I felt Heather's arm around my shoulders as she whispered in my ear. "I hope that you don't mind. I may have meddled just a little bit."

I looked at her, uncertain of her meaning. She had tears in her own eyes from Brooklyn's engaging performance. "Meddled? What do you mean?"

She just shrugged with a smile and clapped her hands together as the entire cast of dancers took to the stage for their standing ovation.

Adam was walking off the stage at this point, heading straight for me. He approached me, and, before I could say anything, he grabbed my hand and pulled me behind him as we made our way toward the lobby. People seated near the center aisle were glancing curiously in our direction. Once we reached a quiet corner of the lobby, Adam stopped to face me.

"Adam, what are…?"

He pulled me against him as he leaned down to kiss me. I lost all train of thought as I melted into him, feeling his heart beat in time with my own. My senses caught up with me, and I pushed him back, my hands against his chest. "Adam, stop. I can't keep doing this."

He put his hands on mine, still resting on his chest, an amused expression on his face. "Doing what, Kendi?" he asked.

"This." After freeing one hand from his grasp, I pointed to him, to me.

"Why, Kendi? Why can't you keep doing this?"

Confused by the absurdity of his questions, I answered him as bluntly as I could. "Because it's killing me, Adam. This back and forth."

"Why is it killing you, Kendi?"

I was becoming infuriated by the minute. What kind of game was he playing? "Because it is," I said a little louder than I meant to, trying to push away from him. He held my hands tighter against his chest.

"Why?" he asked again, still with an amused expression but with more passion in his voice.

"Adam. Just…because. Let me go." I was angry. My cheeks were hot, tears stinging my eyes. And he just kept pressing.

"Tell me why this is killing you?" he asked earnestly, his face inches from mine despite my best attempt to put space between us.

"Because I love you, *dammit*! Is that what you want to hear?" I shouted, immediately shocked by my admission. Before I could react, his mouth was pressed against mine. I surrendered to his warm lips, passion flooding my heart from the conflicting anger and love that I felt in that moment.

Pulling back just enough to look into my eyes, Adam whispered, "That is exactly what I wanted to hear."

I was flustered. "Adam, what are you doing here, and what is this all about? You made your feelings perfectly clear the last time I saw you."

"Did I? Because I think that I was anything but clear."

"I'm so confused right now," I admitted.

"Kendi, the last time I saw you, I was overwhelmed with my feelings for you. I had no idea how you felt about me. I thought that you were in love with what's-his-name. And you had this new life at the beach and your residency… everything that you have always wanted. I didn't want to get in the way of that. It killed me to leave you that night, but I thought that it was for the best…for you."

"So what changed?"

"Heather told me that you weren't in a relationship anymore and that you had told her that you loved me. The next thing I knew, the pianist for the recital broke her leg, and Heather was begging me to fill in. I haven't been able to think about anything but you since that night, and I knew that I had to come."

I searched his eyes for more, wondering what it was that he was trying to tell me. He brought his hand to my face, looking intently into my eyes. "Just so we're clear. I love you, Kendi. I've loved you all this time, I've never stopped loving you, and I will always love you."

People were starting to spill into the lobby from the auditorium, but Adam and I stood in the corner as if we were the only two people in the world.

"I love you too, Adam."

He wrapped his arms around my waist, lifting me up as he spun me around. When he stopped, I slowly slid down his body until our lips met. Still holding me inches from the floor, he kissed me gently through the smile splayed on his lips. Emotions washed over me as images of each moment that we had shared, each moment of our long and convoluted past, played through my mind in rapid sequence—bringing us to this moment.

I wasn't sure where we went from here, but I wasn't letting anything stand in our way again. I ran my hands through his thick curls, pulling him closer to me, knowing without a doubt that he was the last man I was ever going to kiss.

Acknowledgments

I would like to thank my amazing husband, Eric, for proving to me every day that fairytale endings really do exist, for being the reason I wake up each day and pinch myself to make sure that I am not dreaming and really am this happy, and for showing me that although marriage can be tough, love is easy. Thank you for your unending love and support on this journey and for picking up the slack with a smile while I buried my head in my laptop breathing life into this story. I couldn't have done it without you!

To my two wonderful and amazing kiddos, for your patience and love while Mommy was busy "working". Everything I do is always for you in the end. You are my world!

To my Mom, Diane, and sister, Christy, thank you for loving this story as much as I do! Your encouragement kept me going-thank you for believing in me! I love you both! My Dad, Larry, for always loving me like your own. Your unconditional love and constant support has been a precious gift throughout my life! To my brother, Alan, I love you and feel so blessed to have you in my life!

To my dear friend, Tabatha Harris, thank you for staying up late many nights to read this story as I wrote it and for the long texts full of positive feedback at midnight no less! It was so great to have someone to talk to about these characters that were consuming my every thought!

To all my beta readers: Jen Atler-Ammazzalorso, Jen McCloskey, Molly Ursini, Debbie Bayley, and Lindsey Hille. Your feedback was essential and gave me the confidence to put it out there for others to read! Thank you for taking the time to read this book with an open mind!

And I can't leave out the girls ~ you know who you are ~ my dearest friends that I couldn't imagine my life without, the ones who breathe life into my soul each and every day and make every step of the way more bearable and a helluva lot more fun!

Lastly, I would like to thank every single life experience that I have had and all the amazing people that I have encountered along the way... as a writer I can't help but draw from it all!

If you enjoyed this book please review it on amazon.com. Look me up on facebook: www.facebook.com/AuthorL.D.Cedergreen. I would love to hear your feedback!

About the Author

L.D. Cedergreen, author of *Ripple*, is a former RT(R), wife and mother of two. She currently resides in Southern California with her family. She can be contacted through her facebook page: www.facebook.com/AuthorL.D.Cedergreen. She loves to hear from her readers.

Made in the USA
San Bernardino, CA
27 March 2014